The Complete Series

Sloane Howell

LORI,
MAY THE FORCE BE WITH YOU!

SLOANE

PANTY WHISPERER
The Complete Series

Sloane Howell

Copyright © 2016 Sloane Howell
Content Editor: Chrissy
Copy Editor: Spell Bound
Cover Design: Mr. Aaron
Stock photos courtesy of shutterstock.com, Adobe Stock,
and thinkstock.com
Fonts courtesty of dafont.com

ISBN-13: 978-1533248206
IBSN-10: 1533248206

NOTE FROM AUTHOR

Joel is back! I'm sorry that it took so long for me to bring him to you. I had to think long and hard about how to approach wrapping up this series. When I published the first short story, I didn't think anyone would ever really read it. I was wrong

I received message after message wanting more of Joel. So I wrote another five short stories as quickly as possible. I added a few characters and tried to form an overall plot in the process. I received more messages. People still wanted more.

So I wrote a novella with a cliffhanger, because I had other projects I was working on. I soon realized that Joel was here to stay, and his story needed to be finished.

Fast forward a year and four months after writing the first story and I noticed I'd become a far better writer. I wanted to make changes to the originals.

I thought about it for a few days and then I couldn't help myself. I wanted everything to flow as close to a novel as possible and it was impossible without editing the other stories. Without boring you any longer with my ramblings, here are the new and improved—hotter, funnier versions of the man they call the Panty Whisperer. I hope you enjoy...

VOLUME 1

INTRO

THE MAJORITY OF men want sex just to get off. They blow their load, roll over, and fall asleep. That's not my style. I want you to remember my face. I want you to remember every inch of me.

And you will.

I want to watch your eyes roll up in your head, your toes cramp up while curling under your feet, your thighs trembling around my face, begging for my stiff cock inside your hot, wet pussy.

Every time you tease your clit, longing for your hair to be pulled, while squeezing those quivering pussy walls around your slippery fingers, you'll be wishing it was me inside of you, drilling balls deep into that aching cunt while you dig your nails into the sheets. I want to own your mind for the rest of your life.

The thought of me will be a thirst you can't quench, a drug you can't have, an itch that can't be scratched, no matter how hard you try. Nobody will send a shock of neural ecstasy from your pulsating little cunt to the tips of your toes the way I will. Care to bet me?

JESSICA MOORE

MOST PEOPLE HAVE something they're good at: math, sports, music, art. I wasn't born with some common talent. I'm a master of making women come. I don't know why, or how it happened, it's just built into my DNA. I've always been able to talk to women and get them to do whatever I want. Ever since I was a teenager, if there was a girl nobody could bed, I got there first.

My name is Joel Hannover. Well, actually, that's a bit of a lie. Joel is my middle name. My first name is Herbert. I hate that name. It's like my parents were trying to cock block me from conception.

I work as an accounting software consultant. It sounds fancy like I should be good with math or computers. Nothing could be further from the truth. I'm a salesman. My job, however, is perfect for my hobby. Most accounting departments are comprised of women. Women that most people think are boring or uneventful.

I meet these women every day. Insecure, dressed conservatively, hiding their beautiful bodies behind layers of clothing, afraid a few pounds of baby weight might still show. They're ladies who work crossword puzzles, and process numbers and transactions. It's all a façade though. These women are just like any others. Sexual creatures who want to have all of their desires met and all of their needs fulfilled.

They're practically begging for someone to explore them, to bring them out of their shell, and release the sexual tension that has saturated their entire being, afraid to break free. They get their rocks off reading erotica, watching porn, or using the shower head in a manner it was not intended for. I can't allow this. They need someone to open their mind, and release their fantasies into the wild. Someone to spread their thighs and take them to places they never knew possible, where all of their darkest fantasies reside. This is the environment where I thrive.

Meet Jessica Moore: mid-thirties, married with two kids, unhappy.

Fucking hot.

She's a senior fixed asset analyst at a company that's implementing my firm's new software. She is amazingly sexy and wasting away in a bad marriage that is held together solely for the kids. We've been working together on this project for about two weeks now and have grown somewhat close.

She cracks a smile as I walk through the door to her office. "Good morning."

"Jessica—" I pause for a moment and eye her curvy hips and round breasts. "—you look nice." She looks hot as fuck, if I'm being honest.

Jessica bites her lip and smiles. I want to put my cock in that beautiful mouth so badly. I have to have her. I've been observing her for the last two weeks, processing every bit of information she provides. She loves Starbucks, romantic comedies, and has an adventurous side to her that she's afraid to act on. Well, she didn't exactly say that, but like I said before, I can sense these things. It's an innate ability. "Did you have a good weekend?"

"Completely boring, didn't do much of anything. Philip went hunting and left me with the kids. So we had a movie night on Saturday. You?"

I can't really tell her I filmed myself banging two twenty-year-old co-eds, and then watched it while going a second round with them. "Oh, I had a movie night myself. New indie film, you wouldn't have heard of it."

Hey, you didn't lie to her.

I can't stop staring at her black, mid-length skirt hugging tight around her hips. I get the slightest peek at her tanned cleavage protruding through her low-cut red top as she reaches into the bottom of a file cabinet. She's dressed up today, and it's for me; we both know it. The first day I was here she wore mom jeans and a sweater.

Her wavy brunette hair is pulled back into a pony tail, and her bright-blue eyes send my stomach churning in knots every time I catch a glimpse of them. It's obvious that she works out and watches her figure, but she's got these curves that send blood straight to my dick. I have to fuck this woman. No, I want to make this woman come harder than she ever has in her life, if she ever has at all. She deserves it. She works hard and is a good mother.

I'm going to plow her so hard she wants to scream but the words won't come out. I can tell she wants it, constantly eyeing my six-foot-two frame, wondering what I'm packing in my slacks. It's not ten inches, but it gets the job done. A massive cock is overrated anyway. I'm not trying to scar her for life.

I pull a caramel macchiato with no whipped cream out from behind my back and set it down on the desk in front of her. It's all about paying attention to details.

"Oh my god. You're my hero. Seriously." She takes a sip. "I'm a slave to caffeine."

"I know how it goes."

Only my drug of choice is that yearning pussy that's heating up for me in your panties while you eye fuck the shit out of me.

Soon.

"So, what's on the agenda for today?" She walks back behind her desk.

"Just a follow up consult, half a day. Make sure all the modules are functioning the way you like, and then I'm out of your hair."

Her head drops a little and she stares down at the desk for a moment before looking back up at me. "Well, I'm taking you to lunch before you leave. On the company, if that's okay?"

"I can't say no to a free meal." I laugh, knowing what I'll be dining on. It's under that skirt of hers. Today is a day she'll remember for the rest of her life. She just doesn't know it yet.

Most of the morning is uneventful, working out kinks in the software. Lunch can't get here fast enough.

"Hey, can you take a look at this? I'm not sure this menu is exactly how we'd like it." She turns back to me, then back to her screen.

I lean over her shoulder, perching up near her ear. God, she smells amazing. I try to look at the screen, but all I can focus on is a black lace bra corralling a pair of 38D breasts. She knows exactly what she's doing, breaking out the sexy underwear for my last day here, longing for them to end up on the floor. "I think we should switch options three and four on this window."

"Shouldn't be a problem." I don't even look at the fucking screen. My eyes are busy, working down those creamy thighs with her knees pressed together, calves running down to a pair of black heels, legs crossed at the ankles.

I look up at the screen and try to buy myself some extra time. "Well, wait, what if we moved option two, and had a separate pop-up option for four?" I don't even know if my words made sense or not, and I can tell she doesn't care. She starts to speak and I exhale lightly across her neck.

"Hmm, I—" Her voice cracks a little as her eyes close, the tiny hairs on her neck standing at attention from my warm breath.

I interrupt her. "No, never mind. I think I like your idea better." I breathe into her ear as I raise my head up.

I spy her brushing her hands across her legs and onto her knees as I walk away. She doesn't think I notice, but I do. I can't stop thinking about how wet her cunt is right now, her lips begging for my cock to drive into them. It's going to be a long lunch.

I ride with her to the restaurant, but don't make any moves. I want to tease her as long as possible. It's a long-term investment for the eruption that will take place between her legs later, when I press the buttons in every erogenous zone in her brain. The clacking of her heels on the tile floor of the restaurant and her ass swaying back and forth in that skirt have my cock rock hard against the zipper of my pants. She knows she's driving me crazy too. Jessica thinks she might know what's coming, but there's enough uncertainty to keep her wondering if she'll merely be dreaming about fucking me when she rubs one out later.

I pull her chair out for her, to her surprise. "Sorry if that makes you uncomfortable. My mom drilled the behavior into me since I was a boy."

"Aww. A mama's boy? I think it's sweet that she taught you to be a gentleman." She blushes.

"Yeah, she's old school. Guys sometimes look at me funny, but it always seems to work in my favor with the ladies." I flash her a devilish grin as I sit down.

The sexual tension is building, and for some reason seeing her wedding ring makes me want her more, as if it makes the game more of a challenge. I mean, I don't go out seeking married women, but I don't turn them down either. I didn't make any promises to anyone to remain faithful, that's their issue.

She's staring at me with those seductive blue eyes again. Goddamn they drive me crazy. I'm a sucker for beautiful eyes. Her hair pulled back makes them pop even more. I want that red lipstick smeared all over my cock while I stare into them.

"So, what are you having?" she asks.

Definitely not the salad you will order. I can tell she'll order one before the words leave her mouth. It's a funny thing. Honestly, if she ordered a cheeseburger or steak it'd probably turn me on even more. I'll order something decent, but not something that will make her feel bad for ordering salad. Grilled chicken or salmon is usually the go to.

"Oh, I think I'll have the lemon pepper chicken." I look over to see a guy tearing into a cheeseburger. *Fucker.* But it's a price I'm willing to pay to get inside Jessica.

We laugh for a while, trading war stories about work, bad relationships, all the while flirting. Instinctively, I reach for the check when it comes.

"I told you it's on the company." She shoves my hand away, but not before holding on to it an extra split second.

"Sorry, it's a force of habit." Yeah right. I know exactly what I'm doing. She's sharp, so I'm sure she's caught on to some of the bullshit. It's still worth it, as long as I don't overdo it.

The drive back is the longest of my life. I can see her subtly squirming in her seat, anticipating what will come next, afraid that it's going to end, and she's going to be left with nothing but her hand and a cold shower. A memory of what might have been. I smile at the thought and glance over at her.

Don't worry, Jessica. You're going to get everything you want and then some. Just wait.

Tension is building in my balls already as we pull into the parking garage. I'm on the verge of exploding in my pants. This is what I live for, the moments right before. All the anticipation, the sweaty palms, the stomach butterflies, my prick growing hard in my slacks, the animalistic instincts of wanting to drill the woman sitting two feet away, separated only by a console and some cup holders.

Finally, we pull into the parking space, staring at each other momentarily before opening our doors. I pretend to be a little upset that she opened the door for herself.

"I'm so sorry. I'm not used to the royal treatment. My husband would have been inside the building by now."

"Well, why don't you make up for it and walk me to my car?"

That gets a giggle out of her. It's cheesy as fuck, but she eats it up. Jessica holds out her arm to escort me, and I take it. I feel my forearm rub against her tight hard nipple and soft breast. It sends a warm sensation straight to my cock.

The sound of her heels clacking on the concrete as we near my car has my pulse racing. I can see her biting her lip, knowing this is the moment for her. I can practically see everything she is thinking.

Is he really going to fuck me in his car, or in the dark corner of this busy parking garage? Why did he park all the way back here anyway? Did he plan this out?

You're goddamn right I did, Jessica.

We approach my '67 Fastback in the corner and she gasps. I've had it since I was 17 and restored it myself. Classic muscle cars are an aphrodisiac if there ever was one. She releases my arm to walk in front of me. Her ass is driving me wild in that skirt, I want to bite it and hear her squeal.

"Is that a '67?"

Jesus Christ, she knows her cars. I'm now rock hard. "Sure is."

She's walking faster, and I match her pace as she turns to the driver's side door.

"I have to check this out." She runs her hand down the sleek metal in the sexiest way possible.

It's time.

I walk up behind her and press my palm to the small of her back before smoothing it down to her ass. Her eyes close as she presses her tits up against the window, hands resting at the top of the car. I lean in close, next to her ear. "I have to check you out." My voice is a whisper as I watch people get in and out of their cars, nothing between us and them but my Mustang. "I know you want this." I whisper in her ear as I dig my fingers into her ass.

"But, I'm married." Her words are a muttered gasp. She moans lightly as I run my hand up her skirt. She's trying to tease me. She'll find out who's in control momentarily.

"You sure? Last chance?" I exhale in her ear, and walk my fingers up her inner-thigh.

She won't resist anymore. "I think we both know the answer to that."

I rub my fingers back and forth on her hot, wet panties, circling around her clit. A shudder rips through her shoulders. I whisper in her ear again while breathing down her neck. "This is what you've wanted all week, isn't it? Me, behind you, my hand up your skirt, playing with this pussy? Look at all these people. They have no idea I'm about to shove my fingers inside you."

I lean forward and watch as she opens her eyes to see all the people in front of us who have no idea what we're doing. I can see the spark in her eyes as the heat rushes through her veins like a strong narcotic. "You've been dreaming about my fingers inside this tight little cunt, knowing you could lose your job if you get caught. But you don't care, do you? You want it too bad. You need me finger fucking this needy pussy, don't you?"

I slip my thumb inside of her, two fingers swirling on her clit.

"Oh my fucking god, yes." She coos, and spreads her thighs, giving me more access.

I roll one of her tight nipples between my fingers before running my hand over her breast. I can feel Jessica's heartbeat on my thumb inside of her, panties cocked to the side. I focus on her clit, still running my fingers over it in small circles.

"Keep an eye out." I drop to my knees slowly.

"What?" She glances back and down to me as I raise her skirt up, releasing her beautiful peach-shaped ass with black lace panties covering the upper half. She looks back up immediately before closing her eyes, finally giving in to the possibility of being discovered.

I massage her ass cheeks over her panties—I know she wore them specifically for this moment—before pulling them down around her knees, revealing her swollen, pink entrance, already wet and glistening between her thighs. I take my time, working up the back of her tan legs, teasing her slit with the tip of my tongue, before burying my nose in her ass, and darting my tongue into her.

Jessica lets out a slight squeal, and then covers her mouth, looking around to see if anyone noticed. A family of four is walking through the parking lot, oblivious to me tasting her sweet pussy a few cars down. I pick up the pace, flicking my tongue on her clit and probing her while she squirms against the car door, wanting to shout but knowing she can't.

I grip her ass, and turn her around to face me, staring eye-level at her pink, freshly shaved cunt. I can see the lust in her eyes, and it fills me with a sense of power and satisfaction, knowing that she is going to finally open her mind and release all of the tension that's been building for years in every bone in her body. I yank her pussy to my mouth, which sends her bending over me in surprise.

"Oh my god, oh my god." Her words are jumbled under her breath.

I start working my fingers up her inner thigh while teasing her bump with my tongue, licking her wetness that flows down onto my face. The closer my fingers get, the tighter she squeezes her legs together. I lean back and look up to her eyes. "Relax. You're about to experience something you've never felt before."

She loosens, and her legs slowly spread as I work my fingers in, still teasing my tongue on her clit and watching her paw at her breasts. Neither of us give a fuck about getting caught at this point. The attraction is too strong. Her eyes roll back as I take my two fingers to the hilt, curling them up to the ridge I find deep inside. Her walls squeeze tight around my fingers, and I imagine what they'll feel like around my cock later.

Wow, this pussy is tight. She definitely hasn't had it in a while.

The suctioning noise of my fingers pumping in and out of her echoes off the concrete walls surrounding us. My fingers are drenched as she grips the back of my scalp, the insides of her arms pressing those beautiful tits together. I snake my tongue over her and work it in circles as my fingers hammer away deep inside of her.

"Goddamn it, Joel, fuck!" Her words are a little too loud for comfort, but it doesn't slow me down. She's on the edge and doesn't realize what's on the other side. She's always been too afraid to let go and take the plunge. I'm about to take her there.

I lift up my pinky finger. My entire hand and her thighs are shimmering, and covered in Jessica's wetness. I slide my pinky finger between the crack of her ass with each thrust of my fingers, before teasing her tight little puckered asshole with it.

"Holy. Fuck." She's panting, barely able to breathe. Her hips fly back and try to push her ass through the car door, barely able to handle the intense nerve firings ripping to her core. I keep my head buried into her, my mouth latched on to her pussy, increasing the tempo of my tongue and fingers. I remove my head from between her legs for a brief second.

"Just let it happen," I whisper, before diving back in, lashing my tongue across her pussy.

"Okay, okay. Oh my fucking god!" She covers her mouth, trying not to scream as my pinky slides slightly inside of her asshole, and I start rubbing over her g-spot in small circles, my fingers fully plunged into the depths of her.

She's now bucking her hips into my face, fully engrossed in her fantasy. A shudder starts in her legs and shoots through her. Her entire body tenses as her thighs squeeze around my face, her nails digging into my scalp. Her pussy clamps around my fingers like a vise and she convulses against my face, before letting go and coming all over my lips, unable to make a sound. I savor every drop as time freezes for her, all of her sexual energy channeled into her pulsating clit, then shooting to her extremities. She finally relaxes a little, her beautiful breasts rising and falling with each deep breath.

I stand up slowly to meet her with a smile, running my fingers across her tight nipples just to see a shiver jolt through her torso. "You are a genius." A huge smile spreads across her face. "Holy fuck!"

I've unleashed the beast. It's inside of every woman, she just doesn't know it.

She throws me up against the car, and my cock immediately rises to attention as she rubs her palm over it. Her eyes widen as she feels my length in her hand, growing more and more the tighter she squeezes. "I have a few things I want to do to you."

"Do it then." I grin.

She drops to her knees and unbuckles my belt, then pulls it apart with her teeth, one of my weaknesses that I find ridiculously hot. Her bright, blue eyes staring up at me have my balls roiling with tension, and I haven't even been inside her yet.

She unzips my pants and pulls my briefs down with them in one quick motion, releasing my cock like a spring-loaded weapon. "Oh my." She strokes the length of my prick slowly with one hand, the other rubbing on her beautiful tits over her shirt.

She teases my tip with her tongue. A tingling sensation shoots through my legs as soon as her warm tongue curls around the head of my cock. "You've wanted to suck that dick, haven't you?" I stare down at her skirt that's hiked up over her beautiful ass.

She nods, taking me a little farther into her mouth, those blue eyes locked on mine, logging away every reaction in her memory. The inside of her cheeks closing around the head of my cock sends my head flying backward. She's surprisingly better than I thought she'd be. Accountants, they have a wild side to them.

She's now hit her groove, stroking and sucking in one smooth, rhythmic motion. It feels amazing. I can't stop staring at those ruby-red lips spread tight around my stiff prick, smearing her lipstick on the length of it. Suddenly, she lifts my cock and presses it to my stomach, before diving onto my balls and sucking on one and then the other, all the while stroking my cock with her palm.

"You like that, don't you?" She pauses for a moment. I'm not going to lie; it feels fucking amazing. Apparently, I don't answer her fast enough as she spits all over my balls, and takes one in her mouth, sucking forcefully on it.

Goddamn. I'm contemplating letting her have control of this whole ordeal. She might fuck even better than I thought.

"Hell yes, just like that."

"I saw you staring at my tits in the office. You've been teasing me with this dick all week. You want to fuck them. Don't you?"

I grin. What have I created? This woman is incredible, radiating sexual confidence. I'm going to change her life. "Thought you'd never ask."

She looks around as if she's suddenly worried about someone seeing her pull her tits out. Never mind the fact that she just smothered her face with my balls. Before I know it, she has her bra pulled out through her sleeve, and she's lifted her shirt up, releasing a beautiful pair of natural tits that bounce slightly. I want to bury my face between them and never come out.

She squeezes them together and lets her spit slowly fall into her cleavage. "You like these?"

"They're fucking perfect."

"I can't wait to watch you fuck them." She spits on my cock, then scoops under her tits with one arm, her free hand palming my shaft. She slaps the head of my dick on each one, then teases at her nipples with it. I'm about to explode every time her tight pearls rub against my swollen head.

"You like it when I slap your cock on these big fucking tits?"

"Hell yes."

Then she slaps it on her cheek and her tongue a few times, sucking the tip for a moment. Before I know it, she has those gorgeous breasts wrapped around the length of me, bobbing up and down.

God I love my dick between her tits.

She slides me back and forth between them, increasing and decreasing the tempo at will. I fist her ponytail in one hand, and cage her throat with the other. Her eyes grow wide as I thrust my cock back and forth between her tits.

I have to get inside of her. It's uncontrollable.

I grab her under her arms and yank her to her feet. She lets out a slight squeal that turns to a moan as I flip her around and shove her up against the side of the car. Her legs spread, offering her ass to me. "You want my cock inside you?" I smack her ass and dig in with my fingers, as I lean in next to her ear.

"Please."

I slap my dick on her ass from the side, watching the unsuspecting people come in and out of the building. "You've been dreaming about this all week haven't you? This big fucking dick in your tight cunt. It's been driving you crazy. Hasn't it?"

"Mmhmm." She nods.

"Ask me for it."

"Can I have your cock?"

"How bad do you want it?" I grip her by the hair and she moans.

I rub my dick underneath her, back and forth between her soaking wet lips, coating it with her wetness.

"Give it to me. Please. I want to come on your cock."

I pull back on her hair and her face tilts toward the ceiling. Her tits press against the car window as I tease my head around the edge of her pussy. I slowly push into her, watching my cock disappear an inch at a time.

Goddamn. She's so fucking tight and wet.

She's moaning and I haven't even given it all to her yet. I can't wait for her hot walls to spasm around me.

I work about three quarters into her and I start to speed up. Surprisingly, nobody has even turned a head in our direction. I lean in next to her ear. "You ready for me to fuck this pussy?"

"God yes!"

I grip her around the waist and go into jackhammer mode. She starts to scream and bites down on her forearm that is resting on the car. My pelvis is ramming into her ass cheeks, smacking into her as I plunge balls deep. Her tits shake against the glass.

"You like that shit?"

She can't even respond. I grab her ponytail and smack her ass with my free hand, leaving a red hand print.

"You like that? You like being fucked like a naughty little slut?"

"Jesus, I'm going to come again."

"Yeah, come all over this fucking dick you've been craving."

Her hot cunt closes in on me. Her eager pussy clenching for more. She's going to make me blow my load. I reach around and play with her clit, working tiny circles around it while ramming her full speed. Her thighs start to tremble. It's all too familiar now. She knows what she's capable of, and she needs it. I push her past the breaking point and her pussy clamps down on me, her ass and hips vibrating out of control as she bucks back into my cock.

I hear a moan and she pauses, unable to speak. Number two is a success. Her mouth opens to scream but no words come out, just a slight squeal and heavy, deep breaths.

13

I flip her around and lift her against the car, working my cock back inside of her. The car is supporting most of her weight as her tits smash against me.

"Are you going to come for me?" She grips my tie in her right hand.

"Soon."

"I want it on my face." She yanks me closer by the tie, those blue eyes locked on mine. I picture her on her knees, looking at me with those eyes, while I blast her face with my warm load. It sends me into a frenzy. I start pounding into her. The smacking sounds of me ramming her, coupled with my balls slapping up against her tight little asshole, have me in another world.

Tension builds inside me as I continue to fuck her as fast and as hard as possible. I can feel my load inching its way up my shaft as she starts convulsing on my prick with orgasm number three. When she squeezes that slick little cunt around me, it's all over.

"Get on your knees." I slip my prick out into my palm and start stroking it furiously.

She kneels down and looks up at me, her mouth open wide with her tongue sticking out, those gorgeous blue eyes locked back on mine once more, begging for every ounce.

The head of my cock is expanding like a balloon. I can't speak. I can only nod to give her a warning before thrusting and letting loose. I spray across her nose and up under one of her eyes, grunting with each thrust. Her eyes close as I explode all over her. Each stroke of my cock sends a new stream into her mouth and onto her forehead, some of it dripping down to her tits. The sight of her face covered in my hot come makes my balls ache as my pelvis and thighs quiver. Finally, I finish, releasing the last of it onto her soft, pink tongue.

I grab a tee shirt from inside the car. She cleans up the tip of my cock and shaft, before wiping the rest from her face and tits.

I can't lie. I fuck all the time, but it never gets old. Every unique conquest is etched into my mind, a memory I'll keep forever. Each orgasm is like a symphony, in a different location, with different instruments. I look back down into those huge, satisfied blue eyes. A huge grin spreads across her face.

"That was amazing." My breath is labored as I admire her beautiful face.

"You think?" She giggles. "I didn't even know that was fucking possible. Who are you?"

The panty whisperer.

14

VOLUME 2

HOLLY JACKSON

HOLLY JACKSON IS perfectly imperfect. Nothing really stands out about her. Her breasts are small to average size, normal ass, pale complexion, uneventful brown eyes, and yet it all works together to create this work of living art that radiates sexiness. If she could only see herself the way I see her.

She will.

Holly is the controller at a company I'm consulting with. We've been cohorts the last few weeks as I've observed and logged away every possible piece of information about her. Single, no kids, incredibly intelligent, and she's a workhorse, which makes her come off as a bitch to some people. It's something she doesn't like about herself. I know this, because she's told me.

We've been doing the usual flirting every day. The necessary banter to get to know one another in a fun way. But fuck, I've never had to work so hard at this job in my life. This chick is no nonsense in the office. It'll still be worth it.

Today is Friday, my last day here. It's also the day I'll ask Holly if she wants to have dinner, and she'll say yes. I'm going to unlock that conservative demeanor of hers, because the women who put up walls around themselves are the wildest, most exciting on the planet.

I walk into Holly's office with a breakfast quiche. I overheard her tell someone how much she loves them. I'm proud of myself for not eating it on the way to the office. Damn thing smells amazing. Fortunately, I had some self-control and resisted. For the pussy, of course.

"Good morning."

I set the bag down in front of her and she doesn't even look up.

"Are you trying to bribe me? So you can leave early today?" The corners of her mouth turn up in a smile, the reaction I was hoping for.

"I'd never do such a thing. Hell, I wish I could work longer."

"You're so full of it."

Her smile is gorgeous and it makes my morning. Her moans will make my evening.

She opens the bag. "Oh my god. These things are the best. You're a good man, Joel Hannover." She tries to look serious, but chuckles. "I just get so wrapped up in work and numbers I forget about everything, including eating."

Of course you think they're the best. Do you think I got lucky? I learned long ago that women find men who pay attention very sexy. They eat that shit up.

She walks out of the room. Her tight ass rocking back and forth in her skirt sends a warm sensation to my cock. This woman needs to be pleasured. I don't mean some lazy one night stand. That shit is for asshole amateurs. She needs to be pushed to the limit of her mind, and then have breakfast cooked for her the next morning. She deserves to be treated like the goddess she is, not slaving away in a boring, workaholic life. She's going to remember tonight for the rest of her life. If only she knew what I have in store for her.

The flirting has slowly intensified each day, like a good novel. The sexual tension is building towards tonight's climax. A movement by either of us sends sweat to the palms, heat to the face, tingling to the stomach. I can tell it's making her uncomfortable. Good. This is what I live for.

We spend most of the morning working. I can tell she's getting anxious. I haven't asked her out or made any type of move. With every tick of the clock I can sense the disappointment growing in the pit of her stomach.

Don't worry, Holly. You're going to get everything you've ever dreamed of. Every inch of me will be yours.

She stands and walks to the file cabinet.

"What are you looking for?" I ask.

"The payroll procedures file."

"Oh yeah. I wasn't sure where it went. I think I stuck it in the cabinet where you keep all the miscellaneous research folders."

She's fumbling through files. I can tell she's growing irritated by the way she is slamming drawers shut. She's irritated that her files are out of order. Irritated that I haven't once hinted about asking her out, even though I've been driving her crazy all week long. Irritated she hasn't been sexually pleased in a long time.

"I can't find it."

I'm staring at her skirt hugging her in all the right places. She's even cuter when she's flustered. This woman is going to be a wild ride. She has my dick bulging in my pants.

Never waste a good erection.

18

I walk up behind her and peer over her shoulder, pretending to help. I lean in and press my cock up against her ass, talking in her ear.

"I could have sworn I put it right *here*."

I shift my hips slightly, giving her a little feel of what's to come. A slight shudder runs through her arched back. All I can think about is how wet that pussy must be. I want to tear into it right now, but the anticipation is where the fun resides. It makes the reward so much greater. I walk over to my seat, watching her from the corner of my eye. She adjusts her skirt a little and wipes the palms of her hands down her hips before walking back over to her seat.

"Oh, my bad. It's over here on the desk. I swear I put it in the file cabinet. Sorry."

I look at her and smile. She's biting her lip and I'm not going to be able to tease her much longer.

The rest of the day is pretty normal, but she's catching on to the bullshit, and I can tell she isn't going to take it much longer. I'm worried she might bite my head off like a praying mantis if I don't make a move.

"You know—"

Her eyes light up.

"I was thinking that once work is done today, we won't really have any professional ties. Maybe we could grab dinner?"

Her cheeks flush with red hues and she tries to play it cool, but she can barely keep from squirming in her seat. She smiles and stutters, yet manages to get a few words out. "Umm, yes. I would like that."

"Awesome. I'll pick you up at seven. Text me your address." I stand up from the chair and walk to the door.

"There's still five minutes of work left."

I glance back and she has her hands on her sexy little hips. I throw her a wink. "That's what the quiche was for."

I'm cruising in the Fastback, drawing looks at every corner. She really is a thing of beauty. Highland green like Steve McQueen's in *Bullitt*, only his was a '68. I don't know if I've ever loved a woman more than this car, well, other than my mom. It's the only car I've driven since I was 17.

I pull up to Holly's house. I'm certain she heard me and is standing by the door. They always are. She'll make me wait 30 seconds before she answers, so as not to appear desperate.

I walk up and knock. Sure enough, 30 seconds later the door opens, and she looks gorgeous. I have flowers, of course. She's getting the whole package tonight. Her dress is black and mid-length. It would be conservative for most, but it's probably the sexiest thing in her closet. It doesn't matter. She looks smoking hot in it, and it's going to end up on the floor.

I open the car door for her like a gentleman, courtesy of Mrs. Hannover who would wallop me with a cast iron skillet if I behaved any differently. She's impressed, but I think it's more with the car than my chivalrous nature.

I walk around and get in the driver's seat. Right now is my favorite part of the evening. When I turn the key, her panties are going to melt. I can see her waiting. I fire up the Fastback, and my baby continues her winning streak. The vibrations under the hood send her squirming in her seat. Sorry for ruining your panties, Holly. I'll just have to rip those off of you.

Soon.

"Wow. I am in *love* with this car."

"She's taken." I flash her a grin.

I pop the clutch and hammer it about halfway, enough to get a rush of adrenaline running through Holly as her back is forced against the seat. It's standard procedure for my dates. I quickly slow back down to cruising speed.

"Oh my fucking god." She immediately covers her mouth, like it's a sin to drop an f-bomb.

Won't be the last time she says that phrase tonight.

"Holly?"

"Yeah?"

I lean over next to her. "It's okay to say fuck in front of me. We're grown-ups now."

She punches me in the arm playfully as I laugh. There's that smile.

"You have a smart mouth on you, you know that?"

You're going to find out how smart my fucking mouth is. Very soon.

"I know. I probably kid too much."

"No, it suits you. It's cute. You don't overdo it." She twirls her hair with her index finger.

"Well thank you. I'm glad someone appreciates it."

We pull up to the restaurant—it's on the first floor of a large hotel—and I reluctantly hand my keys to the valet. I'm not happy about it. I usually avoid these guys.

Holly must sense my frustration. "Aww, are you afraid she's going to cheat on you in the parking garage?"

I cover my mouth and gasp. "She would *never*."

Holly smiles and it sets me at ease a little. I love watching women genuinely laugh, especially those who take life far too seriously. She smiles and wraps her arm around the inside of mine as we walk to the table. Good. She's feeling more confident, more certain that hot, deprived pussy is going to be filled with this cock, instead of two fingers in a lonely bathtub.

Dinner is full of jokes and laughter. She orders a steak, medium-rare, and I want to bend her over the table to express my gratitude for her appreciation of meat. I love a woman who orders a steak and knows how it should be cooked. I had a date order a steak well-done once, and put ketchup on it. I never looked at her the same again.

The check comes and she tries to reach for it, a noble gesture on her part.

"If you want to hold my hand, all you have to do is ask." I smile.

I pull the check back over to me as her hand slides down mine. She blushes and sinks back in her chair.

"Sorry. I'm just used to picking up the bill."

"Jesus, what kind of guys do you date?" I stare at her like she's a strange looking insect.

"Homeless derelicts, apparently."

"So, tell me something about you. Something nobody knows." I lean in toward her.

"Oh, we're going to play that game?" She stares at me.

Who is this woman? Four hours ago she was an uptight dictator.

"I'm an adrenaline junkie. I went skydiving once and it was incredible."

"Do you do many exciting things?" I take a sip of water.

"No. I'm always at work. It's really all I do, if you couldn't tell." She laughs.

"You know what you need? A vacation, doing a bunch of daredevil shit." I smile.

"I don't have time—"

"Make time. You only get one shot at life. You work too hard. Make it count for something."

I have to use this to my advantage. I'm now on a mission to take her on a thrill ride, an erotic roller coaster of sorts. My heart races at the thought. "I have an idea. I'll be right back. Don't move."

I get up and head to the front of the restaurant. I have a buddy who works here, and I need a set of keys. Yes, it's all part of my plan.

When I return, I'm ducked down like some kind of secret agent. I lean over into Holly's ear. "Come on. I want to show you something."

Her eyes grow wide and she takes my hand.

We're riding up the hotel elevator, and the tension is already building in my stomach. Part of me wants to rip her dress off and pound her up against the wall. It's not a bad move. I've done it before. I have something much more exhilarating in store for her though.

We approach the 30th floor, and I tell her to close her eyes. She doesn't resist. The elevator door opens and I guide her down a hallway. I pull out the keys, open a door, and we step out onto the roof that overlooks the city skyline. She's not the first to visit this rooftop, but she is the first to receive this kind of treatment.

"Can I open my eyes yet?" Her hands shake, and my grin widens.

"No. Just wait. It'll be worth it."

She has no idea what she's about to experience. The sounds of cars rushing past rise to my ears and the urban smells grow intense with each wind gust that rushes between the buildings.

I walk her over to the edge of the rooftop. There's a small wall about three feet high on the edge of the building. She faces away from me, and I stare at her once more in her black dress. I have to get inside this woman.

Soon.

"Keep your eyes closed, and relax." It's more of a command than a request.

I breathe heavily in her ear, and exhale my warm breath down her neck and shoulder.

"What are you doing?" she whispers.

"Exactly what you want me to do. What you've wanted me to do all week."

"Oh really? What's that?" She giggles.

Her eyes are closed and her chin is tilted up as the night air rushes over our faces. I run my hand over her ass and pull up her dress, inching my fingers slowly towards where she needs them. She squirms and squeezes her legs together.

"Just let it happen." I nibble on her ear lobe.

She parts her legs as my fingers caress the insides of her thighs, massaging around her entrance. I brush my knuckles up against her. She exhales. Loud.

"Keep your eyes closed. Enjoy the moment."

I drop to my knees and shove her dress up over her toned ass to reveal a sexy black thong. Yeah, she came prepared. My right hand reaches around the front and I start to tease her little bump in small circles. She moans and playfully tries to push her ass away from my face. She needs to learn who's in charge. It's time for her to get what she came for.

I pull her thong to the side with my left hand and bury my nose in her ass, running my tongue the length of her slit and then swirl it around her swollen pink entry.

"Fuck." It's a breathy moan.

That's right.

I stop momentarily and marvel at her ass, slapping lightly as I massage it. She coos again. I take both hands and spread her cheeks apart, darting my warm tongue into her little puckered asshole, teasing the tight ridges.

"Oh my god." She bites out.

"Keep your eyes closed." I continue to flick my tongue around her asshole as I slide my hand up toward her cunt. I tease around her before slowly snaking my fingers inside, one at a time.

Goddamn she is so fucking wet and tight. My cock is so hard I might pass out. I imagine how amazing it will feel when she squeezes those walls around me, refusing to let me out of her.

My fingers slide farther into her, exploring everything, leaving nothing unpleased.

"Harder." She whispers into the night.

I'm not one to say no to requests.

"Like this?" I start ramming my fingers to the hilt and she clamps down around them like a vise. Her pussy is coating my hand with her wetness and I'm running my fingers around the ridge I've found deep inside of her, feeling every one of her reactions to my touch, knowing she'll spend the rest of her life dreaming and fantasizing about this moment.

"Yes." Her legs stiffen.

She's holding back. Still afraid to let go. I have to push her past her breaking point.

"Relax. Let me please you."

Her thighs loosen and I turn up the heat. I go to town on her needy little cunt, ramming the fuck out of it with my middle and index finger. I rub her wetness around her asshole with my thumb, teasing it while I enjoy her reactions. She's about to release.

"I'm going to come." She's nodding and moaning. The sound is muffled, like she's biting down on her arm.

Goddamn right you are.

I time her moans with the smacking sound of my fingers hammering her pussy. Right when she's on the edge, I bury my thumb inside of her wet little asshole and give her what she deserves. She starts shuddering and convulsing. I can feel the energy ripping through her thighs, down into her toes, and up through her shoulders as she tightens around my fingers.

I don't even give her time to catch her breath. I want that pussy, now. I flip her around and her freshly orgasmed, bare pussy is in front of me at eye level. Standing up, I smack both hands on her ass and scoot her up onto the ledge. Her eyes are still closed, and her dress is hiked to her hips. I rip her panties off and shove them in my pocket before taking my pants to my ankles.

My dick wobbles free in the night air.

"I want it." Her chest heaves up and down as she pants, still not having recovered from coming on my fingers.

I've set another one free. She's cock hungry and ready. I line the head of my cock up with her eager cunt and shove it into her. Usually I take my time and go in for the slow entry, but I can tell she wants it rough. I was right.

"Fuck!" She bites into her arm when I go into her.

I start pumping. Hard and fast, the way she wants it.

"Fuck my pussy," she moans.

Jesus Christ! I may blow my load in a matter of seconds at her words, as they fuel my hips to speed up. I pound my thighs into her, and her tight little hole feels fucking amazing as she grips me with her legs. I wrap my arms around her back and lean her out over the edge of the building. It's an extremely gutsy move, but it's about to pay some fucking dividends.

She moans as I fuck her as deep and hard as possible. I lean down to her ear. "Open your eyes."

She slowly pries her eyes open and turns her head to see the busy street 30 stories down. Fear rushes over her face momentarily and she claws at my shoulders, her body tensing around me. It pulls me deeper into her as her walls constrict. I groan as her hot cunt hugs tight around my cock. The fear on her face quickly turns to pure ecstasy as the adrenaline courses through her veins.

How's that for a fucking thrill?

"You like that?" I ask with a smile.

Her petite body quivers, tightening as I pound her as deep and hard as possible. She leans her head back and goes limp in my arms, completely trusting me, as I keep ramming her over and over. My balls slap against her asshole as she reaches back for her hair.

"Fuck!"

I lift her up, slip my cock out of her, and start slapping my hard dick on her little cunt, teasing back and forth on her swollen clit. Her eyes are locked on mine, fear and elation running through her body. I flip her around and fist her hair, yanking her ear up to my mouth.

"You want to get fucked hard?" I say through gritted teeth.

"Jesus Christ." She can barely breathe.

I yank her hair harder and bite down on the shell of her ear.

"Yes." She nods.

"You want me to pound this cunt from behind?" I reach around with my free hand and slap my hand across her pussy, then tease her clit in lazy circles.

"Oh my god." Her head flies back and I tighten my grip in her hair while I lick up her neck and back to her ear.

"Yeah. Rough from the back is how you want it. Isn't it?" I fist my cock and slide it under her pussy. I can feel the heat on my shaft, but I fight the urge to take what's mine. I growl into her ear. "Yeah, I fucking thought so. You like when I tell you how you want to get fucked?" I tease back and forth underneath her again.

"Mmhmm." She nods, her body trembling in my hands.

I squeeze her hair tighter and slap my cock up into her clit. She moans.

"Tell me you're a little whore." I tease the head of my dick through her wet folds.

"Fuck." She moans.

I let go of my dick and slap her across the ass, leaving her pale skin red. My dick grows harder at the sight.

She winces, but pushes her ass back to me. "I-I'm a little whore."

I reach down and run my hand across her pussy. I breathe into her ear. Her pussy is so hot and ready for me that I can barely contain myself. I turn her head and press my lips to hers, our tongues intertwining as I shove my fingers inside of her. She moans into my mouth as I take them as deep as possible into her core.

I slip them out of her and release her from the kiss, then reach up and shove my fingers into her mouth. "Can you taste how bad your pussy wants my fucking dick?"

Her head bobs on my fingers, her eyes wide and locked onto mine. She swirls her tongue around them as I slip them out of her mouth.

"I'm your little whore, Joel. Please fuck me." She whispers through her labored breaths.

Jesus.

This fucking woman. I shove her forward so that she's bent over the wall and smack her ass again.

She squeals.

I fist my cock and slap it on her bright red ass cheek, then run it underneath her and up and down her ass crack. I reach underneath and paw at her perky little tits through her dress and squeeze hard on one of her tight nipples.

She tries to rise up and I shove her back down and line my cock up with her pink pussy.

"You asked for this."

I lean over her back and grab her by the hair, pulling her head up to me. I bite down on her shoulder and plunge into her from behind, then start ramming her up against the wall. Her head drops when I let go of her hair, and she's looking down at the street below. I can feel the energy and heat ripping from every limb in her body down into her pussy. She starts bucking her ass up against me and I pound it right back in perfect rhythm, shaking her whole body. Gripping her around the waist, I start railing her as hard and fast as humanly possible.

She's trying to scream, but can barely get any words out as I grab her hair and yank her up toward my face. I clap my hand over her mouth, and fuck her to the rhythm of the screams that build in her lungs and land against my palm.

She's in heaven. I can tell she's never been fucked like this before, only dreamed about it while wrapped up in her bed sheets.

My mouth is next to her ear. "Tell me. Tell me what you want. I already know what it is."

The sound of our bodies slapping together echoes off the brick walls of the building. I take my hand off her mouth and smack her ass again. She tightens around my cock and moans.

"I want your cock in my ass." Her words are a jumbled mess, the sound of her voice vibrating from how fast I'm fucking her.

"What's that? Couldn't hear you."

She moans something like a whimper. "I want you to fuck my ass."

A wry smile spreads across my face, her words music to my ears. I could tell she wanted it dark and dirty the first day I met her.

I let my spit drip down in between her ass cheeks, while still pummeling her from behind. I work my natural lube into her clenched asshole with my thumb while she reaches back and spreads her ass for me. I'm getting it nice and wet as I slip my cock out of her.

I drop down to my knees.

"Play with that pussy. Give me a show."

She rubs her hand back and forth over her mound, cooing and moaning up at the bright, full moon. I spread her ass cheeks, revealing that beautiful asshole that's about to have my cock buried deep inside of it. I spit all over it and shove my tongue inside. She jerks suddenly and starts rubbing her clit harder and faster. I get her nice and wet, darting my tongue in and out.

I work my fingers inside, readying her for her wildest fantasy, then grab a small container of lube from my jacket pocket. I'd planned ahead. I squirt some on her ass and my fingers, then start working it in slowly. She's moaning as I take my fingers in and out of her, her tight hole loosening more each time I press them in.

"You ready?"

She nods. "Please."

Now, the plunge maneuver doesn't work on the asshole. That's a good way to send her to the hospital while catching a case of blue balls in the waiting room. No, slow and steady is the way to enter the back door. I tease the engorged head of my cock up against her. I start to ease my way in, back and forth.

She tightens at first, but quickly relaxes and lets me inside of her. I grab the lube and squeeze more out on to the shaft of my dick, slowly teasing my head in and out of her. The last thing I want to do is hurt this incredible woman. She utters a slight squeal as I watch my cock slowly disappear.

Oh my god, it is so fucking tight.

This isn't going to last long.

"You feel so fucking good." I grab the sides of her hips.

She coos. "You like it?"

"God yes. You want me to fuck it?"

She nods. "Hard."

"I know." I dig my fingers into her hips and start to pick up the intensity. My prick has now spread the lube through every inch of her. She's completely relaxed and it's time to go to town.

27

I speed up, slowly increasing the tempo as her head flies back up to the night and she moans louder with each thrust. This woman is all about being fucked in her ass. The harder I pound her, the happier it makes her. I love every minute of it.

She reaches back and spreads her ass cheeks wide, letting me feel the depths of her. My balls are slapping against her hot cunt and I'm not going to last much longer.

"I'm going to fucking come."

"I'm getting close." I grunt, as I feel my balls start to tense up.

"Make me come." Her voice is eager, and incredibly hot.

I don't even respond. I just keep fucking her as hard as I can, trying not to blow before she gets off. She starts to tremble. Her ass clamps down on me, and I slam into her. She wraps up number three, her asshole spasming around my cock as I feel her pussy come underneath me.

I reach down and grab her lightly by the throat, and pull her up close to my face so I can see her eyes.

"Where do you want it?" I smack her bright red ass cheek, but this time her eyes light up with excitement.

"Blow it all over my dirty little hole." She grins as her eyes roll back.

Motherfucker! It's time.

"Spread those fucking ass cheeks, *wide*." It's a command as I grind my jaw.

She does as I say.

My cock swells inside of her and my load rushes from my balls into the head of my dick. I can't hold out much longer. I pull out of her ass and start stroking it furiously.

"Keep 'em spread!"

She looks back at me with those big brown eyes, her hands gripped on her pale ass cheeks dotted with freckles, covered in redness from being spanked like a whore. She yanks her cheeks further apart, giving me a perfect view of her pink hole, her beautiful pussy beneath it, still glistening and streaming down her legs.

My head tilts toward the moon and I belt out a grunt. My first wave is a direct hit and shoots straight onto her. Elation covers her face as my hot jizz lashes across her asshole and pussy. I keep stroking, emptying my balls completely. Some of it lands on her ass cheeks and sprays up to her lower back as I mark her as mine.

I'm still convulsing, fisting my cock as I thrust a few more times, shaking out every last drop. I reach out with my fingers and scoop some of it onto them. Leaning over to her, she opens wide, and I bury my fingers into her mouth as she licks them clean, savoring every drop with that filthy tongue of hers.

I pull her up and flip her around to me before planting a long soft kiss on her lips, then lean into her ear and whisper. "Did you enjoy the dessert?"

She grips my forearm with her nails. "You are a fucking god."

No. No I'm not. I'm the panty whisperer.

VOLUME 3

HANNAH SMITHEE

TOMMY BLACKWELL HAS been my best friend for the past 20 years. He's a good looking guy, early 30s, light-brown hair, in decent shape. The thing with Tommy is that he still acts like we're in sixth grade. The man is a genius, but nobody would ever know it when first talking to him. He takes nothing in life seriously. It's one of the things I love about him. It's also one of the things I hate about him. He happens to be absolutely hilarious, which helps his cause, especially with the ladies. Women love a good sense of humor, and he has more than enough for all of them.

It's weird. Most guys with his level of intelligence are socially inept. I had professors that were smart like that. I couldn't understand a word they'd say. Conversations were just awkward. I'd have Tommy teach me calculus and it was a bunch of 'shits' and 'fucks' coupled with a crystal clear understanding and explanation of the concepts.

I got him a job at my company because I thought maybe it'd turn him into an adult. Poor thinking on my part, but he's actually damn good at it. He's great with the numbers, and his personality scores him all kinds of points with clients. He'll call me from titty bars, hammered out of his mind with executives for multi-million dollar accounts, and they always sign on the dotted line. It's ridiculous.

We're both in the office this week so we decide to grab lunch at the cafeteria. I walk around the corner.

"Hey look, it's the Panty Whisperer." His words boom throughout the building, alerting everyone in earshot to my presence.

I shake my head, expecting nothing less from him.

"You still call yourself that, right?" He smiles.

"You should know. You gave me the name in high school." I sit down at the table across from him.

"Bullshit, that title is self-proclaimed, you arrogant bastard." He laughs, looking around to verify that people heard him.

What do you do? I have to smile and roll with it. "You're such a dick. Some things never change. How's life?"

"Good, good. You?" He cuts me off before I can reply. "Have you seen the new intern walking around? Jesus, dude. She's on fire—

probably 21, junior at the college. You'll know when you see her. She has an ass that would launch a thousand ships."

This piques my interest. I prefer pleasuring women my own age, but I always take delight in ruining a younger woman's sexual encounters for the rest of her life. The frat boys just don't quite measure up.

"Oh yeah? Accounting major?" I raise my eyebrows.

"Yeah, her name is Hannah Smithee. No, no, no, wait, maybe it's Hannah Titties? Or Hannah Bent Knees? Fuck man, I can't remember."

Jesus. People are staring at us now and my face has to be pink. He's the only person on earth who can get this kind of reaction out of me.

"You do realize we are at work, right?"

He ignores my question. "Went by and saw your mom the other day."

"Oh yeah? She loves your sorry ass. No idea why. I'm going to church with her this weekend."

"Yeah, I know. She told me. I bet she's praying for you to find a wife right now and have some grandkids." He mocks me in a falsetto. "When are you going to settle down, Herbert? Find a nice young woman to marry and give your poor mother some grandbabies? When are you going to stop banging the jezebels and repent of your sins?"

Good god, I nearly choke on my drink I'm laughing so hard. I have to change the subject.

"So, you gonna make a run at Hannah?" I flash another smile.

"Are you?"

"Oh, I dunno. Maybe."

"Then no."

"What? Why? You don't want to compete with this?" I lean back and give my abs a quick rub.

He looks at me like I'm stupid. This should be great.

"Let me break this down for you—"

I can't wait to hear this high-level analysis of our women-bedding skills.

"Now take me, I'm a solid B-plus—an 8.5 if you will—in the sack. Hell, maybe even an A-minus if I trim the ol' dick beard up and give the illusion of an extra inch or two. Herbert Hannover is the fucking Good Will Hunting of banging. Why would I go up against him? Sorry, I don't fuck from a position of weakness."

"Oh, we're using poker analogies now?"

"Exactly, Sir! *Poke her* analogies to be precise. I forgive you for your pronunciation error."

We both start laughing uncontrollably and people start to stare. We don't care at this point. He continues, barely able to keep a straight face.

"One does not follow up Herbert Hannover in the bedroom. It's a Newtonian law of coitus."

"A what?" I shoot him a blank stare.

"I'm not about to look like an amateur, fucking your leftovers. You're an impossible standard to live up to." He breaks out his Emperor Palpatine voice. It's creepy and eerily precise. "Search your feelings, Herbert, you will know it to be true."

Jesus Christ, this guy. I can't stop laughing. "You're fucking crazy. Anyway, I better get back to work. Great catching up. Let's grab drinks next week."

"Let's do it."

I start to walk away and he says, "Love you, buddy."

I shake my head. "Love you too."

I'm sitting at my desk going through paperwork, wanting to blow my brains out. I look up and Hannah walks past. Tommy wasn't lying. At about five-foot-six, her height is the only thing average about her. She has blonde hair and blue eyes. She's tan and absolutely gorgeous. A pair of khaki pants shape her ass and hips perfectly, and a tight-fitting red shirt showcases a set of perky 34C breasts, but still leaves a little to the imagination.

I glance up and Tommy is in the distance. His hands are on his desk and he is pretending to jackhammer his desk drawer. I damn near shoot water out of my nose as Hannah walks up to me.

"Are you Joel?" She smiles.

Her lips are gorgeous, and they'd look fantastic wrapped around my cock.

"I am. Nice to meet you. You must be the new intern."

She blushes a little. They usually do. It's not my fault.

"Yeah, for the week anyway. It's an assignment for class. I have some files for you."

She sets them down on my desk. I'm now very interested. I usually have a rule about not shitting where I eat. No office hookups. The last thing I need is to feel awkward every time I'm at work. Interns are an entirely different story, as long as they aren't the boss's daughter. I do have limits. But the others, well, I feel they deserve some kind of parting gift.

"Well that's cool. Should look good on your resume." I can't stop staring at her eyes.

"That's what I'm hoping." A 'please fuck me' smile spreads across her face.

"So, do you know someone in the office? How'd you end up here?" I tap some keys on the keyboard and pull up my email, so as not to appear too interested. But I am most definitely listening. It's time to gather some intelligence.

"No, it's all set up through the college. Maybe you could show me around? I don't really know anyone." She chews on one of her fingernails and rocks her hips slightly.

I can't stop glancing over, her needy pussy just a few feet from my face, covered only by a thin layer of khaki material and no panties. I checked for the lines earlier when I sized up her ass in those pants.

Oh, I'm going to show you something.

"Well, I'm a little busy today. Maybe we can grab a drink after work? I can tell you all about the place."

"Oh my gosh, that would be great. I'm so nervous. It's my first real job. I don't want to screw it up." She bites on her lip and I want to drag her into a closet and tell her all about the place right now.

"No worries. I'm sure you'll fit in just fine."

I stare up at those eyes of hers once more. *I'll fit in you just fine.*

"Why don't you meet me back here around 4:30? I know a place we can go right around the corner."

"It's a date." Her words go up a note, and her face is tinged a pink hue.

This is going to be a fun week. Her ass sways back and forth in those khakis as she walks away, slightly peeking over her shoulder and smiling. She's used to driving the boys at college crazy, but the hot ones always get tired of 20-year-olds shaking on top of them for two minutes and then rolling over. They all want a mature man to teach them the ways of the bedroom.

Now honestly, I could fuck Hannah later this afternoon. But that's just boring and then it would be weird all week. For some reason women always grow attached after a little roll in the sheets. It'll be more fun to tease her. Make that pussy yearn in her panties every day, then give her a memory that will haunt her sex life for the rest of her existence.

Goddamn, that ass though. It'll be hard to hold out all week. I can't wait to wrap those legs around my head and bury my face into that cunt while she comes all over my tongue. My cock is stiff as a fucking board and I'm going to have to hang out at the desk for a few minutes to get things in order down there.

"Hey buddy!" I damn near fall over in my chair. Tommy is standing right behind me laughing his ass off.

"Why don't you stand up and give us a show in that circus tent ya got going on down there?" He's laughing, and even I have to smile as I glance around to make sure nobody hears him.

"You're such a dick. But an honest one, I'll give you that. That girl has a fucking body on her, Jesus."

"Told you man. I saw the look too. She's probably in the bathroom wringing those panties out as we speak."

I shrug. "What can I say? It's what I do."

"Guess you'll be busy tonight. Was going to see if you wanted to hang." He stares at the floor.

"Nah man, I'm free. I'll take care of that Friday, after I lay the groundwork all week." I hit send on an email.

"You work way too hard at this. Complete lack of efficiency in your game, Sir." He checks the screen on his phone.

"Oh, it'll be worth it. You should take notes." I look up at him and smile.

"Shit. I guess it's not being cocky if it's true. I'll catch you tonight, swing by around seven? Play some fuckin' Halo?"

"Sounds good, man. I'll catch you then."

I give him a fist bump and he walks off. I'm certain he's going somewhere to avoid work.

It's 4:30 and my little fuck project is standing at my desk, looking around. I walk up to her.

"Sorry to keep you waiting. You ready to go?"

"Yes. Can't wait to get out of here." She brushes her palms down her hips.

Sorry to disappoint, Hannah, but you're going to be performing solo until Friday. Rules are rules.

I hold the door open for her on the way out, and she frowns. They always do.

"So it's just right up here around the corner?" She points to the end of the block as people stream out of buildings in skirts and suits.

"Yeah, it's a cool little place. Not too loud, where we can hear each other talk." I put my hand on her lower back and guide her out of someone's path.

I can feel her tremble a bit as she smiles at me. "Sounds perfect."

We finally reach the place and walk in. I lead her to the back and she orders a vodka and Red Bull. I'm immediately reminded of her age. I order a Glenfiddich on the rocks.

"So, you're an accounting major?" I turn back to those blue eyes after the waitress walks away.

"Yeah, my dad is a CPA and there's not a lot of promise in a fashion degree."

We both chuckle.

"This is true. So what do they have you doing?"

"Grunt work. Filing and running errands."

Her eyes are amazing. I thought they were bright blue at first but there are hints of a smoky gray that make them very unique. She keeps talking and all I can think about is staring at those eyes while she tries to swallow my dick.

The conversation isn't as bad as I thought it'd be. She's pretty bright, and not just another airhead with a nice ass. Not that there is anything wrong with that, but it's nice to be able to hold a conversation without a bunch of 'likes' and 'totallys' and 'oh my gods' that usually accompany the sorority types. Well, I don't mind the latter so much—when they're moaning it.

"You'll do fine, I promise. Just get used to the guys in the building ogling you. We don't get a lot of beautiful interns in the office. You'll probably get hit on quite a bit."

She blushes. "Well, that's sweet. I'm sure it won't be as bad as at school. The boys there are so immature."

I like where this is headed. She's about to tell me how she prefers older men.

"It's why I don't date college guys. Nothing but dick and fart jokes."

I'm a soothsayer, using my powers for evil.

"Oh yeah, what kind of guys do you date?"

She grins and leans slightly toward me. "Older, mature men."

"Is that so?"

The flirting has officially begun and she is eating it up. Her cheeks are turning pink, she's flipping her hair around, might as well have a sign on her head that says 'fuck me, Joel.'

"Yes—" She pauses while the waitress sets our drinks down. Hannah stirs her drink and licks her lips. "So, tell me about you. Are you married?"

"Nope."

"Girlfriend?"

"Nope."

"Aww, why not? You're a nice guy—" She takes a large, slow drink. Her lips around the straw have my dick warring with my zipper for freedom. "—and cute too."

She's getting bold, I like it. Vodka Red Bulls will do that to a 21-year-old co-ed.

"Well, that's nice of you to say. Humoring an old man."

"I'm not joking." She reaches out and grabs my hand and laughs momentarily, before slowly sliding it back over to her side of the table.

Interesting, she's more forward than I thought. It should make the week fun.

We laugh for a while and finish up our drinks. I walk her back to her car.

"Don't sweat it. You'll do great. You okay to drive?"

"Oh yeah, I'm fine."

Damn right you are fine.

My dick is about to explode. *Must have self-control, stick to the plan.*

I give her a peck on the cheek and thank her for a nice time. She hovers for more, but I walk away before I throw her up against her car and show her how a real man treats a woman.

I can sense the excitement, and the disappointment as I'm walking to my car. I know she sees me get in the Fastback and that pussy is calling my name more than ever. Enjoy your fingers tonight, Hannah.

The next morning is fairly mundane. I actually get some work done. Tommy is nowhere to be found. Shocker. We played Halo until two in the morning. He probably called in.

Hannah walks up and I can tell she needed more than her fingers last night. She's in a tight little skirt today with a button-up blouse.

Her tits are nearly on full display and it's not making things any easier on my crotch situation.

I'm flattered you dressed up for me, Hannah. I truly am. But rules are rules. You have to wait until Friday like all the other interns.

"Hey there." Confidence radiates from her.

"Hey, you. Make it home okay?" I pretend to forget her name, a timeless classic, then look at my screen to check emails, though I can still see her in my peripheral vision.

"Yes." She frowns slightly.

"They give you an actual assignment today? Or just having you fetch more files?"

"Still fetching files." She leans over my desk, her tits right in the corner of my eye, and whispers. "You weren't lying. I caught Bob and a few others checking my ass out earlier."

Jesus, I can barely concentrate. She's bent over my desk and I should be behind her right now, pulling her hair and smacking her ass, my name on her lips. Not stuck in this chair with a lap full of hard dick.

"Well, it's not a bad view." I lean back and my eyes dart to her ass in that skirt. I want to bury my face into that fucking thing.

She slaps me on my shoulder playfully. "Joel!"

I like the way she calls my name. I could get used to it. I think I *will* get used to it.

"You're bad!" she says.

"Sorry, couldn't help myself." I grin.

"Mmhmm." She rolls her eyes, but arches her back just enough to show me more of her breasts. "You want to grab a drink again?"

"Can't tonight, sorry." I am an oak.

Disappointment runs across her face as she drops her head down slightly.

"Have to go see my mom. Can I get a rain check?"

"Of course. We can do it another night." She stands up and adjusts her skirt into place.

"Sounds good." I ogle her ass as she rocks it back and forth for me.

Sorry Hannah, it's going to be those fingers again tonight. It's coming soon though. I promise.

I was out of the office on Wednesday. Had to go to a client's place. They're trying to fuck up my game. It's okay though, I'll recover. It was probably a good thing to spend a day away from Hannah. The flirting is getting intense and I don't want my dick to start thinking for me. It does that from time to time.

Of course Hannah happens to walk by within 30 minutes of me sitting down at my desk on Thursday. She's in a skirt again with a tight, low-cut blue top and black heels.

"Missed you yesterday." She winks.

"Yeah, I had a last-minute client meeting."

"Thanks for leaving me all alone." Her flirting is going to earn her a smack on the ass if she isn't careful. Or maybe that's what she's hoping for.

"I'm sure you got plenty of attention to hold you over. You have quite the fan club." I nod to three guys checking her out while she talks to me.

"Yeah, well, not from anyone I wanted attention from." She leans over my desk again.

Motherfucker. This girl, I swear. I think I'm going to have some fun with her today. My dick isn't taking no for an answer.

"Is that so?"

I can tell the flirting is getting to her. She's biting her nails. I'm anxious to see just how brave she's going to get. She leans over by my ear, giving the boys behind me a show.

Her breath is warm in my ear, and she whispers, "You jealous of their view?"

Well, my cock just shot to the ceiling in a fraction of a second.

I start to lean back and have a look and she stops me with a hand on my shoulder.

I look at her hand and then back to her eyes, and whisper under my breath. "Maybe."

"You going to do something about it?" Her nails dig into my shoulder.

Those fucking eyes of hers coupled with her incessant flirting, are too much. It's time to take action.

"Follow me." My words are a growl under my breath.

Her eyebrows rise. I walk through the bullpen of cubicles and she's on my heels. Glancing around to make sure nobody is watching, I grab her by the arm and shove her into a maintenance closet near the stairwell.

As soon as I walk in she attacks me, and our lips lock onto each other, tongues circling furiously. My hand goes straight to that ass.

She's actually a decent kisser, but she needs to know who's in control.

I flip her around and press her up against the wall. Hard. I swipe her hair to the side and start breathing on her neck, growling into her ear.

"Is this what you wanted?" I reach down and yank her skirt up over her ass. Jesus Christ, no fucking panties. I am going to have some fun with this one. I reach around her hip and start circling her clit with two fingers, then spread her quivering folds, sliding my fingers back and forth between them. Goddamn she is fucking wet.

She gasps.

"You like the way I touch your pussy, Hannah?"

She nods, moaning slightly.

"You know anyone could walk in here, at any time. You'd lose your internship. You'd fail your class." I speed my fingers up, focusing on her clit, as I press my chest into her back.

She gasps for air and splays her fingers against the wall. "I don't fucking care."

"I bet the college boys don't touch you like this, do they?" I reach around with my left hand, grab one of her breasts, and start teasing at her nipple through her shirt and bra. "Fuck no they don't. Bet they don't make you fucking come either, do they?" I fist her hair and pull her ear next to my mouth. "And a little slut like you needs to come, don't you?"

She nods and I slide two fingers inside of her. My cock juts up against her ass when her heat squeezes tight on my fingers. Her thighs quake around my hand.

I squeeze her hair tighter at the thought of making myself wait until tomorrow to fuck. "Yeah you fucking need to come. The college boys don't treat this pussy right. They don't know what it needs, do they?"

My slippery fingers explore every inch of her aching cunt, and each time I hit the right spot I feel a jolt of ecstasy rip through her body. She doesn't answer my question. I slip my fingers out of her and smack her ass.

"No." Her voice cracks.

"And you want me to make you come? Don't you?" I smack her ass again, harder this time.

She moans at the impact, and then nods.

"That's a good girl." Sucking down the side of her neck, I stop at her shoulder and bite down on it.

"Fucking hell." Her words are a whisper through heavy breaths.

I release her hair and drop to my knees, then grip the backs of her thighs. "Spread your fucking legs."

She does as I say and I knead her ass roughly with my fingers before spreading it apart. She tries to push it back into me, but I want to make her wait a little longer while I stare at how gorgeous it is. It's a fucking work of art.

"Did you like teasing me with this fucking ass of yours all week?" My thumbs inch closer to her pussy, massaging her inner thighs.

"Mmhmm." Her legs start to shudder as one of my thumbs grazes her shaved cunt.

"Yeah. Now it's my fucking turn." I lean in and tease the tip of my tongue the length of her slit.

She gasps and tries to shove her ass back into me for more. I let go of her and then slap both hands on her, and hold her right where she is, this time spreading her even wider.

"Keep your fucking ass still. I'll eat your pussy when I see fit. Got it?" I dig my fingers in hard enough to leave marks.

"Yes." She's panting, and I grin.

Sometimes you have to break them a little before you give them what they want.

"Yes what?" I bite down on her ass.

"Yes, Sir." Her words are a whimper and her panting intensifies.

"Better." I slide my tongue up the insides of her thighs, brushing it against her slick folds, feeling her legs and ass start to quake around my face.

"You ready to come for me?"

"God yes."

I reach around to the front of her thighs and yank her back toward my face, so that she's bent over at an angle now.

"Fuck." She coos.

"Spread that pussy for me."

She reaches down and parts her dark pink folds with two fingers, exposing her clit. I flick my tongue on it gently and she squeals like it's the first time anyone's ever tasted her properly. I grip her ass once more, spreading and admiring the view simultaneously. Both of her shaved, bare holes on full display.

It's time.

I lean in and snake across her clit with the tip of my tongue, my nose buried in the depths of her ass. Her head flies back and her ass bucks up against my face as I increase the tempo. She's panting for air, on the verge of screaming as she bites into her forearm pressed on the wall.

I lean back and growl. "Rub that fucking clit."

She starts circling it with two fingers as I watch and listen to her perform.

She's getting close, I can sense it. Her legs and ass are tightening up.

It's time to make her wildest fantasies come true.

I work two fingers inside of her while she circles her clit, then angle the tips of my fingers up to her g-spot and full-on finger fuck her as fast and hard as possible.

Muffled sounds come from her mouth on her forearm.

Good.

She's shaking all over and starts bucking her ass wildly onto my hand. She's about to release all of that sexual energy built up inside of her when I plunge my tongue into her ass and speed up my hand.

Every muscle of hers stiffens and she starts shuddering on my fingers.

I stand up behind her and grab a fistful of hair, then lean over, breathing into her ear as I finger fuck the shit out of her tight cunt.

"Shit!" She squeals when I pull her head back to me. I want to hear her words, her labored breaths, while I master her pussy with my fingers.

Her voice pauses as the orgasm rips through her. Her breaths cease, her hips and ass shaking uncontrollably before finally relaxing.

I hold her up, my mouth next to her ear, fingers still knuckle-deep in her. "You're welcome."

I slip my fingers out of her and pull her skirt back down over her ass. She turns to look at me, her entire body shaking. I lean in as if to kiss her, and then grab hold of the back of her hair once more. Her eyes widen at my grin. I raise my fingers up to her mouth and she takes them both, licking and sucking her sweet nectar off of each one, her eyes locked on me the whole time.

I squeeze my grip on her hair as she reluctantly lets my fingers slip out of her soft, wet lips. I kiss her on the forehead and let go of her.

"Well, if you'll excuse me. I need to be getting back to work now, Hannah."

I own your ass.

She stands there with a look of disbelief, her beautiful tits rising and falling in rhythm with each deep breath as I walk out of the closet.

No cock for you today. That comes later.

It's Friday morning and I'm feeling rather pleased about giving Hannah a little sample of what's to come. She walks over to her desk and finds a card I left for her. She opens it up and there is a hotel key and note inside.

"6:00 p.m., Hilton, room 408. Don't be late if you want to play."

I watch her smile as she reads it, biting at her lower lip. That pussy is on fire right now, I can tell. It's all she'll think about today, imagining her little hole being drilled with my cock. Goddamn, I can't wait to fuck this girl.

Tommy walks up, seemingly out of nowhere. "Did you enjoy your little romp in the closet? You have no self-control. I swear."

"How the hell did you—"

"I know everything, Sir." He smiles.

"Just gave her a little taste. Or was it me that had a little taste?" I chuckle.

"I want some motherfucking details, bitch."

"A gentleman doesn't kiss and tell."

"You're so full of shit." He shakes his head playfully.

"Just wait. She'll get it good tonight. I'll give you the details later so you can have yourself some jerk-off material. Maybe I'll show you the video, if you're a good little boy."

"Oh, you prick. I hate you so much right now." He grins.

I start to walk off.

"See if she has a friend," says Tommy.

"If she does I'm banging that too. Sorry buddy, survival of the fittest."

I see a middle finger fly in the air as I turn the corner.

I have to decide how I want to play this tonight. What type of girl is Hannah? It should be easy. I'm sure the boys at the college have been less than stellar.

All day long she's been eye fucking me. Perhaps I ate that pussy too good. I hope I didn't make her fall in love. It happens sometimes, and it never ends well.

I'm sitting at my desk and the clock reads 4:30. My stomach is always in knots, regardless of how many times I've done this. Goddamn, I love the anticipation. I can't stop thinking about those perfect fucking tits. I haven't had the chance to get a good look at them yet. In two hours they're going to be bouncing in my face in time with Hannah's moans. The thought of it sends blood straight to my cock. I'm anxious to see how well she can suck my dick. If previous actions are any indicator, it's going to be a good night.

The time has come and I pull into the hotel parking garage. My week-long investment is about to pay off. I have a bag with me. I plan on making a little gift for Hannah's enjoyment, and my own of course.

I walk down the hallway, and I can feel my heartbeat in my dick. It intensifies with every step toward the door.

I insert my key and open it. There are lit candles all around the room with the lights dimmed. Rose petals are spread out on the floor. There sits Hannah, cock hungry and ready with a huge smile on her face.

I walk to the bed slowly and she starts to get up.

"Stay there." I hold up my hand to halt her.

I stroll to the corner, open the bag, and pull out my video camera.

"What's that for?" She tries to sound reluctant, but I know it makes her hot and eager. She can't wait to fuck me on camera. I don't respond.

I walk over and hand her a box with a ribbon on it.

"Oh, but I didn't get you anything." She frowns.

"Don't worry." I grin. "It's not for you."

She opens up the box and it's a set of lacy black lingerie.

"How do you know it'll fit?"

"Oh, I sized you up the first time I saw you."

Her eyes widen.

"Go change in the bathroom. I'll wait here."

She walks off with her gift, working that ass and looking back at me smiling. I can feel the tension building in my balls already. This girl is fucking dirty.

I undress down to my boxers and set up on the bed with the camera in my hand. A few minutes pass and she emerges from the bathroom, wrapped in a bath robe. She knows exactly what she's doing.

She eyes me on the bed and flashes a seductive grin. Apparently my ab workouts have been paying off because I can damn near feel the heat from her pussy melting in those fresh black panties under the bath robe.

She slowly starts to untie the cotton belt in the front as she approaches. When she gets to the bed she opens it up to reveal her gorgeous, begging-to-be-fucked body. My cock is rock hard, pointing up at the ceiling, and she licks her lips like she wants a taste. Jesus Christ, her tits corralled tight by the black lace bra look phenomenal as she drops the robe to the floor and starts towards me.

I have the camera trained on her eyes, capturing every one of her reactions. Her mouth is practically watering as she eyes the stiff cock standing at attention in front of her. I set up the camera on the table, making sure I have the perfect shot before returning back to my original position.

She's crawling on her hands and knees toward my dick, but bypasses it to come in for a kiss. As our warm, wet lips press against each other, my hands feel for her tanned ass and she starts grinding her pussy up and down my swollen prick, her soft breasts rubbing across my chest. I can feel the heat from her cunt through the thin layers of fabric separating us. I'm so hard the tip of my cock is slipping inside of her through both sets of underwear.

She releases my bottom lip with her teeth, leans into my ear, and whispers, "Can you feel how wet I am for you? You asshole, making me wait all week for this—" Her nails dig into my scalp as she grips the back of my hair.

Goddamn.

She reaches down and starts rubbing the length of me. I can see the spark in her eyes as she wraps me in the palm of her hand. She starts sizing it up for that mouth of hers, probably wondering if she can fit it all in. She eases back down the bed toward my dick, and wraps her lips around the shaft over my briefs. I'm already about to burst.

"Are you going to play with it all day, or are you going to suck it? It's what you want isn't it?"

She doesn't respond, just keeps feeling every inch, gripping it in her palm and staring at it. She scoots forward on me and arches her back, slowly running her breasts along the sides of my face. She backs her ass over my dick, grinding on me a bit before licking down my chiseled six-pack, dragging her nails down my chest.

She pulls my shorts down and my cock springs free.

"Holy shit."

It bounces back and forth in front of her face. I grin.

She grabs around the base of my shaft and slowly licks up the length of me, locking her eyes onto mine.

"The things I'm going to do to this—" She slaps it against her cheek.

Her warm tongue sends a shiver up my spine as she starts to lick around my swollen head. I want to fuck her mouth so goddamn bad. She's working hard to make sure I enjoy myself, like she has something to prove. I can't stop staring into those eyes of hers.

"Swallow it."

"You sure?"

Her teasing is going to get her in trouble.

"Now." I reach down and gather her hair into a ponytail, gripping it with one hand, making sure I get the perfect shot on the camera without her hair in the way.

She keeps teasing me with her tongue. "You want your cock in my mouth?" She licks around the head.

I tighten my grip on her hair, answering her question for her. She moans.

She spits on my shaft and it sends my free hand reaching back for the headboard.

I'm still holding her hair when she plunges her mouth down the length of me, damn near taking it all at once.

"Fuck." I groan, drawing out the word.

She starts bobbing on my cock, taking it down her throat. Jesus Christ. She's sucking me off like a fucking porn star. I can see the excitement course through her body as she strokes on my shaft while sucking up and down on me before taking it all, tightening her lips around the base of my shaft and shaking her head wildly.

She comes back up and lets out a gasp as she releases my cock from her mouth. A smile forms on her face, knowing that she is pleasing me. She keeps stroking me off while staring into my eyes. I can guarantee none of the frat boys she's sucked off at parties have lasted through that. This is not an ordinary college girl.

"You like that shit, old man?"

Oh, you little bitch.

"You didn't just say—"

She buries my cock in her throat again, and I'm about to blow in the back of her mouth already. I can't have that. I manage to control myself as she keeps jamming my dick into my throat, gagging herself on it. I need to take control of this situation.

She's still staring at me, her eyes watering, with those beautiful lips wrapped around me, taking me into the side of her cheek now and sucking hard on the head of my dick. I can see the imprint from the tip of my cock next to her jaw. I tap it a couple times with my free hand.

"You like sucking this dick?" I yank on her hair, forcing her head to tilt up toward me.

She nods and giggles. It's sexy as fuck.

"You want me to shove my cock down your throat? Fuck that dirty mouth of yours?"

She nods and grins once more as I fist her hair and start thrusting my dick into the back of her throat, causing her to gag.

"You fucking like that shit, don't you? Naughty little bitch."

Her eyes are wide and she knows who's in control now. I pull her head up and she gasps for air.

"I want it all," she says.

Jesus.

"You want it all?" I grit my teeth.

I yank her up by the hair again and slap my cock on her cheek.

She giggles and nods again, before taking me in her mouth. I shove her head down on me and thrust my hips into her, giving her every inch as her neck and head start shaking. I thrust a few more times as I force her head down onto me, my balls slapping against her chin. She claws at my legs, hard enough to leave marks.

I need to taste that sweet cunt of hers again. "I want that fucking pussy on my face."

I reach down and grab her under the arms and pick her up in the air. She squeals.

I drop her down on my mouth, hard, while she grabs the top of the headboard. My left hand yanks her panties to the side, revealing her shaved pussy. Her clit is inches from my eyes as I lean up and press my entire mouth to it and suck before giving it a nibble and grazing it with my teeth. Her head flies back toward the ceiling, blonde hair flipping across her shoulders.

"Holy shit." She grinds her wet cunt back and forth on my face.

That's right.

The insides of her thighs are wrapped around my head, and I am in heaven.

I grip her hips tight with my fingers, holding her steady. I suck on her clit and dart my tongue around it as her wetness start to run down the side of my face and land on the sheets. She reaches back and unclasps her bra, releasing those beautiful tits. They bounce perfectly as she tosses her bra to the side. She massages them as I slide my hands to her ass, and she grinds her cunt up and down my mouth with her eyes closed. Her scent is intoxicating and her moans have my balls tense as I reach down and stroke my cock.

I let go of my dick after a few tugs and grab her around the waist with both hands and lift her from my mouth. "You want to get fucked?"

She nods.

"How bad do you want it?" I bring my hand up and start playing with her clit and dart my tongue in and out of her.

She can barely control herself.

"Please. Fuck." She moans.

"You want me to shove my cock in here?" I lick the length of her pussy, flicking my tongue on her clit, then look up at her. "Fuck you till you scream my name and come on my dick like a good little whore?"

"Yes." She nods, her voice eager.

I smack her across the ass and her pussy jolts against my face. I make sure to lick it one last time before she backs off. "Get the fuck up and sit on it then."

She stands up, still hovering over my face while I yank her panties down to her ankles and she kicks them off. She starts to sit on my cock, and I flip her around.

"I want to watch that ass bounce on this fucking dick."

She bends over toward the end of the bed and flashes her pussy in my face before hovering it over my cock. I slap her ass hard and she lets out a squeal that echoes through the room.

"Slap my dick on it."

She reaches back between her legs and grabs a handful of dick. She starts to tease it around her ass and slaps it against her swollen, pink entrance.

"That's a good girl." I palm the base of my shaft and she moves her hands out and plants them on the bed. I slide my cock between her ass cheeks and then under her slick folds, slapping it against her clit.

"Tell me you want it." I tease my head around the edges of her.

"Please put it in me."

I barely part her lips with the tip. "Spread your cunt."

She reaches back and spreads it wide, revealing the warm, pink pussy where my cock wants to be.

"Is this what you want?" She lowers herself on me a little farther.

You're goddamn right it is.

I ease into her slowly as she pushes her ass down onto me and lets out a moan. I watch it disappear inch by inch. Fuck, she is so fucking wet and tight.

I grab the video camera and start to film my cock filling every inch of her.

"Ride that dick."

Her ass bounces up and down on me, clapping against my hips. My eyes close and my head flies back toward the headboard. This girl knows how to fuck. Her warm walls grip tight around my shaft as she takes my cock whole with each bounce.

She's definitely a screamer.

"Oh my god. Fuck my pussy. You like the way I ride your dick?"

You know I do, Hannah.

"Oh my god, fuck me, fuck me!"

I begin thrusting in rhythm as wet flesh smacks together and echoes throughout the room. I can see her breasts bouncing out to the side. I need a better look at them.

"Turn around. I want those fucking titties in my face."

I'll be goddamned if she doesn't swing around in one smooth motion, my cock never leaving her. I'm pointing the camera up at her, getting those perfect, perky breasts in the frame as she paws at her hair and runs her hands over them, taking every inch of me inside of her. She gets up on her feet and starts bouncing up and down, ramming my dick into her as her ass slaps against my legs, her breasts shaking uncontrollably.

"Grind on my fucking cock."

I set the camera on the nightstand and grab her hips, pressing her down on top of me, going balls-deep as she squeezes her walls around my dick. She grabs her hair with both hands and arches back, pushing her beautiful tits out in the air as she rocks her hips back and forth furiously on top of me, moaning and squealing.

"You want more?"

"Fuck yes. Give it to me."

I slap one of her tits and watch it bounce back and forth before gripping her around the waist, pushing her down as hard as I can while I thrust up into her, shoving my cock as far inside her as humanly possible. She goes crazy, her hips bucking, grinding her clit against me.

"You like that shit?"

"I'm gonna come."

Yeah you are.

"Do it then! Come on my cock, you dirty bitch."

I slap one of her tits again, harder this time, and then palm both of her breasts and squeeze her nipples.

She's grinding me as fast as she possibly can with her eyes closed, barely able to breathe.

I reach up and wrap my arms around her back. I yank her down to me, smashing her tits against my chest while her ass keeps bouncing on top of me. Her head is next to mine and I exhale into her ear, nibbling on her earlobe. I get up on the balls of my feet and start pumping into her as she bites down on my shoulder and screams into it. It sends a wave of pleasure down to my stiff dick, fueling my hips as I keep pounding into her. My balls slap up against her tight, clenched asshole.

Her mouth is in my ear. "I'm going to fucking come."

Her words vibrate, and it sounds like she's stuttering, I'm pounding her so fast and hard.

I dig my fingers into her cheeks with one hand, and lightly slap the side of her face. Her eyes get big.

"Do it then."

I full-on fuck into the depths of her harder and faster than I've ever fucked in my life, and she starts to tremble on top of me, trying to push away. She looks like she's about to lose control.

"Let it happen. Come on my dick, now." It's an order, not a request.

She gives in to the pleasure. I can feel the energy building in her core. Her eyes roll back slightly and her toes curl as the nerve endings in her body start firing on all cylinders. Her pussy walls quake and then clamp down on me as her entire body jolts multiple times.

She pushes against me and I let her go. A scream catches in her throat, and the words won't come as she convulses on my dick.

She slaps me across the face—I'm surprised at how much it turns me on—before she starts riding my cock like a mad woman, bouncing as hard as she can and taking it all inside of her.

"Jesus fucking Christ." I grunt, which elicits a wide smile from her.

She slaps me again.

"You like it when I ride this dick hard? This pussy wrapped around your cock, and these big fucking tits in your face?" She grits her teeth and leans down, smothering my face with her soft breasts.

Adrenaline courses through my veins. This is a pleasant surprise. I haven't been this turned on in a long time. I'm about to blow my load inside of her. I take one of her tits in my mouth, and bite down on her nipple, before shoving her off of me and standing up on the side of the bed. She's lying on her back, staring at me with those big eyes, practically begging for me to finish her off.

"You going to stand there or are you going to fuck this pussy?" She rubs her fingers on her clit in little semicircles.

"Get your fucking ass over here." I reach around her legs and yank her to the edge of the bed.

She squeals and slaps her palm on her mound. I lift one of her legs with one hand and smack her ass as hard as I can.

"You want to get fucked like a whore?"

"God yes." She squirms against the bedsheets.

I reach down and dig my fingers into her thighs and shove her legs apart. "Spread your fucking legs."

Leaning over the top of her, I grab a handful of hair and squeeze it so hard my knuckles turn pale. She squirms. I slap my cock up and down on her clit, sliding over the top of it with my shaft.

I lean down and run my teeth up her neck, before hovering next to her ear. "Where do you want me to come, Hannah?" I trace the curve of her cheek with my index finger. "On this pretty fucking face of yours?" I slide my fingers across her lips and then shove them into her mouth. "In your mouth, like a little slut?" I exhale into her ear and little pebbles form down the skin on her neck. I reach down and slap my hand on one of her tits, and then roll her nipple between my index finger and thumb. "Come on these fucking tits?" Her hips rise off the bed, knowing my hand is coming for her pussy next. I slide down to it and she shudders, my words in her ear stimulating every nerve in her body. I slip two fingers inside and take them deep.

She gasps as I curl them up and run them along the ridges inside of her. "Or should I blow in your cunt? And watch you take it all like a filthy fucking slut?" I slide my fingers out of her.

She moans at the last bit. Loud. I know what her answer is.

I bite down on her shoulder and shove my cock to the hilt, burying it as far and as deep as possible. I return to her ear and growl into it. "Remember this shit. Because nobody will ever fuck you as hard as I'm about to."

I feel her body tense underneath me at my words. Her pussy squeezes around my cock like a vise and she starts to pant as I push harder into her, my cock deeper than it's ever been inside of her.

She starts to scream and I clap my hand over her mouth and watch her eyes grow wide. I rise up and put my free hand around her throat, and start pounding her pussy as hard as I can.

She's trying to scream and her voice is vibrating against my palm from being rammed at such a rapid pace. Her eyes widen and I stare into them as I pump my cock so hard, my thighs are destined to leave bruises on her ass.

My hips smash into her and send her breasts in every direction. She cups both of them, moaning into my hand as I fuck her so rough she won't be able to walk tomorrow. My balls start to tense and my load is inching up my shaft.

She starts shaking and I feel her tighten around me as her eyes roll back. Her hips arch off the bed and I grip her around the waist and thrust my cock as deep as humanly possible. It's her most intense orgasm yet. Her pussy constricts so tightly I lose control.

My legs start to tremble and I go full bore, pumping in and out of her like a madman. She starts shaking, another orgasm rolling through her body, and she can barely breathe now as she claws at the sheets.

"Fucking take it." I grunt, barely able to speak as my cock kicks hard inside of her, and I release. Hot spurts of come shoot into the depths of her. I pull out and fist my cock, still pumping it as one last wave lashes across her freshly-fucked pussy.

My vision gets blurry for a second, and fuzzy stars pass in front of my face. I stroke the last little bit from my cock and let it drip down onto her quivering cunt.

I finally collapse on top of her, kissing along her neck as she drags her nails lightly across my shoulder blades. Our sweaty bodies stick together as we catch our breath. I brush my hand across her cheek and drop a kiss on her forehead before getting to my feet.

I stand there, our eyes locked on one another for a moment.

She stares up at me in amazement, knowing she'll never be fucked like that again as long as she lives.

Her cheeks turn pink, and she covers her face, as if suddenly embarrassed. "Oh my fucking god. That was—just. I want a copy of that video. You are fucking amazing."

I know, Hannah. That's why they call me the panty whisperer.

VOLUME 4

OLIVIA ROTH

TOMMY AND I are both in the office again this week, so we decide to meet up for a drink after work. Now he may say otherwise, but I don't go out actively seeking ass, especially when I'm hanging out with my friends. That's just rude. When I hang out with someone it's to hang out with them. That's not to say if a piece of ass finds me, that I am going to turn it down.

This day is dragging, and I can definitely use a scotch. The clock is ticking down at the speed of a snail, and I can practically taste the Glenfiddich. Finally, it's 4:30 and I head out to meet him.

I walk through the door of our usual watering hole and haven't even spotted him yet when he hollers from across the room.

"Hey Herbert, over here buddy."

He has a shit-eating grin covering his face because he knows how much I hate that name. I learned long ago to just ignore it; otherwise, it only gets worse.

I walk up and give him a fist bump. He already has a drink waiting for me so I let the name calling slide.

"What's up?" I have a seat.

"Jack shit. It's going to be a long week. Beedernuts is driving me up the wall."

John Beeder is the VP of our department, and the guy really is a true asshole. I can empathize with Tommy, but it's hard to feel sorry for him because he invites so much conflict. He has a hard time keeping his mouth shut.

"Yeah, I told you to avoid that prick at all costs." I reach for my scotch.

"Fuck him." Tommy stares off in the corner.

"What is it?"

"Oh, couple of chicks over there, eye fucking you of course. I don't know why I don't hang out with ugly motherfuckers. It'd give me a decided advantage." He chuckles.

"Oh really?" I start to turn around.

"Don't even think about it Whisperer. The boys are hanging out right now."

"You're the asshole that pointed it out. Fine, I won't look. Happy?"

"As a matter of fact I am. Keep your fucking light saber in your pants, Obi Wan."

We both belt out a laugh. I never tire of *Star Wars* references.

We chat for a while, bitching about work, trading war stories. I have to take a piss and it's going to mean making eye contact with the girls in the corner. Tommy's eyebrows narrow as I start to get up, and he's staring me down the entire time I walk by the girls' table.

They smile at me and blush, of course. I give them a quick wink.

One of the girls is a skinny redhead, and I have my eye on her. It may be stereotypical to say they have a crazy streak, but it usually rings true. I'm not sure what it is about her, maybe it's just the scotch, but she's going to get it. The girls look like they're in their late twenties, probably hanging out and bitching about how unfulfilled they are in the bedroom. *A guy can wish, right?*

When I walk out of the bathroom, I head to their table. Tommy scoffs and asks for the check. I feel bad, but I can't shake this redhead from my mind. Her friend is giving me the 'fuck me' eyes too, but I'm not interested in her. She looks boring.

"Hey ladies." I walk up to their table.

"Hi," says the redhead.

"Hey, see that guy over there? The one asking for his check?"

"Ummm, yeah." She looks surprised.

"Do me a favor and throw up the Star Trek hand gesture at him. You know the one I'm talking about?"

They start giggling.

"Yeah, I know it, hang on."

Tommy glances over and she gives him the ol' 'live long and prosper' hand gesture of the Vulcans. I don't even turn around to look. I just wait for it.

"Trekkies? You fuckin' kiddin' me?" His voice booms through the bar. I'm laughing so fucking hard inside it's killing me.

"That was absolutely perfect. Thank you. Now, if you'll excuse me, I need to go tend to my friend before he has an aneurysm." I start to turn and head back to our table.

"But you just got here." Her voice is needy.

"Give me five minutes." I walk over towards Tommy and he looks pissed.

"Thought the bros were hanging out, Judas? Selling out for 30 pieces of pussy, aren't you?"

"It was just a joke. Calm down Jar Jar." I flip him the bird.

"*Nobody* calls me Jar Jar." He tries not to laugh.

"I'm here, bro. Let's grab another one."

"Nah, fuck it. I already tabbed out. I was just fuckin' with you. You're going to nail that redhead anyway. I can see it in her eyes."

"Yeah, I think you're right." I glance back over to her.

"Catch you tomorrow?"

"Yeah, buddy."

I give him a quick fist bump and he heads to the door.

"So, what are your names?" I walk up to the table.

They both turn red and giddy.

"I'm Olivia," says the redhead.

"Jennifer," says the other.

"Joel. Nice to meet you."

"Yes it is," says Olivia in a flirtatious tone. I'm already imagining grabbing hold of that red hair and pounding her from behind.

My cock must be thinking the same thing, because he's readying himself for battle in my pants.

"Sorry about the Vulcan earlier. He's in a foul mood."

"Why?" asks Olivia, pretending to be interested.

"Oh, the doc botched his sex change. Gave him a micro penis."

They both nearly shoot their drinks out of their noses. If only Tommy were still here.

"You're a funny man, Joel." Olivia runs her hand onto mine.

That's right. Wait until that hand is fisting your hair later.

I don't have to wait long. Her hand goes under the table and starts up my thigh, working its way towards my erection. Redheaded and crazy, confirmed.

Her friend can definitely see she isn't going to win the prize.

"Well guys, I'm getting tired. I'm going to head out."

"Okay," says Olivia almost instantly.

Fuck, this chick wants it bad. She's practically giving her friend the boot. I'm not working for it at all. It's almost too easy. The crazy look in her eyes makes up for the lack of a challenge.

Jennifer gets up and leaves after paying her bill. I scoot over next to Olivia and make myself comfortable. She stares me in the eye, rubbing up and down my stiff prick over my slacks. I feel I should return the favor. I work my hand down between her legs. She squirms a bit at the first touch but quickly relaxes and parts them for me. She has a skirt on and I'm working my way under it.

I take her hand and remove it from my cock so I can get in closer to her. I lean in next to her ear.

"It's all about you right now."

Yeah, right.

I start circling her clit and she's already wet as fuck. Closing her eyes, she lets me work my magic as I slide into her panties. She rests her hand on top of mine as I take two fingers and work them inside of her. Squirming ensues on her part.

I lean in to her ear. "I'm going to make you come in front of all of these people."

Her eyes widen and she mumbles. "Fuck."

I'm at an awkward angle but her hot cunt is making me forget my troubles. I'm not about to stop. I increase the tempo, running my thumb on her clit in little circles while sinking my fingers into her and gripping upward. She lets out a small moan and covers her mouth.

The waitress walks up and she tries to pull my hand out of her skirt, but I shove my fingers even deeper.

"You guys need anything?" she asks.

"No." Olivia squeaks at the waitress as I smile.

"I'm okay for now," I say.

"Okay, well just let me know."

The waitress walks away and I whisper, "Is there something you need, Olivia? Just ask for it and I'll give it to you."

"Your cock."

"What's that? I couldn't hear you."

She attempts to glare at me, but she's too dick hungry to look mad.

"I want your fucking cock in me."

I'm next to her ear. "Not before I get you off under this table."

I start flicking her clit with my thumb and working my fingers while she silently gasps for air, moaning under her breath.

"You almost there?"

She nods quickly. That's right.

Her thighs are quivering around my hand and I can feel the energy ripping through her legs.

"Shh." I look her in the eye while I continue finger fucking her tight cunt under the table.

She starts to buck her hips on my hand, trying to remain stoic above the table.

"Come for me, now." I growl into her ear.

She lets loose and comes all over my fingers. Her chest heaves and falls with each quick breath, and her legs stiffen. She shudders from the waist down, and tries to stifle her moans.

Her orgasm finally subsides and she is eyeing me like a predator as I slip my fingers out of her slick pussy. "I need you right now."

Well that's music to my ears.

"Follow me." I grab her hand and lead her toward the restroom, looking around to make sure nobody sees us.

She opens the door to the ladies' room and it's empty. I'm keeping a look out and all of a sudden I'm yanked into the bathroom. She locks the door behind us and stands there staring at me, still breathing heavily.

She drops to her knees—so that she's eye level with my cock—and yanks me over to her by the back of my legs. She rips my belt loose and undoes my button and zipper. Before I know it, my pants are at my ankles and she is staring my cock down like it'll be her last meal. She takes it in her hand and teases the tip with her tongue while staring up at me.

"I want to taste you."

I immediately grow another inch in her hand.

"Do what you want with it."

"You want it in my mouth?" She continues stroking me.

It's a stupid question. "Fuck yes."

She takes me in her mouth and starts sucking me off hard, stroking my cock with both hands.

My head flies back toward the ceiling.

She spits all over the tip and starts fondling my balls before taking all of me into her mouth, then releases my cock for a moment and looks back up at me. "Fuck my mouth."

"Gladly." I grip the back of her hair and start fucking that dirty mouth of hers while she gags on my dick. I'm relentless, and she loves it. I grip her hair even tighter and ram my cock farther down her throat. The harder I fuck her mouth, the more excited her eyes grow.

I start to pull out to give her a breather and she swallows it whole, shaking her mouth on the base of my shaft.

"Fucking hell." My hand snakes through her hair.

She leans back and spits down the length of me, stroking me back and forth. It feels amazing. Her tiny hands make me look huge.

"I want your cock in me." She continues stroking me off.

I yank her up by her armpits and shove her against the door.

"How do you want it?"

"Hard. Fuck me hard." She groans.

I'm about to give her everything she's wishing for. I hike her skirt up over her tight, pale ass. I'm amped up. I love a girl who likes it rough and isn't afraid to ask for it.

"Spread your fucking legs." I sweep the inside of her right leg, and she spreads, showing me that dark pink pussy I'm about to put my cock inside.

I bend down to her ear and whisper, "You want this cock in your pussy?"

I fist my dick and slap her ass with it, rubbing it up and down on her ass cheek and under her needy cunt.

"Fuck yes."

I slap her ass hard, leaving a pale handprint that quickly turns red when the blood rushes back to her ass.

She coos.

I lick my hand and slap it over her pussy, rubbing my palm over her entrance, my fingers circling her clit. I fist her hair into a ponytail with my other hand.

"Spread your cunt for me."

She reaches down and parts her swollen lips.

I hold my cock around the base and press it into her slowly, leaning over her shoulder so I can see her eyes close. She claws her nails into the door.

"Sh-shit." I'm only in about three quarters and she can barely take it. That won't do.

I pull my cock back out of her and quickly plunge it back in. She moans loud enough for the whole bar to hear, neither of us giving a fuck at this point.

"Yeah, you like that shit. Don't you?"

I pull back out and ram it into her again, loving hearing her moan and beg for more. I repeat this three more times and on the fourth I plow into her and start pummeling her from behind. She bites into her arm, her petite frame shaking with each thrust.

I reach around and yank her shirt up, exposing two small, perky breasts. I grab one of them and squeeze her hard nipple while I continue pounding her pussy from behind. My pelvis is slapping into her ass. The smacking sounds of her wet cunt echo through the bathroom.

She's in another world right now.

I fist her hair and yank her ear up near my mouth. "You gonna come for me?"

"Yes. I'm so close. Please don't stop. Keep fucking me." She reaches back and digs her nails into my thigh.

"Do it then. Come on my dick."

I feel her tighten a little as she bites down on her arm once more. I start railing her harder and faster and she squeals, staring back at me before her eyes roll up in her head.

"Fuck. I'm coming." She starts to scream and I slap my hand over her mouth and yank on her hair.

I slam balls-deep into her, and she is on cloud nine, having the most intense orgasm of her life. She starts bucking her hips back into me and I can feel her screaming into my hand. I grip her hair even tighter and slide my hand from her mouth to her neck, still pumping into her slick cunt as hard as I can. She clamps down on me, refusing to release it. I fucking lose it. I'm about to blow.

"Get on your fucking knees." My words come through gritted teeth.

I slip my dick out of her and it's glistening, coated in her wetness. I start stroking it off as she drops down to her knees in front of me, her back up against the door.

She sticks her chin out in the air while I pump my prick furiously with my hand. I nod quickly and she opens her mouth.

My legs and ass start to spasm, and I can't hold out any longer as my load rushes to the head of my cock. I release, and it sprays across her cheek. The second wave hits her square in the mouth, and I can tell she loves every bit of it. She holds out her tongue as I squeeze out every last ounce, standing there in a daze, light-headed.

I slap my swollen head on her tongue a few times and then rub it along her cheek, wiping up my come with it. She starts licking it off of the tip of my prick and then swallows the head of my cock. I can feel her tongue cleaning all of it while I'm inside of her mouth.

I finally slip out of her. She holds out her tongue with a puddle of my jizz squarely in the middle of it, then closes and swallows it all. She opens back up to show me it's gone.

"You are one dirty bitch." I give her a post-fuck smile.

"That was fucking amazing." She gasps for air.

I hoist her back up under her arms, and she shimmies her skirt back down over her ass. I grab some paper towels and help her get the rest out of her hair.

We walk back out to the table—hair disheveled, both sweaty and panting. The waitress and a few others stare at us.

"Sorry, she lost a contact." I flash them a huge grin.

Olivia starts giggling as we near our table and I throw some cash down for my tab.

"Sorry, I have to get going. I have some stuff to get done in the morning."

She looks down at the ground and gives me a pouty lip. I don't like where this is going.

"You're leaving me already?"

"I'm really sorry. I have to get some sleep."

"But—"

I cut her off before she says something about wanting to go on a date, or even worse, that she loves me. Yes, it happens.

"Hang on." I grab a pen from the waitress and scribble down a fake number. I'm not even sure it has the right amount of digits.

"Give me a call, okay?"

"Okay." She's back to smiling.

Success.

Goddamn, I dodged a bullet there. I walk out of the bar into the cool night air, feeling like a new man.

You have to be more careful, Joel. The panty whisperer is nobody's boyfriend.

VOLUME 5

JOEL HANNOVER

"CALM DOWN LIVI."

She sobs in front of me.

"I don't know why he would do that? Why would he give me a fake number?" Olivia is in tears.

Well, maybe if you didn't bang every decent looking guy who smiles at you. "I don't know, sweetie. Come here."

I wrap her up in a hug. She is a mess, and this guy is a fucking asshole. I mean, she shouldn't be fucking guys in the bathroom of bars and expect a relationship, but he could have at least humored her, let her down easy.

"I fucking hate him. We have to make him pay for this." She weeps into my shoulder, again.

Man, this guy did a number on her. Olivia is a sweet girl and the best of friends. I've known her since we were ten years old. But dealing with men is not her strong suit. She has no self-control. She falls hard as soon as she meets somebody, and always gives it up way too soon.

"Just give it time. You'll find a good guy."

"No, fuck him! Fuck that asshole. You have to get even with him for me. If anyone can, it's you. Guys always fall for you."

I really wish she'd make them work harder for it. She's a pretty girl with a lot to offer. Not to mention, watching them squirm in anticipation makes it way more fun.

She smiles, and I don't like where this is going.

"We're going to make him fall in love with you. And you're going to crush him." She paces back and forth across the living room.

"Look Liv, I think you're just upset and living in the moment. Just calm down and give it some time."

My words don't even register. She just stares at me. I have to say something. "Come on. I'm really busy. I have work and umm—"

"Please. For me?" She's begging now.

Great.

I can see I have no choice. She's not going to drop this. This is so childish, and I don't know why I'm about to agree to it. Maybe because she's always been there for me, and I have to admit, teaching this prick a lesson sounds pretty fun. He's clearly an arrogant douchebag.

"Fine. I'll do it."

She starts jumping up and down, clapping her hands. "Thank you!"

She's lucky I love her to death.

"The waitress said he's in there all the time. It's at McConnell's. Take Brandi with you. He's already met Jennifer. He had a friend with him last time and she can keep him occupied."

"Am I supposed to sit there every night? Waiting for a guy who may or may not come in? I have no idea what he looks like."

All I get is a stare in return. "You'll know when you see him. Trust me. He'll hit on you."

"Fine, but you're paying my bar tab for the week." I fold my arms across my chest.

"I will. I promise."

What am I getting myself into?

Brandi and I walk into the bar and head over to a corner booth. I'm in some jeans and a tight-fitting top. Nothing too over-the-top sexy, but it'll get the job done. Getting all dolled up isn't really my style.

We're ogled by a group of older men as we walk in. I smile to be polite, and we head to a table and sit down.

The waitress walks over and I order a scotch on the rocks. Brandi orders some kind of girly drink that will probably come with umbrellas and fruit.

"I can't believe I agreed to this shit. We don't even know what this guy looks like."

"He's fucking gorgeous. That's what Livi said anyway. She couldn't believe he even talked to them. Said he's about six-foot-two, built like an Olympic swimmer, brown hair, green eyes. Early thirties."

We'll see how fucking gorgeous he is. Olivia likes to embellish.

"So she really fucked him in the bar?" My lips mash into a thin line.

"In the bathroom. Well, according to her, he got her off under the booth, and then fucked her in the bathroom."

"Wow."

"She said it was incredible. Best she's ever had, by far."

What is she? This guy's cheerleader? We'll see how beautiful this asshole is when I'm done with him.

We've been there about an hour when Brandi starts tapping my shoulder repeatedly.

"Oh shit. Oh my god. That has to be him, act cool."

Act cool? I'm surprised she didn't wear some One Direction fan girl shirt.

Thank god this asshole turned up on the first night. Maybe my whole week won't be ruined. I turn around to see what all the fuss is about, and he pierces me with a pair of emerald-green eyes. Goddamn, they were telling the truth if that's him. He is a beautiful specimen if there ever was one. Fuck, he's hot.

"Wow." I bite my bottom lip, but stop as soon as I notice what I'm doing.

"He's fucking gorgeous." Brandi swoons in the booth.

It doesn't matter. I'm still going to teach this guy a lesson for fucking my friend over. A few unfamiliar butterflies rush into my stomach as I see him and his friend look over at us. I don't usually get nervous around men. I wipe my palms down my jeans. He turns back to talk to some people. I'm assuming they're regulars, but he keeps glancing back to me.

"He's coming over. He's coming over." Brandi is practically squealing, and I want to strap a muzzle on her.

"I got it. Just relax."

"Hi ladies." Fuck, even his voice is hot.

"Hello," says Brandi.

"I'm Joel."

Confirmation. It's him. Jesus my palms are still clammy. What in the hell?

"Ladies," says his friend.

I need to flirt with his friend. That always drives them crazy. His friend is semi-cute. I'd probably find him more attractive if he wasn't standing next to the most beautiful man I've ever seen.

I ignore Joel completely and look up at his friend. "What's your name?"

He looks shaken up a bit.

"Umm, Tommy." His eyebrows rise and then fall. He looks like he's sizing me up.

"Well, umm Tommy. I could use a drink. Wanna go grab one?"

"I'm Joel." The handsome asshole cuts in.

"Yeah, that's great." I turn back to Tommy. "So how about that drink?" I wink at him. He shrugs at Joel.

I can tell I'm getting to the beautiful, green-eyed asshole.

"Why, I'd be delighted my lady." He offers his arm for me to take hold of. It's pretty cute, only because I can tell he's joking and rubbing it in Joel's face.

I grab his arm and head off to the bar, leaving Joel with Brandi. I peek back and his jaw is damn near on the floor. I'm sure to shake my ass a little as I walk away, give him something to jerk off to later.

Tommy and I get to the bar and he orders two scotches.

"So, I don't think I got your name?" He leans on the bar top.

"Oh, sorry. I'm Quinn."

"Nice to meet you, Quinn."

"Do you work out?" I start rubbing on his arm. It's pretty obvious what I'm doing, but guys are dumb. Joel is biting his lip at the table with Brandi, and continues to constantly glance over at us. I look back and Tommy is staring at me, but he's not checking me out. He appears confused.

"What?" I ask.

"Really? What the fuck is going on here?" He stares long and hard at me.

Maybe he's more astute than I thought. I'm going to play dumb anyway. "What do you mean?"

"Enough with the bullshit. You're a 12, and I'm an 8.5—most of the time." He cracks a smile. Must be an inside joke. "Joel over there—he's a 12. Something is going on and I want to know what it is. You trying to make him jealous?"

This guy is sharp, and it makes him more attractive.

"Okay, you got me. But—you're easily a 9.5." I grin.

He still doesn't buy into my bullshit. "He did something to you, didn't he?"

I look down at the floor without thinking. It's an obvious tell.

"Your friend. He did something to one of your friends. You're getting back at him. Devilish fucking women, I swear. It's the redhead isn't it?" He smiles as if he knows he's correct.

"Hey, don't be an asshole. And how could you possibly know that?"

70

"Hah! I knew it. She's the only girl he's recently hooked up with in here. He's been working off-site." He starts laughing and my thoughts are a jumbled mess. I don't know whether to knock his ass out or laugh with him.

"Well, you don't have to be a dickhead about it."

Fuck, I've ruined the whole thing. Oh well, I have better shit to do anyway.

"Don't make me wash your mouth out with soap, Quinn. You're better than that."

I start laughing. This guy is a riot.

"Look, if you want to get back at him, it's cool with me. His ass could use a reality check. But he better not find out that I know."

I smile. "Deal."

"Now go back to feeling my arm. That shit makes me feel strong and manly."

I nearly shoot scotch out of my mouth. I like Tommy. I can tell he's a good friend.

"So here's the deal—"

"I don't even wanna know. I want to hear about it from him later. Just know he's a good guy. He just likes the ladies, a little too much sometimes."

"He is one beautiful fucker, isn't he?" I gaze over at Joel, trying not to look interested.

Tommy props up his chin on his hands, elbows on the bar top, looking like he has a schoolgirl crush. "Oh yes, he's just dreamy. McDreamy loverballs."

"You should have your own TV show, seriously." I almost snort.

"So what's up with Brandi? She's cute." He looks to the table.

"She's super sweet, but I know someone who'd be better for you."

"You don't understand. I'm in a drought. It's like the Great Depression in my pants. Fucking Dust Bowl status."

I try to stifle my laughter. "Trust me, okay?"

"Well thanks, and just so you know, Joel is relentless. He won't stop until he gets you."

"I'm planning on it."

We're over at the table, and I'm flirting with Tommy. He's playing along and I think it's making Brandi a little jealous.

Joel keeps trying to get close to me, and I keep scooting away, pretending he's not even there. God, his fucking eyes though, and those lips, and that gorgeous smile. My panties are in a fucking knot, and they are not even close to being dry. I find myself being jealous of Livi. I wouldn't mind having him go to town on me under the table. It's been a while.

Must remain strong.

Finally, the unavoidable happens. Joel is standing next to me. I keep giving him one or two word answers to everything he asks. His face reddens each time. Fucker.

"So, what do you do, Quinn?" His eyes are searing into me.

"Marketing."

"Oh yeah, anything specific?"

"Not really."

I can tell he's used to having girls gush over him.

That's right, you handsome bastard. I'm going to leave your balls blue and aching.

He reaches for his drink and rubs up against my hand, it's obviously on purpose. It sends a wave of nerves firing through my body. I'm flustered, but manage to play it cool and pull my hand away.

"Sorry about that. It was an accident."

No it fucking wasn't, you arrogant prick. Somehow the topic of sex comes up and Joel looks like he's in heaven. I stare at him and pretend to look disgusted, even though I'd like to take him somewhere private and fuck his brains out.

They're all trading war stories. I can't take much more of hearing Joel. It's making me hot and simultaneously irritated. I find myself jealous of Olivia again. If only I'd gotten to him first, then I could have him. Now, I never will.

Some time has passed and I've grown more comfortable around Joel. Perhaps a little too comfortable. I've had three scotches, and I'm starting to loosen up. I decide it's time to start the flirting. I have to make him think he's getting laid tonight.

"I'm going to get another drink. Joel. You want to come? You look a little dry." I look to his rocks glass.

"Absolutely."

I throw Tommy a wink and he smiles.

We walk up to the bar, and I start to order. Joel puts his hand on my lower back, trying to be nonchalant about it. It sends a shudder up through my shoulders. I hope he didn't feel it. I love the way he touches me.

He leans over my shoulder, his words a whisper in my ear. "Can you grab me a Glenfiddich on the rocks?"

He lingers, exhaling down my neck and my panties are officially ruined. This fucker. I think it's my turn to play.

"Sure babe, you got it." I bend far over the bar to get the guy's attention. When I lean back I put my ass right in his crotch and rub it gently on his hard prick.

I hear him grunt a little. My ass has that effect sometimes.

"Oops, sorry about that."

"Don't worry about it."

"You should register that thing as a deadly weapon." I nod towards the bulge in his pants.

"I could say the same about that ass of yours."

I giggle a little. *Jesus, stop acting like a girl.* This guy is getting into my head, and that's not how this works.

"You want to get out of here?" he asks.

"What about Tommy?"

"He's a big boy. He has a driver's license."

"You'd just bail on your friend? Isn't that kind of shitty?" My hands ball up into fists.

"Not to leave with you. He'd understand."

What a prick. He's going to pay for that as well.

"So you're going to give me a ride home?" The green eyes are getting to me.

"Sure, I'll give you a *ride*."

My eyebrows perk up, and I feign interest. What a cheesy line. You're better than that, Joel.

"Ohh, a *ride* huh?"

"Yes, ma'am."

"What kind of *ride*?"

"Just a ride to your house. I'll *drive* you home."

Does this shit really work? I'm losing respect for every victim of his corny lines. "I think that sounds—fun. What kind of car do you drive?"

His eyes light up. "A '67 Fastback."

My pussy kicks up a few degrees. *Must recover.*

"That's a fast car. My ex-boyfriend had a '67. A Shelby GT 500."

He stares down at the ground.

What's wrong Joel? You jealous? Feeling inadequate now?

My last boyfriend drove a Prius and was a tool bag, but he doesn't need to know that. You don't need to know that if it weren't for Olivia, I'd probably fuck your brains out. Ride you on the hood of that muscle car and making you scream my name over and over.

"That's umm, a nice car. I love Shelby's."

That's right, bitch.

"Oh my god, I was so in love with his car. He was a surgeon at the children's hospital. We were actually engaged, so technically he was my fiancé."

He keeps tugging at his collar. I'm laughing on the inside. I don't know if it's a good idea to have him give me a ride home though. His car is guaranteed to make me all hot and wanting, and then there is no telling what might happen.

"Sounds like a great guy."

"He was, but he decided to marry his job. He went to work in Africa. Doctors Without Borders was his calling. I couldn't stand in the way."

Where do I come up with this shit? I can't believe he's still standing there. I've one-upped everything about him. I need to flirt a little more to balance it out.

I grab his tie playfully. "I love this tie. It looks good on you."

"Is that so?"

"Yeah. I know something else that would look good on you."

"What's that?" he asks.

I lean in to his ear and whisper, "It's a secret."

"Oh really?" He whispers back.

"Mmhmm." I nod slowly and smile.

I grab the two scotches that are sitting on the bar. "We better get back now."

I brush my ass up against his perfect cock as I walk by. His eyes close and he sighs. *I own your ass, Joel.* He'll be jerking off for weeks. No amount of pussy will compare to the thought of having me, and he will *not* be having me.

It's getting late, and I'm actually getting tired. Well, mentally tired. I could stay up and watch Joel squirm all night. It's obvious

he's not used to this kind of treatment. Maybe if a woman told him no once in a while he wouldn't think he could fuck whomever he pleases. Cocky bastard.

"Guys, I'm gonna have to get home and get to bed." I stand up from the booth.

"I'll give you a ride. Tommy, you're good, right?" Joel winks at me.

"Yeah boss, good to go," says Tommy.

"Well, okay then. Brandi, I'll see you tomorrow?" I ask.

"Yep, see you then."

I walk by Tommy and whisper in his ear. "Do not hook up with her. I will find you a good girl, okay?"

"You promise?" he asks.

I love that guy. He's such a good friend. I'm sure Joel's probably a good friend to him as well, just an asshole when it comes to a girl's feelings.

I look at Joel and smile.

Ready for your balls to ache, big guy?

We walk out to his car. When I see it I almost lose my shit right then and there. It is fucking beautiful. It should be illegal for a man as hot as him to drive such a gorgeous beast.

I try not to look impressed, but it's difficult. He opens the door for me. It's actually kind of nice.

I mean to say thank you, but all I can do is sit there and anticipate him firing up the engine.

He turns the key, and she explodes under the hood. Rumbling energy rushes through the seats and through my body. I want to yank his pants off and fuck his brains out. I can't stop looking over at his dick and he knows it. God, the thought of it just a few feet away has me hotter than I've ever been in my life.

I have to remind myself every two seconds to think of Livi. She would murder me if I fucked him. Seriously, she's pretty crazy. I might just wake up with a knife to my throat.

"It's a rush, isn't it? Riding in this car?"

"It's okay."

His hands tighten on the steering wheel. It's not the reaction he was hoping for.

"Where do you live?"

"Fifth and Nashville."

"Well, all right then."

He hammers the gas and it forces my back against my seat. I'm so fucking aroused. I can see his eyes glancing occasionally to my tits.

They get attention wherever I go, and the rumbling of all eight cylinders has them shaking non-stop, even with a bra.

It's time to do a number on this guy, for Livi of course. I'm going to drive this fucker insane. I've had just enough booze to get dirty, and it'll help get rid of the urge to ride his cock all fucking night.

"Your car makes me so fucking wet when we go fast."

He swerves a little and I smile as he squirms in his seat.

"Sorry, I can't fucking help myself. I'm so goddamn horny right now. It's been a while."

I run my hands up to my tits and tweak my nipples, then moan as the vibrations of the car have my clit buzzing.

I move another hand down my stomach slowly and he watches it disappear into my jeans. I have my eyes closed, secretly imagining him touching me, running his tongue along my thighs and up to my pussy.

I start to rub on my clit, trying to imagine it's his fingers and forget that it's my own. I open my eyes wide and stare right at him. He's shifting in his seat and I imagine him fucking me. I remember every inch of his cock from rubbing my ass against it, and I think about taking it in and out of my mouth, and feeling it inside me.

He reaches over for my left breast and I smack his hand away.

"Just enjoy the show, you lucky bastard." I run my hand up my shirt and paw at my breasts over the top of my bra.

"Is this why you wanted to get me alone in your car? To get me all fucking hot?"

"Hell yes it is."

I unbutton my pants and pull them to my knees along with my panties.

I shove my hips up in the air and grind on my fingers, circling my clit, while he stares down at me. He swerves again and almost takes out a mailbox. I'm moaning loud as I imagine him shoving his cock into me over and over. I can feel the tension swirling down to my core. I can't believe I'm playing with myself in front of this guy. I've never done anything like this before.

I start hammering my fingers in and out, and my wetness streams down my thighs to his seat.

"Oh, fuck." I moan.

He starts to say something and stutters. Apparently, he's never had a woman finger fuck herself in front of him. I thought this guy was some kind of master in the bedroom?

He reaches over again, this time going for my pussy. I take my other hand out of my shirt and smack his hand away again.

"Bad boy. Wait your fucking turn."

I look over and see him pumping his hand on his cock over his pants. Watching him stroke his dick, knowing how bad he wants to fuck me, makes me want him even more. I look up and realize I'm going to have to get off soon. My house is coming up.

"Oh shit, I'm about to come."

I start circling my tight nub with my thumb and slide my fingers in and out of my pussy. I'm about to come all over the seat of this beautiful car and I don't care one bit.

I pull my fingers out and slap my hand on my slit, before putting them back inside me, hammering myself even harder than before. I'm streaming all over his seat. He doesn't care one bit. He's too busy watching me finger bang myself right in front of his face.

"Oh fuck, I'm coming Joel."

I reach with my left arm and grab hold of his forearm as I convulse in his seat, my fingers as deep as they can possibly go. I pause as I squeeze myself around them and my legs straighten into the floorboard. An intense surge of tingling and heat radiates through my body and rips to my toes and fingertips. It is fucking intense, and I dig my nails into his arm so hard that I draw some blood.

"Oh my god!" I squeal.

I'm panting, trying to catch my breath.

I finally wrap up as we pull down my street.

"That's me right there," I say, panting uncontrollably.

I point to my house and he pulls up in front. He starts to lean over as if it's time for him to join in. I push him away and pull my panties and jeans over my hips and button them back up. I give him a quick pat on the cheek and then stare down at the blood on his arm. He looks like a confused little boy who just had his favorite toy taken away.

"Thanks for the ride. I had a great time."

I hop out of the car and start to walk inside. He sits there, awestruck. Wow, I don't think I've ever had an orgasm like that. He is one beautiful bastard. I'm sad that I'll never get to fuck him. Actually, I'm not sure if I could handle it or not. I could barely contain myself getting off in front of him.

I turn around and stare at him through the open window.

"Oh, by the way, Olivia says to go fuck yourself. Prick!"

I shoot him the finger and walk to the house, shaking my ass as I head up the steps, then look back to see his mouth gaping in disbelief.

I walk inside and wait by the door, imagining him sitting there, wondering what the fuck just happened.

He hammers the gas and drives away, making me hot all over again. I can see why they call him the panty whisperer, but he's not getting in these panties. *Ever!*

VOLUME 6

CHAPTER 1
JOEL

"**S**WEET MOTHER OF Leia's tits! Have you looked in a mirror?" Tommy navigates his way through various foam restaurant containers, cutting through the smell of rotting takeout and shame. "Oh, goddamn. This is worse than I thought. It smells like Honey Boo Boo's mom shit up your living room, bro."

I snarl at him. "What?"

I set down my Xbox controller and sigh, shooting a blank stare in his direction.

"Jesus, look at your stomach. It looks like the quarter pounders have been kind to you." He starts to chuckle as he gazes in disbelief.

"What the hell is so funny?" My blank stare turns into a glare.

"Nothing." He shakes his head.

"No, you opened your mouth. Say what you have to say."

"Oh, you know, just thinking about all the Panty Whisperer victims, looking just like this for weeks after a taste of ol' Herbert."

"I've never made anyone feel like this." I pause for a moment. "I'm doing fucking great by the way. I'm just taking some time off from work and relaxing. I work hard. I'm allowed to take some vacation time and fuck off."

He stares at me the way an irritated mother looks at her children when she doesn't buy any of the bullshit coming from their mouths.

"Mmhmm, ol' Quinn, she slayed the giant. You have to get over her, bro." He folds his arms across his chest.

"I'm not getting over anyone. Is there a reason you're here? You're fucking up my little eco-system."

"Yeah, it's definitely an eco-system. There is shit growing in these boxes. I can smell it. Get your ass up and take a shower, you nasty bastard. We have to get you back out on the prowl."

He kicks a pile of trash against the couch and stands in front of the television, staring right at me with a look of haughty derision, his nose constantly wrinkling as he takes in the smell that has invaded the apartment. I'm oblivious to it. I can see there is no getting rid of this persistent asshole.

"Fuck it! Fine."

I'm not sure what we're going to do that's so important at 11 a.m. on a weekday, but he seems to have a plan of some sort. He continues to stare without saying a word, nothing but a hidden smirk behind a somewhat genuine look of concern. He lifts an arm and points to the shower. "Go! I'll wait here, sweetie."

"Jesus Christ. I hate you." I get up and start toward the hall.

"You love me, Herbert. You don't mean that."

I saunter down the hallway towards the bathroom. Each step feels like I'm stepping into quicksand as I make my way to the bathroom, like cinder blocks are tied to my feet.

What an asshole. I was perfectly happy sitting there playing GTA5 and eating everything in sight. I fumble through my toiletry kit and I'm afraid to look in the mirror. I finally muster up the courage to remove the shirt I've been wearing the past week and damn near puke on myself.

For fuck's sake, I look like the guy at the end of *Super Size Me*.

I stand for a moment and stare in amazement at my stomach. Just a few weeks ago it was a chiseled six-pack, and now it has been reduced to an unrecognizable blob, moving and shaking in whichever direction it pleases with each breath.

That bitch.

I don't know what the fuck is going on, but I can't get that girl off my mind. One second it was all going as planned and then suddenly she's telling me to fuck off as she walks away. What is that shit all about? I tell myself it's the rejection, my competitive side showing. But hell, it seemed like it was more than that, like we had a connection. I know she felt it too, regardless of what happened.

She was smart, witty, and absolutely beautiful. But there was something more. It was like I knew her. There was mystery, intrigue, something behind those eyes, and I wanted to know her. I wanted more than to get her into bed.

Tommy beats on the door, and I jolt backwards. My hand knocks my toothbrush to the cold tile, and I snap out of my imaginary pity party.

"Fuck, dude. What the hell?" I glare at the door.

"Everything okay in there, Jabba the Gut?"

"Jesus Christ. Can I have a minute to get ready?" I chuckle for a second. That shit is pretty funny. "Nice one, by the way."

"Thanks man. I've been trying to think of a way to use it for like ten minutes." He laughs.

"You executed it nicely, babydoll."

"Thanks, hon. Hurry the fuck up and don't use any sharp objects on yourself. I worry about your ass. Like you might start cutting or something."

"I could never harm a face as pretty as the one I'm looking at."

"That sounds like my good little bitch. It's nice to have you back, Sir. Now hurry. I'm worried about your takeout boxes coming to life, and I left my Geiger counter at home."

This fucking guy.

I hop in the shower and let the hot water stream over my head and face. I don't know what the deal is. I haven't been able to get off the couch. I want to eat everything in sight. My arms and legs feel like they weigh a hundred pounds each. Things are dull, and nothing is interesting. I've neglected my poor car. She hasn't been driven in weeks.

Finally, I step out of the shower into a cloud of steam that remains suspended in the air, slowly drifting inches below the ceiling. I do feel much better, like a new person. Until I look down. Fuck, I need to go running, this is unacceptable. I'm not even going to step on the scale.

I throw on my last pair of clean clothes and burn a few calories trying to button my jeans. I can hear Tommy laughing at my predicament in the other room.

"I think I might call a hazmat team to come in while we're gone. Or maybe we can just set this place on fire." I laugh as I walk around the corner.

"Something man. This shit is ridiculous. Grab a trash bag." He starts shifting the trash into piles.

"I didn't really mean we need to throw my shit away."

He stares at me like I am an idiot. "Dude, we're going to get rid of the garbage and drop your clothes at the cleaners."

"Ahh, good idea." I walk over and start to help.

We spend the next 30 minutes gathering two trash bags full of takeout boxes and empty ice cream containers. I lower my head and look at the floor as he walks by holding them, staring me down like I'm a filthy filth monger.

He tosses them outside and turns to me. "Alright, Whisperer. Are you ready for the next step?"

"Ha, what's that?"

"Walking out the front door. I mean if you're not ready, I understand. Baby steps are key. I don't want to overwhelm you." He holds up both hands as if he's trying to keep me calm and relaxed.

"Shut the fuck up." I punch him in the shoulder and open the door. "Oh fucking hell."

It's like the sun has me in an interrogation room. I damn near feel like I'm going blind, as little fuzzy stars pass in front of my face. I'm disoriented momentarily and think I might pass out.

"You ok there, Paul? Having a defining moment in your life?"

"Paul?" I look at him like he's speaking a foreign language.

"The Apostle? Road to Damascus? Goddamn, you ever read the Bible?"

I shake my head and laugh. "You are the most blasphemous person I've ever met."

He starts the mocking. "Your poor, poor mother. What a disappointment." He shakes his head and walks toward the car.

"Where you going? I need to get my baby out of the garage."

"Not in that condition, Sir!" He hollers and bugs his eyes out at me, a fake angry look on his face. "You lose five pounds before you even think of showing your face around her!"

"You make a valid point. She deserves better."

He continues to bug his eyes at me and stares as if he's looking into my soul. "Yeah." He nods. "Goddamn right she does."

We drop my clothes off at the dry cleaners and get back on the road. Tommy takes a familiar exit off the highway and cringes. All at once, the dots start to connect.

"No, no, we are not going there right now." I shake my head at him.

"I was given strict instructions from a power much greater than all the panty whispering fairies in your little pecker. You should've answered your phone when people tried to call."

"Seriously, bro. I can't right now."

"It's fucking happening. Man up, pussy." He grins at my discomfort.

"Fuck me." I squirm in my seat. My stomach cramps up as we pull down the road. I roll down the window to take in some of the air and let the warmth rush across my face as we coast down the street that looks exactly as it did 20 years ago. It's the same people doing the same things in their front yards, only the kids playing in the grass are now grandkids.

Tommy eases on the brake and there she is, standing in the grass, her arms folded, and a scowl across her face. My chest tightens and I can't even look at her.

My mother is not a woman to be trifled with. My father passed away when I was young, and she raised me by herself. She's petite, about five-foot-three with curly brown hair and blue eyes. She looks like the sweetest and nicest woman someone would ever meet. I love her more than anything.

But when she's angry, it's best to stay out of her way. This woman would whip a grown man's ass without flinching. I finally glance in her direction and notice her foot tapping on the ground. It's not a good sign.

Tommy pulls up, and for the first time today he looks genuinely serious. We get out of the car, and her stare burns into my skull.

Tommy steps out and walks over to give her a hug.

"Thank you, Thomas." Her voice is monotone. She gives Tommy a slight peck on the cheek as he wraps his arms around her. Her eyes remain trained on me the entire time.

"You're welcome, Mom." Tommy releases her and backs away.

I might just shit my pants if I have to watch her stare at me much longer. It doesn't matter how old I get, when Mom is disappointed there will be hell to pay.

"Over here, now." Her words are not in a pleasant tone.

The scent of fresh cut grass and summer heat seeps into my nostrils and my shoulders slump as I saunter over to her. It's like I'm seven all over again. I have to be a foot taller than her and it's like I'm looking up at her from the ground. Once in front of her, I stare into a familiar pair of eyes. Memories of my childhood flash through my mind. It's the woman who made me.

My hands fumble around in my empty pockets as she reaches up and squeezes my cheeks together with one hand like a vise.

"Herbert Hannover, when your mother calls, you answer the phone. Do you understand me, boy?"

"Yes, Ma'am." I want to look at anything but her, but I can't.

There's a pause.

Finally, I let it all out. "I'm sorry. I was in a messed up place, and I'm just, very, very sorry."

Her small arms wrap around me and she crushes me with the strength of ten grizzly bears. I can barely breathe, but I don't care. It's the best I've felt in weeks. Her upper body trembles as I lean down and let her kiss me on the cheek. Guilt seeps from my pores.

She whispers in my ear. "I love you, Bubs."

"I love you too, Mom."

She releases me, and oxygen rushes into my lungs. Tommy chuckles when she's not looking in his direction. He's been on the receiving end of Mom's hugs as well. They can murder a man's soul and make him feel like the most loved person on the planet at the same time.

"Come on inside now, boys. I'll make something to eat, and you can tell me about the girl."

There's no secret that can be kept from moms. They always know what's going on with their sons.

Tommy whispers in my ear as he walks by, a shocked look spread across his face. "How does she do that? She's the fucking Oracle, bro."

"Watch your language, Thomas. I'll wash your mouth out with Dial dish soap. You understand me?" She doesn't even turn around.

His eyes look like they may pop out of his head. "Sorry, Mom."

We both rush to get ahead of her, fighting for position to open the door before she can do it herself.

She smiles. "Now those are the two young men that I raised."

We follow her inside.

Family pictures hang on the walls in old cracked wooden frames. Tommy's smile can be seen in many of them. He's been a member of my family since we were about five. His dad passed around the same time as mine, and his mother worked as an engineer to support their family, sometimes working long hours. Somehow, Tommy remained socially normal in a family full of geniuses.

They're nice, but it's difficult to have conversations with them. Tommy is fluent in their language, but not me. He used to get mad when Mom would scold him for making a B while I was congratulated for the same grade.

"*We all have different levels of ability, Thomas,*" she would say.

"Hey bro, you think the Nintendo is still around here? Need to grab that shit before we leave. Play some fucking Tecmo Bowl later."

It's not a bad idea, except for the fact Mom probably sold it off in a garage sale. We were always encouraged to play outside and only allowed to play video games as a reward for good behavior. At Tommy's house a Nintendo was laughed at as inferior. They were always writing their own games in BASIC and doing all kinds of shit I didn't understand.

Tommy could've done it easily, but he was never very interested. It's funny because he's the only one who works in the software industry. Not that I would call what he does, working.

Mom walks around the corner with a plate of sandwiches and sets them down on the worn oak coffee table. She smacks Tommy's hand as he reaches for one of them.

"Have we said grace yet? What is wrong with you boys? It's like you've lost your damn minds."

I laugh and Tommy glares at me.

"Herbert doesn't even know who Paul is." His words are in a child's voice.

Mom gasps. I can't tell if she is being serious or playing along. "Excuse me?"

"I know who Paul is. He saw the bright light on the road to Damascus." I shoot Tommy a nice wide 'fuck you' grin as his face turns pink.

Mom smiles. She sees right through all of our bullshit antics. It doesn't stop us.

"So. Tell me Herbert. What exactly happened to Paul on the road to Damascus? What *really* happened that day?"

"W-well—" I stutter and glare at the prick while he leans back and cheeses on the couch.

Mom cuts me off. "You boys quit fooling around. I want to hear about the girl."

"It's nothing, seriously. No big deal."

"Is that right? No big deal? That's why you didn't answer your mother's calls? Had her worried sick about you? No, I want to hear an actual reason you would let me sit here thinking the worst. That's not how you were raised."

"Fine. Okay? There's a girl. It didn't work out."

The corners of their mouths turn up in unison. I hate this shit. They can't get enough. I've never dated a woman more than a few months, and I've certainly never been in love.

"Both of you need to quit. I liked her. It's nothing. I'm over it. Can we please move on?"

Their grins have morphed into huge smiles, and I can see two white sets of teeth.

"Your faces are going to cramp up if you smile any wider, Jesus." I freeze in my seat as Mom's smile turns to ice, sending a shiver up my spine.

Fuck me. People don't say the Lord's name like that in her house. I can't believe I just did that. Tommy was nearly catatonic, and is now covering his mouth, trying not to laugh his ass off.

I hold my hands up and lean back away from her. "I'm sorry. I don't know why that just happened."

She stands and points a finger at both of us as I slink into the couch.

"Probably because you speak that way when you're not in this house. Boy, I will lay your ass out if you ever do that again. Chasing girls around will be the least of your worries. Got me?"

"Yes Ma'am."

Tommy's face is tomato red.

She leans down and smacks him in the chest. It looks like his lungs cave in. I burst with laughter and quickly compose myself when she shoots me a look. She turns back to Tommy and points at him.

"Don't think I don't know you do it too. Sitting there laughing like you're innocent. I will put a whipping on both of you clowns. Turn your asses red as watermelons." She sits and turns to me. "*Now*, Herbert. Tell me about my future daughter-in-law."

Son of a bitch.

They both erupt in laughter. I sit there and stare in disbelief, shaking my head. "You're both hilarious. You know that?" I get up and walk toward the kitchen to get something to drink. I know what's coming next as I stare at both of them.

"Are you guys registered at the Pottery Barn? I saw they had some nice salad bowls on clearance. I mean, I'm working with a budget here." Tommy tries to keep a straight face while I stare lasers at him, before turning and walking into the kitchen.

When I disappear, I hear them burst into laughter.

I shouldn't be surprised. This is the way it was growing up. I couldn't have asked for a better childhood.

A few hours pass, and it seems like minutes. It's been good to be home. We're about to head out the door, and Tommy walks to the car. Mom grabs me by the hand.

"I just want you to be happy." She puts a hand on my cheek.

"I know."

"Don't give up on her. If you think she's the one. At least try."

"It's complicated. I don't even know her. It doesn't make any sense." I sigh.

"You know her better than you think. Sometimes things just happen and it can't be explained. You just know."

"I'll think about it, okay? I don't think she feels the same way."

"Well, you won't ever know if you don't find out. I love you, Bubs." She gives me a hug.

"Love you too."

She releases me from the death hug, and I walk out to the car.

"I love you too, Thomas. Keep him in line." She stands in the driveway and waves.

"You know I will, Mom. Love you!"

We pull away.

As we cruise down the street, I turn to Tommy. "Thanks."

"You'd do the same." He pauses and looks over at me. "Check out the back seat."

I turn around and there sits the Nintendo with Tecmo Bowl next to it. "Dude, fuck yes! You swiped it from the house?"

"Nah, Mom brought it out to me. She said to make your fat ass exercise before you're allowed to play."

CHAPTER 2
QUINN

I'M SITTING AT a table in Starbucks when I nearly shoot piping hot white mocha out of my nose. Tommy ducks in the door wearing a trench coat, sunglasses, and a hat. It has to be 90 degrees outside. His head is on a swivel as he bumps into people on the way to the table.

I whisper under my breath. "What the fuck are you doing?"

"What the fuck, Quinn? You didn't wear a disguise? We talked about this on the phone for fuck's sake." He stands in front of the table, and I worry people are going to think he's robbing the place.

We continue whispering for some reason.

"I thought you were kidding. What the hell? You look like an idiot."

"I can't be seen with you, woman. You know that. Hence, the disguise."

He twirls around like he's a Victoria's Secret model before striking a pose on a fictitious runway. I need to take advantage of this conversation to ask about Joel. It's like a dagger to the stomach when I think about what I did to him, but he needed a reality check.

I halt the whispering and speak at a normal volume. "Seriously? Because of the Joel thing. He hates me that much?"

I hope he doesn't hate me. What the hell is my problem? Why do I feel sorry for him? He's a fucking player. Not worth my time.

"He's pretty shaken up. Gained some weight. Think he might be depressed." Tommy finally sits down.

"Poor guy."

Poor guy? Get your shit together, Quinn. You sound like a desperate groupie for some celebrity.

"I mean, umm, yeah, that's too bad. Hope he feels better soon." I shrug and look away.

Tommy stares at me, too fucking intelligent for his own good. He takes off the terrible disguise, leans toward me, and props his elbows on the table. "So, you like Joel. Interesting."

"What? Why in the hell would you think that?" My face heats up, and it has to be turning pink.

There's that sarcastic stare of his again. I look up and see Megan. Thank god.

"There's Megan." I smile and wave her over. I promised Tommy I would set him up with someone. My matchmaking skills are superb, because Megan is perfect for him. I look over, and he's sweating bullets.

"Pull yourself together. Since when are you the nervous type?"

"I don't know. I think it's the disguise I'm wearing. You've got my ass all flustered over here. I can't think straight with the clandestine spy operation and that fine specimen of a woman walking this way." He taps his fingers furiously on the table.

I look down at his hand, then back up to him. "Jesus. Well, do me a favor and don't call her a specimen when she gets here, okay?"

He better not fuck this up. I want to look hot in my bridesmaid dress.

"Hey, Megan." I smile.

"Hey, how are you?" she asks.

"Great. This is Tommy. He's my friend I told you about."

Tommy stands up, but not before wiping his sweaty ass palms down his legs.

"Hello, me lady, how art thou this morrow?" His voice is some god awful Olde English accent.

I mouth "what in the fu—" from behind Megan where he can see. He shrugs as if he has no control over his actions. Megan is smiling. It's a good thing Tommy is cute. My face is in the palm of my hand at this point. It's a total disaster.

Please play that shit off as a joke.

"Oh, why hello, good Sir." Megan reciprocates with some kind of awkward curtsy.

She's wearing a black mid-length dress, and her wavy brunette hair is flowing over her shoulders. She has long legs that go for days down to a pair of black pumps. She's gorgeous, but also insanely smart. I don't understand what she's talking about when we talk about work. She's the director of IT at the marketing firm and graduated from Stanford with some degree in smart people computer stuff.

At least her reaction seems to have Tommy at ease. Maybe he will act normal now.

She sits down next to me. They're both silent, and I need to help them break the ice, apparently.

"Tommy works for a firm that specializes in accounting software. *Right, Tommy?*" I shoot a stare in his direction, trying to get him to start a conversation.

"Yeah, I don't really work much. I try to shirk my duties whenever possible."

Goddamn it. Women don't like lazy men, especially those who wear it as a badge of honor. This is going horribly wrong. Megan is ambitious and driven. Tommy tries to skate by with minimal effort. Maybe it was a bad idea.

"Oh yeah? How do you get away with it?" Megan leans in, apparently interested in his ways of laziness.

She must find him attractive. It's the only explanation.

"It's not hard. People are easy to read. I recognize patterns. Our software is a joke. Easy to learn. I show people modules that will be most useful and they love the hell out of me. I just steer them away from those that have the most bugs."

"Interesting. So you're not a programmer?"

"Hell no. I'd blow my brains out writing accounting software."

Megan laughs. What the hell is going on here? I'm cringing with every word. Surely he realizes this woman's life is programming computers and he says he'd blow his brains out?

"So, how do you know it has bugs?" Megan twirls a lock of her hair around her finger.

I convince myself I'm in the Twilight Zone.

"I spotted them when they showed me the source code."

She laughs but has a curious look about her. "You spotted the bugs? Looking at it once? Bullshit."

"Umm. Okay? I didn't spot all the bugs looking at it once." He shrugs.

There's the confident sarcasm I've been waiting for.

Megan appears intrigued. "Okay, seriously? You really spotted them?"

"I can spot an infinite loop a mile away. Especially in Python. Most of those pricks are amateur script kiddies that think they're hackers."

"Is it all written in Python?"

"No. There's one decent coder there who actually listens to me. I told him which parts to write in C. I edited some of it for him. It made the program lightning fast. I really should've leveraged that deal better. I didn't get a damn thing come to think of it."

Megan keeps giggling like a schoolgirl.

I look over at Tommy. I give him a thumbs up when Megan isn't watching.

"Also, if I free up time at work, I can flame all the wannabe George Lucas fanboys on YouTube."

Megan leans toward Tommy. "I know right. This fucker on Facebook tried to make an argument for Jar Jar's existence the other day."

I seriously do not know what in the fuck is going on at this point. But they are both smiling, so I feel like it's going well. I'm also shocked that she said "fuck." I've never heard her talk like that.

"Jar Jar Binks is a fucking abomination who should be tortured Law-Abiding-Citizen-style. Abrams had better bury that fucker or I will troll the balls off his Twitter feed." Tommy beams with pride at his declaration.

"We need to have a *Star Wars* night and compare notes on George Lucas edits that warrant hatred and contempt." Megan starts twirling her hair again.

"That sounds like the greatest date of all time." Tommy winks at me like it's a suave maneuver.

I roll my eyes, but it appears to be working as Megan swoons in her chair.

"It's a date then. Here's my card. It has my number. Hope it's sooner than later." She smiles at Tommy and her face is all kinds of pink.

"You have to get back to work?" I ask.

"Yeah. Big project going on." She looks at Tommy and smiles. "See you soon."

She heads toward the exit, and when she walks out the door Tommy leaps to his feet and dances around, holding her card in front of my face.

"Uhh, Quinn. See that shit? Mackdaddy skills right there, son!"

What the hell? I don't get any credit. I start to interrupt him and he holds a finger to his lips, shushing me like a child.

"Don't interrupt mah mojo." He switches to some kind of android voice and starts doing the robot. "Must. Do. The. C3PO."

People stare at us, and I can't quit laughing. Between his antics and the smell of roasted coffee beans in my nose, it's like heaven.

He keeps gyrating in stiff, jerky movements. "Sir, the possibility of successfully navigating that pussy is approximately 3,720 to 1!"

"Oh my god. Sit down." I can barely catch my breath.

He's still holding her card, staring at it as he looks around at the gawkers. "Sorry folks. Got some digits. You know how it is."

"Well, I'm glad I could help." I shake my head.

"She's perfect. I owe you one."

"Yeah you do."

"I thought I lost her with ye Olde English opener, but she ate it up." He smiles.

"Well, I told you I'd find you a good girl. Didn't I? Now don't fuck it up. I have to work with her."

He's staring back, and I can see the gears turning in his head. "Now, where were we with this Joel conversation? Maybe all four of us could hang out and watch *Star Wars*?"

"I don't think that's going to happen. Not a good idea."

"What the fuck ever. You two are perfect for each other. You need to quit playing all the bullshit games. Stubborn bunch of assholes."

"Hey. I just hooked you up with a ten. Don't call me an asshole. Besides, it's his fault. I'm not going to betray my best friend for a guy. He shouldn't have fucked her over and maybe there'd be a possibility. Not to mention the fact that he bangs everything that walks."

"Oh horse shit. If he hadn't pounded out your friend you would've never met him in the first place. And he would stop his playboy antics if he met the right girl, which is *you*. If he didn't like you he wouldn't be sitting in a pile of filth in his apartment, calling in to work and blowing through his vacation days like Tony Montana through a mountain of coke."

"He's doing what?" I perk up in my seat.

"Shit. Never mind. He's fine. You're right."

My stomach churns. I tell myself it's the coffee, but I know better. "Is he going to be okay?"

"I shouldn't have told you that. Please don't say anything. I finally got him out of the house and took him to his mom's. If he knew I told you, it'd send him right back off the deep end."

"I won't say anything. I promise."

Who the hell would I tell anyway? Tommy heads out the front door and lets in a warm breeze that wafts over my face.

I have to get back to the office.

When I walk outside, a garbage truck pulls up to collect the trash on the street. The rancid smell coupled with the guilt makes me nauseous, and I might vomit. It's going to be a long fucking day.

CHAPTER 3
JOEL

I'M AT WORK and getting back into the swing of things. Quinn still finds her way into every corner of my mind. I've convinced myself that I need to get laid and it will all go away.

It seems like a bad idea but what's the down side? Getting laid? Sounds pretty fool proof to me. I need to think with my brain anyway. My feelings obviously can't be trusted.

There's a woman in finance I've pretty much laid the groundwork for already. Her name is Brittany Mayhew. She's attractive, but not supermodel hot. It should make things pretty easy. I decide to pay her a visit.

I walk around the corner, and she's sitting at her desk. Her brunette hair is in long curls today, and she's wearing a dark-green top that conceals a pair of medium-sized natural breasts. Her ass isn't proportional, but I don't mind. All I can think about right now is slamming into it from behind while she moans my name.

She's 32 and divorced, with a kid. I think she needs some excitement in her life. She deserves to be pleasured, and I need to clear my mind. It's a win-win.

She doesn't have one defining feature that stands out, but it all works well together. She's definitely self-conscious about her appearance. Most women are at her age, hell, any age for that matter. I'll never understand it. She's fucking hot and needs to be reminded how beautiful she is.

A sense of impending doom rolls through my stomach, but I ignore it. She looks up at me with a pair of dark-brown eyes and a smile creeps over her face. Her desk is littered with stacks of papers and miscellaneous files, not unusual for most accountants. We've been office flirts for years. Usually I flirt when I need a favor, but sometimes I do it for fun.

"Well, it's about time you stopped by to see me. Where have you been, stranger?"

"Oh you know—out of the office for a bit, working off-site, wishing I was here so I could stop by and see you."

She stands up and has on a mid-length khaki skirt. She looks amazing, way hotter than usual. My cock bulges in my pants, maybe because I haven't fucked anyone in a while. The things I'm going to do to this one, though. She has no idea.

This should be fun. She's practically begging me to take her from behind, fuck her the way she deserves to be fucked. Hard.

After all these years of flirting, it will finally culminate in a hot and steamy office closet. I can't wait to put her up against the wall.

She lowers her black-framed glasses and eye fucks me. "So, I'm the reason you are always swinging by here?"

"Of course, why else would I come by?" I lean against her desk.

It certainly isn't to see her boss. He's an asshole. Works his people to death and he's always creeping on her.

"I don't know." She twirls her hair, basically begging for my dick in her throat.

"Are you busy? Want to go grab some coffee?" I smile.

I can almost feel the heat rushing into her face as she blushes.

"Sure. Why not?"

"Follow me."

I walk in the opposite direction of the break room and I imagine how wet it makes her. Everyone in the office has heard the rumors. She needs to find out for herself though. She needs to experience me.

I stop in front of a maintenance closet, the same one I took Hannah in a few weeks ago. I've never actually fucked in here, and I do love to try new things. I look back and Brittany looks incredibly sexy, excitement radiating from her face. She's already walking with a look of confidence, rocking her hips side-to-side with her chest out. I throw her a wink and walk into the closet.

When she walks through the door we attack each other. Four years of flirting with no pay off will do that to a person. My hands go straight to her ass, yanking her skirt up to reveal a pair of lace panties hugging her cheeks together. I slap one of them forcefully and grip with my fingertips while biting her bottom lip. I grip her hair and yank her head back, exposing her neck. I dive into her throat and suck down to her collarbone.

She's panting, pushing her tits into my chest as I work back up to her ear.

Her hand strokes my cock over my slacks.

"You ready for a taste?" My mouth is next to her ear, hand still fisting her hair.

She doesn't respond and I smack her ass again. She coos and strokes my shaft faster.

"Take it out." My voice is a throaty growl.

She unbuckles my belt and unbuttons my pants slowly. I release her hair and let her do what she needs to. She unzips my pants and yanks them and my briefs down simultaneously. My cock springs free, and she looks up at me.

Her eyes grow wide as she runs her hand up and down me, staring into my eyes through her glasses. "Oh my."

"Get on your fucking knees."

Brittany drops to her knees, still stroking my cock. She seems to enjoy being told what to do, so I take advantage of the situation. She stares up with those big brown eyes, and her warm tongue licks up the length of my shaft.

I groan as she explores every inch of my dick with her tongue.

"I've wanted this for so long." Her voice is a whisper.

I reach down and grab a handful of her hair. "Put it in your mouth."

She licks the length of me again but this time swirls her tongue around the head and takes half of it into her mouth.

I slap her playfully on the cheek and she moans on my cock. "All of it."

She takes me into the back of her mouth, doing as she's told while I stare at the big round ass sticking out the back of her skirt. It's hot as fuck and I'm going to have to be careful not to blow my load too early. I can't miss out on getting inside that pussy. I've put in too much work for it.

She sucks me harder, and my head tilts back toward the wall. She pauses to tease the tip.

"Spit on it." I look down at her eyes.

They're staring back at me and I squeeze her hair in my fist.

A moan rolls off her lips. She smiles and spits all over it. It drips down her chin and along my shaft. She strokes me in smooth, rhythmic motions. It feels fucking amazing, but we don't have a lot of time. I'm going to have to speed this up.

"You want to get fucked?"

She nods and takes me in her mouth again. I turn her head so that my cock is lodged in the side of her mouth, then lightly slap her cheek with my hand.

"You want to get fucked like a dirty little whore? Is that what you want?"

"Uh huh." A mouthful of my dick has her words jumbled and she nods on my cock.

I grab under her arms and yank her up to her feet. A light squeal escapes her lips.

I flip her around and shove her up against the wall. Swiping her hair back over her ear, I lean in next to it, all the while my hand is up her skirt, rubbing her pussy over the top of her panties. I slowly increase the tempo.

I grip the back of her neck, and press the side of her face against the wall, my mouth in her ear.

She gasps. "Fuck."

"You want me to shove my cock in here?" I yank her panties to the side and palm her wet cunt, then run my fingers back and forth through her slick folds.

"Mmhmm."

"Not yet." I shove off of her neck, releasing her from my grip.

I drop to my knees and pull her panties to her ankles. She kicks them to the side.

I spread her ass apart and bury my nose in the middle of it as I lick from her clit to her asshole. She squirms and I slap her ass, hard. Her legs stiffen at the impact and she stills.

I tease her swollen, pink entrance with the tip of my tongue and a shudder rips through her thighs and up her back. She moans and reaches back with both hands to spread that big beautiful ass of hers for me, digging her nails in.

I circle my fingers on her clit while probing my tongue in and out of her, pausing occasionally to run it around the tight ridges of her asshole. She claws her ass harder, spreading it wider.

"I'm gonna come." She can barely breathe.

Yeah you are.

I tease her clit faster with my fingers, still going to town on her puckered asshole with my tongue. She's about to lose control and is trying to remain still. It's time.

I slip two fingers into her hot pussy and start ramming them to the hilt. She loses control, bucking her ass in time to my fingers pumping in and out of her cunt, her ass shaking, her fingers still gripping it tight.

She lets go of her ass and splays her fingers across the wall as her head flies back and her body tenses up, tightening her walls around my fingers as she grinds her ass up and down them.

I take my fingers deeper and shake my head, my tongue lashing her asshole from every angle as I growl.

She belts out a loud moan and convulses on my face, my head buried in her ass and my fingers in her cunt.

Finally, her muscles relax. I can't waste this opportunity.

I stand up and grab one of her wrists in each hand, then yank them back to her ass. "Spread your fucking ass."

She does it, offering up her pink, wet pussy. I slide my cock underneath her, soaking up her wetness that's streaming down the insides of her thighs.

I grab her hair once more and lean in, biting on her earlobe. I want to hear her reaction to what I'm about to do.

"Is this what you want?" I tease the tip of my cock against her clit. She nods, her eyes closed.

"How do you want it?" I slap my cock up against her wet mound. "You want it hard? Like a little whore?"

"Uh huh." She nods again.

I grip her hair tighter and turn her head to face me. "Look at me and tell me."

Her eyes open and I slap my cock up against her clit. They roll back and she moans, before they lock onto mine again. "Please. I want you to fuck me like a little whore."

"Whose little whore are you?" I line my cock up with her entrance.

"I'm your little whore."

"Goddamn right you are."

I turn her head back toward the wall, and lean in next to her before shoving my cock into her wet cunt. Her gasp and squeal is music to my ears as I lean back and start a punishing pace, pumping into her while her ass slaps against my thighs. Leaning back, I keep a tight grip on her hair. I grab her chin with my free hand and turn her head to me so I can see her eyes.

"Look at me when you come."

Tension builds in my balls and I can't hold out much longer. She keeps her eyes locked on mine as I pound her to the hilt.

Her moans grow louder as I increase the tempo.

"You gonna come for me like a good little whore?"

She nods, still staring at me.

"Whose little whore are you?" I use my hand that's on her chin, and slap her playfully on the cheek.

"I'm your little whore."

I grip along the top of her shoulder and dig my fingers into her soft skin, then start yanking her back to me while I pump into her.

She squeals. Loud.

"Yeah, you like it hard, you naughty little bitch. Come on this fucking dick."

I thread my arm through hers and grab hold of the other, then yank her up towards my chest. My other hand slaps on her clit and I work it in rapid strokes.

She gasps as I fuck up into her as hard and as fast as possible, and her body starts to tremble under my touch. She squirms and tries to push away, but I tighten my grip on her arms and lean up next to her face.

I growl into her ear. "That's it. You take every inch of that fucking dick and you come all over it *now*."

Sounds of my thighs punishing her ass cheeks with each thrust, coupled with those of my cock pistoning her wet cunt, ring out through the closet.

"Fuck." She's getting fucked so hard her words vibrate from her lips.

"You gonna come for me?"

She nods, unable to speak.

"Look at me when you come on my cock, you dirty bitch." I smack her on the ass and somehow manage to speed up my hips. I feel my balls tighten and my load start to build. I slap my hand over her mouth and she screams into my palm, looking me dead in the eye, as I fuck her so fast and hard she won't walk straight tomorrow.

Her eyes roll back and her warm walls clench around my shaft as her body seizes against me. She finally recovers a few seconds later and I release my hand from her mouth.

"Where do you want it?"

"My mouth." She's panting and I barely make out her words.

I never get tired of hearing that.

"Naughty bitch. Get on your fucking knees." I slip my cock out of her and start pumping it as she drops down and tilts her chin up. "Stroke that cock off in your mouth."

She takes my dick from my hand, wraps her lips around just the head, and starts pumping it furiously with her hand. I stare down into her eyes and my load builds in the tip of my cock.

I grab her by the hair and fight the urge to fuck her face while I blow in her mouth. I nod to give her a warning, and finally, it's too much to take. I grunt and let loose, emptying my balls in her mouth as she sucks on me and flicks her tongue across my dick, still jerking me off until she gets every drop.

She starts to pull me from her mouth and I push it in another inch.

"Swallow it you little slut." I tighten my grip on her hair.

She moans on my cock as she gulps, then finally slides me out of her mouth and opens up so I can see that it's gone.

"Good girl." I give her another playful tap on the cheek and she smiles.

102

I'm standing there in a euphoric state, a little dizzy from the intensity of the orgasm. Brittany stands up and starts to get dressed.

Suddenly, out of nowhere, a sharp pain of anxiety and regret stabs me in the stomach. I know what's causing it, but I can't admit it to myself. What have I done?

Don't shit where you eat, Joel! Goddamn.

"Oh fuck, Quinn." My brain to mouth filter doesn't catch the words before they escape my lips.

Joel, you stupid bastard, how could I do this to her?

Wait a second. I didn't do anything to her. She's not my girlfriend, or my wife.

Fuck her.

I immediately feel bad for thinking that last bit.

"Joel, Joel."

Brittany's words are like gibberish in my ear as I stand there with a blank stare on my face. I'm oblivious to her. All I can think about is Quinn, now more than ever. My body tries to trick me into thinking I've betrayed her. Why? It doesn't make any sense.

I think I might hurl everywhere. This woman has taken up residence in my head, despite the eviction notice.

"Joel!" Her voice is one level below a scream.

"Yeah, what? What is it?" I snap out of my daze.

"Who the fuck is Quinn?"

"Who?" Maybe I haven't completely snapped out of it. I put my pants back on.

"Quinn!" Her arms are folded and her lips are mashed together, her jaw clenched.

"Nobody. What? What are you talking about?" I buckle my belt.

"You said her name, twice. God, she's your girlfriend isn't she? Or your wife? Jesus Christ, you're married aren't you?"

She looks at me the way kids look at vegetables on their plate.

"I don't have a fucking girlfriend."

How am I going to get out of this? I can't even focus.

"Yeah right, you fucking asshole." She storms out of the room.

I'm in shock. I can't believe that just happened. Goddamn, she's going to tell people I'm a cheating bastard. I honestly feel like one, but it's simply not true.

What have I done? I'm like Buckner in the World Series. This has to be a bad dream.

.

CHAPTER 4
QUINN

"**SO** WHAT DO you think about Tommy?" I ask.

"He's so much fun. We've hung out almost every night this week." Megan grins sheepishly.

"Well, go on. Give me the details."

It's Monday at the office and people are bustling down the halls of the firm. It smells of coffee and depression. Some people look hungover, some sad, but not Megan. She's been smiling a lot this past week and that means Tommy must be doing something right.

"We're taking things slow, just having a lot of fun. I haven't laughed so hard in my life. He's absolutely brilliant too."

"Go on." I nudge her with my elbow, and she blushes.

She leans over to whisper. "It's going very well."

So much for getting some juicy details. She's obviously not going to give them up. She hasn't said a thing about Joel. I know she's met him. I have to stop thinking about him. I hope he's doing better.

Get your shit together, Quinn.

"Well, I have to get going. We have a consultant coming in. I might just blow my brains out." I put my fingers next to my head and pull the trigger.

"Okay, well let's grab lunch later this week. Or hang out. We haven't done that in forever."

"I know. I need a girls' night so bad." I adjust my purse on my shoulder.

"Let's do it then. Just shoot me a text and let me know when works for you."

"Sounds good." I turn on my heel and walk through a row of cubicles full of people trying to look busy.

A couple of guys look up to check me out. I look like a mess but they don't seem to mind. I woke up late and pretty much threw my hair up and slung some clothes on. I forgot that I would be in meetings all day.

I see some of the ladies from my department standing around whispering to each other. It's usually the same gossip—who's cheating on their wife, who's sleeping with who for a promotion, who the bitch of the week is, or the latest episode of Grey's Anatomy.

It's always pretty boring and petty, but I like to stay on their good side. The last thing I want is them talking about me.

I refer to them as the bitch brigade—in my mind of course, and never to their faces. I walk up as they all point and snicker.

"So, what's the dish? Come on, I want the deets!" I want to slap myself hard for saying "deets." It's what I have to do to survive in the workplace though. It makes life less complicated.

The leader, Madeline, and the hideous mole on her upper lip respond.

"Oh, you haven't seen the consultant yet? Delicious!"

Oh goddamn, please don't lick that disgusting mole on your face. She always does this thing when she sees an attractive guy, where she sort of licks her lips and tilts her head back. She has to be pushing 60 and calling her rotund is putting it nicely. Fuck me, there goes the "tilt 'n lick" maneuver. I try not to vomit.

I look over, and Tommy is standing there.

What in the hell?

He's an accounting consultant. There's no way he's here for the marketing department. He spots me and comes walking over at a brisk pace, and he's glaring.

"Well, you can't even let Megan go to work. Can you? She's got that ass whipp—"

He cuts me off mid-sentence.

"We have epic fucking problems, woman."

My mind races. Tommy is attractive and brilliant, but he's not hot enough to elicit a "tilt 'n lick" from the cunt sorceress. All of the neurons in my head begin to fire in a meaningful sequence, and it hits me just as he walks around the corner.

Joel.

Fuck me. No wonder Tommy is here. But why? These bean counters shouldn't be consulting with marketing. They should be down with the number jockeys, making Excel jokes and talking about taxes and shit. Actually, most of the people in accounting are really sweet, even the guys. They're mostly introverts though, so it's fun to fuck with them from time to time. I would take them over the bitch brigade any day.

My body is yanked out of Joel's view before he sees me.

"Jesus Christ, Tommy." I pause for a moment and stare at him. He's sweating bullets. "What the hell is your problem? She making you go to war to get in that skirt or what?"

He starts to lecture me and then chuckles. "Yes, she is actually. But that is beside the fucking point. Joel is here."

"I know. I just saw him. Has he gained weight? He looks a little puffier than I remember."

I start to look around the corner and he yanks me out of view again. He's about to get knocked out.

"Will you fucking focus. Just stop for a second and connect the dots."

I stare at him blankly, and my face heats up. "Look man, I haven't even had my goddamn coffee yet. What the hell kind of quantum entangled conspiracy theory do you have cooked up in your brain right now? I'm worried about you."

"I came to see Megan and I ran into Fatty McGhee out there."

"He has gained weight. I told you. He's still gorgeous though. Bastard." I fold my arms across my chest.

"Well, he's going to meet Megan. He will see you. You get what I'm saying?" He's still staring at me like I'm an idiot.

"Yeah, he meets your girlfriend, and he sees me. It seems pretty obvious. He will talk to women he knows today."

"Man, I swear. Get your shit together. He's going to know I met her through you. Which means he will know I've been hanging out with you. Which will send him flying off the deep end and he will close the goddamned Haagen Dazs factory for good this time." He tugs at the collar on his shirt.

"That's quite a stretch. I mean c'mon."

He's still standing there, staring at me like I'm stupid, and he's about to get dick kicked across the room. It's as if he can sense it too. His knees turn to jello.

"He's my best friend, okay? I should've told him about this shit. I didn't."

"Okay, what do you want me to do? Pretend to be sick and go home?" I shrug.

"That's not a bad idea. Occam's Razor at its finest."

I have no idea what the fuck Occam's Razor is, so I just nod.

"No, no, I have to tell him. I'm just going to tell him. Holy tittyballs, has that lady seen that goddamn mole on her face?" He stares at Madeline and it looks like he just bit into the sourest lemon on the planet.

"It has hair growing out of it. Doesn't it?"

He looks at me and grins. "Yeah it does. That is a hairy fucking supermola. That thing collapsed on itself at some point and blew the fuck up. Stage four shit. Am I right?" He giggles. "She needs to go see George Lucas and have the Death Star laser that fucking thing off. I might puke."

I'm about to choke trying not to laugh, and I'm afraid my cheeks might explode. "You need to watch some new movies. You're going to run out of references."

"You need to watch your mouth. Now, if you'll excuse me, I'm going to go send Joel into a tailspin of chicken wings and filth."

Poor guy. I feel bad for Tommy. I can tell he genuinely cares, but Joel needs to get over it. What? Tommy can't talk to me anymore? If Joel is that petty, Tommy needs a better friend. It's not like I dated him for a year and then dumped him. It was just a little joke. I'm irritated at myself for doing it, but he has to have hurt other women as well. Women who didn't just fuck him in a bathroom of a bar, having their hair pulled and all their wildest fantasies come true.

Jesus Christ. Get it together, Quinn. You have to face him this morning.

Shit.

I suddenly remember how I look today. Of all the days he would see me, I look like this. I'm trying to think of some way I could make myself look presentable, but nothing comes to mind. Fuck it. It's not like we're going anywhere anyway.

I walk back over to the bitch brigade.

"That man is delicious with a capital D. Word is he knows his way around the bedroom too." Madeline rakes her hand through her hair.

"Who told you that?" I say it before I realize the words have escaped my mouth.

Natalie, who I refer to as Madeline's bitch—in my mind of course—responds. "Someone heard it from the boss lady in IT."

Relief washes over me and I have no idea why. Megan must have told someone. Which I'm sure she found out through Tommy, or me. I can't remember. At least I know he hasn't fucked anyone from the office. It's hard enough walking around my house knowing he's banged his way through half of the inhabitants.

"I would let that man do whatever he wanted, *to* whatever he wanted," says Madeline.

I've had about all I can take when I look up and see Joel piercing me with those beautiful green eyes. My chest caves in. If my heart is capable of fluttering, it does that too. It's like a weight is pushing down on the top of my head and anxiety, fear, and excitement are all coursing through me, penetrating every organ in my abdomen. I've never felt this way about a man, ever.

Joel and Tommy walk toward me.

I keep telling myself that I need to get rid of these feelings, because there will never be anything between us. I have to play it tough. I can't let him know that there is any part of me that wants him. That shit is like gold to manipulators like him.

"Quinn." He nods. "Nice to see you again."

I stop breathing when I hear his voice.

Fuck.

Tommy smiles. I look down, and he's tapping his foot up and down rapidly. Say something, Quinn. Why can't I speak? Don't sound like an idiot for the love of god. I glance up at Joel trying to burn into his soul with my retinas.

He returns my stare and then turns to Tommy. "Well, I was nice, Tommy. Like I promised." He turns back to me. "You have a great day, Ma'am."

Tommy's face goes into his palm. My face is on fire. This prick is not going to talk to me like that. Ma'am? Goddamn it! Ma'am? You, arrogant fucker.

I snarl at Joel's back as he starts to walk away. "The kitchen is that way." I point in the opposite direction of where he's walking. "We laid out a gluten free spread. Some of the women get a little bloated around here. If you're worried about that type of thing."

That's right, dick. I fold my arms over my chest and stare at his back as he freezes. You're being an asshole to the wrong chick.

Tommy looks like he's trying not to giggle.

Fortunately, the bitch brigade is out of listening range. But those women are experts at reading body language.

Joel turns around slowly. A forced grin is covering his beautiful face. He walks back and leans in next to my ear. "Well, personally, I find gluten free food to be a tease. I prefer eating the real meal at the other table. While the gluten free finger foods sit jealously, at their lonely table, watching me devour their friends who provide an entire, satisfying meal."

"Oh fuck," whispers Tommy.

Joel leans in closer and I know he can feel the anger radiating from my body.

"Fuck me, please don't—" Tommy whispers again.

"In fact, I might just have to go back for seconds. I don't think I'd have any problem grabbing another plateful." He pushes some stray hair back over my ear, and I want to melt into his hand. Then he opens his fucking mouth again. "I love your hair like this, very natural. Like a messy, working woman type vibe. It suits you."

He smirks and I lose my cool. My eyes wander around the room and nobody is looking. Without realizing it, my fist clenches and I rear back and pummel his balls with a right cross. It's an instinctive self-defense maneuver my dad taught me when I was very young.

He drops his papers all over the ground as he doubles over at the waist, somehow managing to hold onto his laptop. Tommy is damn near catatonic, and then his face turns bright pink and he is covering his mouth, trying not to laugh. Joel is bent over at the waist coughing, trying to figure out what just happened.

I'm still shaking, but the shame of what I just did is building up inside me. This fucking prick just knows how to push my buttons. He gets under my skin like nobody ever has. He makes my blood boil, to the point it's uncontrollable.

I lean in next to his ear and breathe heavily into it. "Eat up, bitch."

I walk off toward my office and can see Tommy tending to Joel in the corner of my eye. Fuck me. I'll probably get fired for that.

What did you just do, Quinn?

CHAPTER 5
JOEL

"NOW HERBERT, I believe Mom wants you to make babies with that woman, not prevent them from being made."

I look up, and Tommy has a huge grin on his face. I know he's right, but I don't know what just came over me. That guy isn't me. I don't do petty shit like that. That girl drives me to the point of insanity.

"Fuck man. I think she knocked my balls up into my stomach." I reach down and see if my balls are still attached when nobody is watching.

"I know, big guy. I know." Tommy pats me on the back as he helps me up.

I slowly straighten myself out and Tommy is trying not to giggle his ass off. I can't blame him. I'm sure it would've been hilarious if I were a spectator.

"You sure you're not mad?" he asks.

"About?"

"Me not telling you about talking to Quinn." He scrubs his hand through his hair.

"Like I said. Mad about what?"

He sighs and relaxes. "Thanks, bro."

"Don't sweat it, man. I mean don't get me wrong, it was a total Lando move. But you had your reasons. Personally, I'd rather be frozen in carbonite right now. It's like my dick just went ten rounds with George Foreman."

"Well not even Ali was crazy enough to rope-a-dope with his cock."

I chuckle and his joking takes my mind off of my swollen balls. She hits like a fucking man.

I suddenly feel sick to my stomach, and it's not from taking a right cross to the nuts. It's the same feeling I got in the closet at work. I immediately want to go and apologize to her. How would that go down though? She'd never believe me.

"Alright, well if you're going to survive, I'm going to go see Megan before I head to the office."

"No worries. I'm going to try and get my dignity back, and hopefully survive this day. Drink after?"

"Can't, hanging out with the ol' lady. Rain check?"

I do my best impersonation of Indiana Jones cracking his whip.

Tommy shakes his head at me. "Yeah right. You gotta actually get it to be whipped."

I shoot him a blank stare. "She's making you work too hard for it."

"That's what I like about her. I'll text you later."

I walk into the conference room, and Quinn's eyes sear a hole in my skull. Time is going by at the pace of a snail. I think that Einstein guy was on to something with his theory of relativity. I plug in my laptop and fire up my PowerPoint presentation. I look around, and it's almost all women. Thank god only one of them is holding me in contempt. There are a few men, but marketing and accounting are usually comprised of females.

I mean sure, I get it, I hurt her friend. I thought I was doing the chick a favor. She's batshit crazy, but I gave her a memory she will never forget. I guarantee nobody has ever gotten her off like that. Quinn needs to grow the fuck up and get over herself.

You are a fucking mess, Sir.

I look up at the room and start my presentation. But there's only one person I can focus on, and she hates my guts.

"Now, many of you are probably wondering why accounting is important to the marketing department."

Quinn rolls her eyes.

Bitch.

"But, you're actually vital to the accounting process. Marketing is on the front lines—securing sales, landing contracts, seeing deals through to completion. You're the first line in capturing information that helps inform management in their decision making processes."

Most of the women are checking me out, probably not hearing a thing I'm saying. Quinn is on her phone, smirking. I grip the edge of the table, hard. She's probably texting Olivia, telling her all kinds of fucked up things. Laughing about what they did to me. How she sucker-punched my fucking junk. I'm sure Tommy has let her know what a mess I was after their little stunt. He's a great friend but he's a little gossip queen sometimes.

The rest of the morning presentation is as awkward as the beginning. I can't get out of this fucking place fast enough.

"Okay, so that pretty much concludes the morning overview of how our software can help integrate and automate a lot of the work you guys do. That way you can focus on doing what you do best—selling, fostering relationships with clients and vendors, and securing new revenue streams. After lunch, I'll be sitting down with different people individually to find out what I can do to make your life easier."

Quinn is practically out the door before I can finish. I can't believe how ridiculous she's acting. Well—I said some pretty mean things to her—but for fuck's sake I was just defending myself from her onslaught. Oh well, what's done is done. I just need to do my job and then I can be rid of her.

Yeah right.

Grabbing my plate and drink, I start walking through the small cafeteria. It's pretty crowded. Their company is quickly outgrowing their building. I weave through the crowd and suddenly Quinn is right in front of me, sitting at a table alone and looking down at her phone. I have to say something. I need to be the bigger person and put the petty shit aside.

Making amends will make this whole ordeal easier. I don't know why I care so much, but I don't want her to hate me. Tommy is also dating her good friend and I'll no doubt have to encounter her outside of work. I need to be a professional regardless, to protect my job.

Instead of doing the mature thing, I look for a way out. But everywhere I turn I'm surrounded by middle-aged women, all talking to each other and oblivious to my predicament.

I take a deep breath. "Look, Quinn—"

She doesn't even look up from her phone. "What is it, Joel? Do your little boys need a hug? The ice machine is across the hall."

What the fuck?

I mean, that shit's pretty funny, but not when it's directed at me.

Why couldn't we have met under normal circumstances? Her quick wit turns me on and she's so fucking hot, even when she doesn't try. How does she just wake up in the morning, roll out of bed, throw on some clothes, put her hair up, and still look like that? I just want her to like me. Even as a friend. I hate knowing that she despises me.

I try to disregard her snarky comment, but something in me just won't let it go.

"What did I do to make you hate me so much?"

"Really? You want to do this right now? While we're at work?" She pushes her plate aside and folds her arms across her chest.

I couldn't care less about where we are at this point. It's killing me. "Yeah. I want to know why you're treating me like this. I didn't do anything to you."

She glares at me and I swear I can see Satan dancing around in her eyes, with flames and shit. Maybe a pitch fork thing.

She gets up and storms out of the cafeteria. Without thinking, I follow after her. It's difficult. She knows this place better than I do and there are people everywhere I turn. I set my plate and drink down on a table and weave through the crowd. I can barely see the top of her head as it disappears around a corner.

I finally make my way through the ruckus and see an exit door closing at the end of the hallway. Hauling ass down the hall, I pause momentarily in front of the door and try to catch my breath. I've been hitting the gym but I definitely have some work to do.

I put my hand on the door and take in a huge breath, pausing for a moment. Then I ease it open and she's sitting there. A tear streams down her cheek. I knew she felt something for me.

She looks up, and her gorgeous blue eyes look lighter in the sun. My collar feels ten times more snug than usual around my neck and I tug at it. I can't help but feel responsible for the tear I just witnessed. I have to do something to take her pain away. Without thinking, I start walking toward her like a man on a mission.

What the fuck are you doing, Joel? Pull yourself together.

She wipes the tear from her face, and a scowl replaces the sadness in her eyes.

"Here for another ass whipping?" She nearly chokes on her words.

Her face reddens more with each step. I've completely lost control of my actions at this point. I don't have a fucking clue what I'm doing. When I get to her my palms flatten on both sides of her face, and I press my lips to hers.

What the fuck are you doing?

Her eyes widen, but she doesn't push me away. She presses back into me and our tongues intertwine. My hands find their way into her hair, and then slide down to the sides of her neck as I taste her on my lips and feel her in my palms. We're both momentarily in another world. It's the best kiss of my life, and I never want to let go of her. It's a new experience, something I've never felt. Colors and energy come alive in everything, and it's like floating on a cloud, invincible from anything that could possibly go wrong. The rest of the world does not exist. For this brief moment in time, I'm in another place, feeling something that's indescribable.

We finally release, and I stare into her eyes. A tear forms, and she pushes me away.

"I-I can't. I can't fucking do this. I'm sorry." She hurries toward the parking lot, and I don't follow her. I can't—physically—my body won't let me.

She disappears into a sea of automobiles.

"Yeah, I'm sorry too."

CHAPTER 6
QUINN

I SIT ON the couch curled up in the fetal position, trying to contemplate what just happened. My brain is running a marathon. Jesus Christ, that kiss. No, I can't do this. What about Livi? What about everything I know about Joel? He's a player—an asshole, yet he won't leave my mind. I want to know what he's thinking, what he's doing. Why'd he have to fucking kiss me? And why does he kiss so fucking good? Livi is going to hate me, and I have to tell her.

Voices from the porch jolt me from my thoughts. What the hell? It's two in the afternoon. I recognize Livi's giggle, and she has someone with her. A key rattles inside the door handle, and I grab a pillow, pulling it close to me.

Livi comes through the door, and a guy falls in behind her. So much for her being in love with Joel. It takes them both about 15 seconds to even realize I'm there.

"Oh, shit. I thought you'd be at work, Quinn."

"Yeah, I came home. Didn't feel well."

The guy she's with checks me out.

Asshole.

Bringing another guy home after just meeting them, Livi? What a shocker. Usually I'd be nice, but I'm just not in the mood.

"This is Christian."

"Sup." He leans over to shake my hand. I smell the douchebag on him from a mile away. "Damn. Two hot chicks livin' here? Bet you ladies have some fun." He slow nods like an idiot.

What a prick.

"You guys want me to go?" I stand up.

"No." He answers immediately before Olivia can say anything. "We was about to have some fun if you wanna join?"

It takes me a moment for his words to sink in. Are you fucking kidding me? Livi's face turns to disappointment knowing her new hook-up is interested in me. I need to be nice even though I'd like to throat punch the sack of shit.

"I'm going to go." I turn and look at the prick. "Forgive me. I've forgotten your name."

I doubt he caught the sarcasm and it was the most diplomatic response I could muster.

Livi's eyes light up. She obviously wants to get rid of me, and I'm going to knock the shit out of this asshole if I stick around much longer. I walk past him and whisper to Olivia. "I need to talk to you for a sec."

She turns to Christian. "Go hang out in my room. I'll be right there."

"Ooh, sounds hot."

I'm not even going to try and talk her out of this. Fuck it.

She plops down on the couch next to me. "He's hot, isn't he?"

I can't help myself. I have to tell the truth. "No, he's not hot. He's an idiot."

"Don't be bitter. God, what's wrong with you?"

"I have to tell you something. I did something, well, kind of. I don't know how to explain it—" I rake my hand through my hair.

"What happened?"

"I saw Joel today." Nerves roll through my stomach.

Her eyes light up. "Really? How'd he look? Fucking gorgeous I'm sure. Did he say anything about me?"

Well, so much for Christian replacing him. This girl is so sweet, but fuck she is dumb when it comes to men. How do I respond? He did mention her, but it was not flattering. I don't have the heart to lie to her. It's time to just rip the Band-Aid off.

I turn and look at her. "He kissed me."

She adjusts herself on the couch and looks as if I just murdered her puppy. "You kissed him?"

That's not what I said, but fuck it.

"Yeah, I guess. It happened so fast."

"How could you do that to me? You're supposed to be my best friend. What the hell?"

My jaw starts to grind. I didn't do anything wrong. At least I think I didn't. The whole incident races through my mind, and my head begins to spin. It all happened so fast. He kissed me, and I kissed him back, but then ran away. What's the big fucking deal? She's the one who got me in this mess.

"Look, he's consulting at my firm. I was being a bitch to him. I left. He followed me out the door and kissed me. I kissed him back for a second, but then pushed him away and left."

"I don't believe you did this. I've always been there for you and then you what? Stab me in the back?"

"You dragged me into this! I didn't want any part of your childish bullshit, remember?" I stare at her.

"Oh, whatever. You've wanted him since you met him. Brandi told me all about it."

Beautiful. Add another bitch to my shit list. I sigh. "What'd she say?"

"That you were all flirty and left with him that night." She glares.

I seriously need to be taking crazy pills. It's time to be honest with Olivia. If she doesn't like it she can kick rocks. I'm pretty much done with her anyway.

"That's what you told me to do. I can't believe I'm having this conversation. You already have a new fuck buddy waiting for you in the bedroom. Fuck it. I do like him. I like him a lot actually. But I haven't acted on it, because of *you*, out of respect for *you*. Even though you're too fucking stupid to realize he used you for sex. And you know what? He probably does like me. But that didn't matter because you're my friend. I didn't want any part of the silly games you wanted to play with a guy you fucked within 10 minutes of meeting, but I did it anyway. *For you!*"

She shakes her head at me. "Well, now the truth comes out. You are so self-righteous. Always perfect. Perfect little Quinn who looks down her nose at everyone. In the meantime she's stealing their men from behind their back. So fucking fake!"

I can't believe what I'm hearing. I'm quickly realizing it wasn't Joel who was the problem. It was her. He was just in the wrong place at the wrong time, and banged the wrong girl.

"You're a fucking psycho. I'm done. Have fun with pencil dick back there."

I ball my hands into fists and stare her down. But it's my own fault. I should know better than to be friends with her. Should know better than to stoop to her petty games. It's like I have this need to fix people. My friends are projects and I'm out to change them. For some reason—like always—I feel the need to apologize though. I was pretty harsh.

"Look, I'm sorry. I tried to do what you wanted me to do. Obviously I fucked it up."

"Yeah, you did. I need some time to think about this. To see if we can still be friends."

"Call me when you figure it out." I stand and walk out the front door, with no idea of where I'm going.

Nice job, Quinn. Enable her some more. Make her think she's in the right. I don't know what my fucking deal is. I always have to be the peacemaker. Jesus Christ, I need a shrink.

I'm at the bar, picking at the cardboard coaster, sitting next to my third scotch in an hour, drinking my sorrows away. It smells like peanuts and fat married guys in here, but I don't mind. The whiskey burns my throat as it goes down, and I love the feeling. It sounds like a terrible place for a single woman to hang out, but it's actually nice and low key. The bartenders know me and it's one of the only places in town where I won't get hit on every two minutes. I fumble through my purse and manage to find my cell.

"Megan. Hey, what's up? I hate to do this to you, but can I borrow your boyfriend for an hour or so?" I run my hand through my hair.

She chuckles on the other end. I'm pretty sure I am the only person on the planet who could get away with asking her a question like that. I can't help it. I need to laugh, and I need an intelligent person's take on my predicament. Tommy knows the situation better than anyone. I pick at my fingers when I think about not asking them both to come, but they'd sit there and stare adoringly into each other's eyes, and I'd most likely vomit on the table.

Thirty minutes pass, and Tommy comes through the door. He's frowning, probably because I pulled him away from his hot new girlfriend. I'm a disappointment to everyone I suppose, but with scotch number four going down, I don't give a fuck about much at all right now.

"You're a cock blocking devil woman. You know that?" He stands in front of the table.

I'm a bit tipsy and laugh a little more than I should. There's just something about Tommy. He's like a funny big brother. I can't help but smile when he's around.

"What's this all about? Why are you halfway to hammered before the sun goes down?"

"I fucked up. I fucked up bad."

He stares at me like I'm wasted, but it's just a slight buzz. So maybe I slurred my words a little. So what?

He takes a seat. "Okay. How did you fuck up?"

"Joel kissed me."

"I know." He chuckles.

"Bullshit."

"I know everything, woman. No secret is safe from me."

I relax a little when he smiles, and I sigh. Why does life have to be this complicated? "I told Olivia. She hates me now. I don't know what the fuck is going on. My life is in some kind of tailspin."

"Let me guess, Olivia acted like a spoiled little bitch? And this surprises you? I swear I thought you were smart." He grins, possibly to hide the sting from his jab.

"Come on. Don't be mean. I need to laugh."

"Well fuck, you need some tough love too, son. Yeah, Joel got a little wild with her. It's who he is, or well—never mind."

"What were you going to say?"

He looks down then back up at me. "It's who he was before he met you."

I scoff. "He doesn't even know me."

Tommy gives me a blank stare. "Stop acting stupid in front of me. Seriously."

I give up and swing my arms up more than any sober person would. "I don't know. I don't know what the hell I'm doing. Everything was so simple, and then he came along. Why did he have to kiss me like that?"

"Look, girl talk isn't really my thing. But I can tell you this—the kid has feelings for you. You obviously have feelings for him. I mean what the fuck? Do I have to spell shit out for you? Give it a try. It's not like you have to get married. Go on a date with him, and see where it goes. This shit is not rocket science. Hell, double with me and Megan. Then you two can talk about girly shit if it doesn't go well, and I'll hang out with fucknuts."

I switch the subject, because I can tell it's making him uncomfortable. But I know he's right. "What girly shit do you think we talk about?"

He exhales a long breath. "Man I don't fucking know. Cosmo quizzes, shoes, celebrity babies—you know, girl shit?"

"You guys are so fucking clueless, I swear." I laugh.

"Truth." He holds out his fist.

I tap my knuckles on his. "Tommy?"

"Yeah?"

"Thank you."

"No problem. You going to be okay? You good to drive?"

"Yeah, get out of here. Go hang out with your hot girlfriend. I'll catch a cab. Treat that girl nice. She's a keeper."

"I wouldn't dare be mean to her. I love my balls too much. I don't think they could take one of your right hooks."

I fake a quick punch and he shoots back in his chair with a look of fear in his eyes. I laugh it up.

"You think you're funny, woman? Fucking around like that? Your ass needs counseling, man. Jesus Christ." He barely gets the words out without laughing.

"Aww, I could never hurt my big teddy bear." I pinch him on the cheek like he's a toddler.

Wow, maybe I am a bit drunk. I need to sober up. He laughs it off, but I can see that he's worried about me. There's no way he could be best friends with the Joel I've created in my head.

"You sure you're good?"

I need to be serious so he can get on with his evening. "I promise. I'm fine. Just blowing off a little steam, but I'm about to head home. Thank you, Tommy."

"Anytime. You call me if you need anything, okay?"

"I promise."

I finish off scotch number five and catch a cab back to the house. Dear god, please let the queen bitch and dickhead not be there. No such luck. I see a car parked in the driveway, as I hop out and pay the cabbie.

I'm sobering up, and I feel a headache coming on. I shouldn't have drunk that much.

Handing the cabbie his money, I say thanks and walk up the driveway.

I stand there and marvel at Christian's car for a moment. It definitely suits him. A 90s model Prelude with one of those loud exhaust pipes. It has all kinds of Asian decals on it.

"Fucking idiot. I bet he has neon lights under this piece of shit." I chuckle to myself.

I contemplate doing something to it, but I have enough drama in my life. It would be petty. Fun, but petty.

I walk through the front door and prepare for the worst. Fortunately, I think they're all fucked out and asleep. I snatch a bottle of Tylenol and take a couple with a glass of water. I don't know if this method actually prevents hangovers, but hopefully I'll at least get some form of placebo effect.

I just want to go to bed and forget the day. No such luck. Cock boy comes strutting around the corner in nothing but boxer briefs. It's like god hates me.

"Sup?" He nods his head up in the air as he says it.

"Nothing. Going to bed."

"Your friend is a wild one. Redheads, right?" He smiles.

This is why we don't keep guns in the house. "Whatever."

"She's passed out but I could still go a few rounds. You want some company?" He stretches his arms toward the ceiling.

Is that a line? In what world does that fucking work on any woman? Livi's standards have gone to shit. This guy couldn't get laid in a gay bar wearing a sequined shirt. I can't believe that combination of words actually came out of his mouth.

"What the hell is wrong with you? No, I don't want to fuck you. I don't even want to look at you." I scoff at him.

"Yo, you don't have to be a bitch about it." His voice is harsh.

"What'd you just call me?" I think maybe I should've stopped at scotch number three. I'm about to blow a gasket on this fucker.

"You heard me. Don't be a bitch." He takes a step toward me.

Try something, you motherfucker. You picked the wrong one today. "You're going to see bitch if you open your goddamn mouth again. I'm not in the mood."

"Yo, I think you need to be put in your place. Bet you like it like that, huh?"

I grit my teeth. "I'm not going to say it again. Get out of my way, *now*."

He sticks his chest out in front of me like he's a bad ass. "The fuck you gonna do if I don't?"

I move to walk around him and he steps in my path.

I stare hate into his eyes. "You step at me again and I'll defend myself. You've been warned."

"Fuck you." He takes another step toward me.

I've had it. I reach over on the counter and grab a fork that is sitting there and stick it straight into his upper right arm.

"Ahh, goddamn!" He squeals and grabs his arm, then falls to the floor as I walk around him.

"Yo, you crazy fuckin' bitch, you stabbed me. I'm callin' tha fuckin' cops."

I chuckle. "To tell them you threatened little old me and got dropped like a pussy?"

He sits there, clutching at his arm. It's barely even bleeding. Where are the real men in this world? I pull out my phone and snap a picture of him while he flops around on the kitchen tile. Tommy won't believe me if I don't have evidence. I look at him and smirk. "Nice barbed wire, brah."

I nod to the shitty looking tattoo on his arm and walk towards my bedroom. What an asshole. I have to admit I'm pretty happy with myself as I lie in bed and hear him pull out of the driveway in his little Honda with a weed eater for a motor. I'm probably going to need a new place to live.

CHAPTER 7
JOEL

I STILL DON'T know what the hell I was thinking.

You can't just kiss that girl. You fucked up.

I mean, she kissed me back for a second, but she's the kind of girl that will go home and analyze everything about what she did, think things through. She probably hates herself right now. I know women more than anything. I can always tell what they're thinking. What they want. She hates herself the more she thinks about it. Her only logical conclusion is that I'm an asshole who takes advantage of women.

I can understand how it might look that way, but it's never been my intention.

I stroll down the hall for day two of the longest week of my life. The offices are more colorful and people dress more casual in marketing. The sounds of voices actually carry across the room. I quickly realize what's different. It's been bothering me the entire time I've been here. In accounting departments, there are always printers running. I miss the sound of the printers.

I'm supposed to meet with some members of management to see how I can make their lives easier and their departments more efficient. It really means I'm supposed to sell them some bullshit they probably don't need, but I have to convince them otherwise.

I scan the room looking for Quinn, just wanting a quick glimpse of her. Where did she go? She just disappeared yesterday. I haven't seen her since. Get your goddamn head in the game, Herbert. This is my career. I can't have my mind occupied by some schoolboy crush.

People carry on like nothing is out of the ordinary. If they were only inside my head right now. I see a couple of ladies—probably in their thirties or forties—checking me out as they pass files back and forth to one another. They really must not get many men down here. I smile to be polite.

The smell of coffee draws me in its direction. I need some caffeine and it's fucking frigid in this office. Someone has commandeered the thermostat and made it their plan to renovate this place into an igloo.

Voices grow louder as I near the breakroom. It's the same in every office. I can only imagine how much productivity is lost in the first 30 minutes of the day. I can't say that my office is any different. People are naturally programmed to walk in, turn on their computer, and then do nothing for the next half hour.

I follow the aroma, and it energizes me with each breath as I turn the corner. I take two steps, and there is Quinn. Jesus Christ. My throat starts to close off, and my palms start sweating. I'm not sure what to do because no woman has ever turned me into a bumbling idiot when I see her, sitting at the table across from the coffee machine. I freeze stiff in my tracks and stare. She looks up from what she's doing, and our eyes meet. There's something different about her today.

She doesn't advertise it, but something about her is off. Her posture, the way she looks at everything. I'm paralyzed, can't move. I can't do anything but stare at her. She has on khaki pants and a red top that hugs tight against her curves perfectly. Her dirty blonde curls drape over her shoulders. I've only ever seen her thrown together—jeans, tee shirt, hair up. She's so fucking beautiful, even when she looks depressed. She *is* definitely the girl you take home to meet your mother.

I don't want to rock the boat any more than I already have. "Sorry, I'll come back."

"No, it's okay. Get your coffee." She actually musters a smile for me and some of the tension releases in my muscles.

I hope she's not in trouble for what happened yesterday. God, what if someone saw her hit me? She'll probably get fired. I can't believe I said that stuff to her. I lean over and get a cup of coffee, then rise back up.

It feels like an eternity as the steam rises from my cup. She's sitting there like she's waiting on me to say something. I want to ask her what's wrong, and why she kissed me back. Did it mean anything? It's like gravity is crushing me into the floor.

My hand starts to tremble. "Ow!" Scalding hot coffee spills over the side of my cup and on my hand.

"Damn, are you okay?" She looks genuinely concerned.

I panic and start to walk away. "Have a good day."

"Sit down."

My heart begins pumping at an alarming rate. I'm pretty sure I just had a hot flash. Can guys even have those? She's turning me into a chick. I turn around and look at her. "Sorry, did you say something?"

She glances back down and doesn't look up from the paper she is reading.

"Don't act stupid. You heard me. Sit down."

It's certainly an improvement from her hitting me in the dick, so I'll take it. My hands still shake when I grab the chair to pull it out.

What in the fuck?

She sets her paper down and looks up at me. Her eyes have dark circles around them.

"I'm sorry for running off and for hitting you."

If anyone else in the world said that to me I'd have some smart-ass comment, especially after how she's treated me. Not that I didn't deserve some of it, but she appears sincere, and I want to be polite.

"It's okay."

"No, it isn't. I really am sorry, though. I don't expect you to forgive me, but I wanted you to know."

"I just, umm, I'm sorry for kissing you like that." I brush my palms down my legs under the table.

Her head drops, and she stares at the table. Fuck, I can't say anything right. She must still be mad about it. What the fuck does that mean? How am I supposed to interpret that?

"It wasn't—the worst thing that's ever happened to me." She lifts her head and a slight smile forms on her lips.

I'm completely out of my element. I should be knocking this out of the park. My hands are still shaking, palms clammy, chest feels like it has a ton of bricks sitting on it. I have no control. Each time I say something I'm taking a risk. I hate it, and it simultaneously excites me. I've never had to work at getting a girl to like me, it's always just happened.

But Quinn doesn't fall for bullshit lines or corny antics.

I decide to shoot straight with her. "Look, if I just know you don't hate me, I can live with that. I never meant to hurt your friend. I really didn't. I swear that's the truth."

"Fuck her." Her hands grip the table.

This is an interesting turn. They must've had a falling out. I try not to chuckle at her choice of words when she realizes what she said.

"I mean don't! I mean, not again anyway, shit." She turns pink in the face and looks away.

We both laugh, but I need to draw her attention away from the fact that I did indeed fuck her friend, pretty hard. My old confidence returns in a way, but it's different this time. It's not confidence that I'm going to get in her pants. That's a long shot at best. But the confidence to talk to her, knowing she's not bulletproof.

"I promise, trust me. It shouldn't have happened in the first place."

I get a text from Tommy just as the conversation is getting good. I can't help but check it though. How do you not read a text when Darth Vader's voice comes through your phone saying "I am your fatherrr"?

I look down to read it.

Tommy: The goose finally buried its beak

I tell Quinn what happened without thinking. "I guess ol' Tommy boy finally found the Holy Grail."

Her eyes widen. "Shut up! Megan finally gave in, huh?"

"Looks like it."

I say aloud what I'm texting back so that Quinn can hear.

Me: I know you're excited Obi Wan, but you might clear it with your ol' lady before you tell people she let you break out your light saber.

"I swear. You boys and your Star Trek quotes." She chuckles.

My face begins to heat up and I realize she's fucking with me. "Don't ever say that to him. He will disown you."

"Yeah, well he shouldn't be telling the world about how he just became a Jedi."

God I love this fucking woman.

Whoa! Get your fucking shit together, Joel. How about you try to be friends with her before you pop the question?

The prophecies from Mom's couch are coming true. I can vividly see her and Tommy teasing me about marriage, about Quinn. Fuckers. I give myself a quick mental slap for saying "fuck" in front of my hypothetical mother.

"I warned him."

"Seriously, Megan is a pretty private person. I don't want to see him fuck it up. He's so happy being with her."

"Yeah, he better be. He betrayed me and hung out with my mortal enemy for a shot with her."

Quinn drops her gaze back down to the table. "Is that what we are? Enemies?"

Her head lifts slowly, and I want to hug her. I don't want her to hurt. It's obvious she doesn't like the way things are going down with the psycho redhead. They must be really close. That doesn't bode well for me. Quinn seems like the type to stick around and remain loyal, even when someone doesn't reciprocate.

"It's not what I want." I take a sip of coffee.

"What do you want?"

"For you not to hate me. I mean, I'd like us to be friends, but I'll settle for being able to be in the same room together."

"We're in the same room right now." She smiles.

I glance around, then back to her face. "I guess we are."

I look to my watch, fuck. I'm supposed to be meeting with Quinn's boss. I don't want to go anywhere though. I just want to sit here and talk to her. I'm not going to be able to focus for shit all damn day.

I shoot Tommy a quick text.

Me: So Quinn and I are getting along

Tommy: Bullshit

Me: She hasn't dick kicked me once

Tommy: We're all hanging out tonight. Don't even reply. You're going!

I set my phone on the table. "Looks like we're all hanging out tonight."

She sighs. "Yeah, I just got a text."

"You know they're going to spend the entire time trying to make us a couple, right?"

She turns away, but I can see her cheeks turn pink. I can tell she likes me, but it'll take way more than a nice little chat to win her over.

She shakes her head. "I know. They'll probably want to do something nerdy too, like watch Star Trek."

It's a trap!

"Like we'd ever want to see that piece of shit, when we could have a *Star Wars* marathon. Am I right?" I smile.

"Oh, good one. Nice redirect." She mocks me for a second, and then stands up from her chair. "Unfortunately, I should go do some work."

"Yeah, I'm late for a meeting with your boss as it is."

"You better go. He's a stickler for punctuality. And I don't think your charm will work on him."

"I think you u-underestimate, I mean, umm, d-don't value. Fucking hell, just—" I pause and collect my thoughts. "Have yourself a great morning." I smile.

Jesus, what a clumsy fucking buffoon. I can't help but think about the scene in Goodfellas when Spider is stuttering all over the place. If Tommy were here he would act the whole thing out. "Spidah, ya stutterin' prick ya!"

I'm laughing my ass off at the mental image of Tommy dancing around. Quinn almost shoots coffee out of her nose at the last thing I said to her.

I shake my head. "I'm sorry."

She smiles and bites her bottom lip. "I like clumsy Joel. He's real. I'll see you later, okay?"

"Looking forward to it."

CHAPTER 8
QUINN

MEGAN AND I are standing in the parking lot of the bowling alley, waiting for the boys to show up. Finally, I can get to know Joel without the Livi situation constantly hanging over my head. A cool breeze sends a few strands of hair across my cheek, but I don't care because the wind makes the heat bearable.

"This is going to be fun." I bite one of my nails.

"I know. We're so excited to hang out with you guys. Tommy won't shut up about it. Hopefully, we can keep the boys' attention. They tend to get distracted around each other."

"They're pretty close, aren't they?" I look around the parking lot for them.

"God yes. It's cute and annoying at the same time. Sometimes it's like babysitting a couple of grown toddlers. It keeps things fun though." She looks over at me. "Don't worry. You'll hear them when they get here."

Fuck. The car. It's not going to help me resist him. At all.

Stop thinking about it.

I look over at Megan. "I hope Joel's the good guy Tommy says he is."

"You like him a lot, don't you?" She grins.

I tense at her question, but I don't see a way to get anything past her.

"Yes. I want to give in so bad. I just know his type. Not his personality type, just the playboy type. You know what I mean? I'm babbling. Please tell me to shut up."

"No, it's cute. I don't know a lot about what happened. Tommy talks a lot but it's hard to pry useful information out of him."

"It was stupid. We were both stupid. I just—"

That car.

The roar of a familiar engine rumbles across the parking lot and interrupts me. The vibrations under my feet reset my brain into "fuck me now" mode. We both look up and there are the boys, pulling through the parking lot in the Mustang. My thighs squeeze together. I'd forgotten how beautiful she is. If it were a man I'd marry it right now.

I look over at Megan and can tell her heart is racing too. I don't think many men besides Joel know what a car like that really does to us. We don't want to get into an expensive, fully loaded Lexus. No, it is gorgeous raw power that does it. For me anyway.

"Good god." Megan's words come from under her breath.

"That car is not going to help me have self-control tonight."

She reaches over and grabs my arm. "Stay strong. I'm here for you."

I laugh at her joking tone.

"Thanks."

"No problem. So—you think he'll take me for a ride in it?" She winks at me, and I push her shoulder playfully.

"Better back off, bitch."

She gasps.

Tommy's window is down and I hear a voice yell, "Sexy bastard coming through! And a fucking beast car."

We both giggle like school girls in a high school parking lot. Joel is revving the engine, knowing what it's doing to us. Prick. I catch a smile from the driver's side. I smile back, but it's not really for him. Well, maybe a little.

They park, and Tommy gets out first. He immediately presses himself against the car and wraps his arms around the windshield. "Oh, I missed you so much, baby."

"Hey!" hollers Megan.

"Hey yourself, woman! She's my first love."

Joel steps out of the car looking hot as hell in a pair of dark denim jeans and a tight, gray v-neck tee. He's always dressed perfectly. I can't help but notice that he's appearing leaner. I wonder if he's working out for me? I know it's presumptuous, but a girl can hope. His smile, and those eyes, and that hair—every one of them styled perfectly as his jawline flexes with his smile.

Everyone's attention immediately turns to Tommy. He's still hugging the car. He starts to dry hump the side of it, and I'm about to lose it, trying not to snort when I laugh. Megan has her mouth covered and pretends she doesn't even know him.

"Tommy!" Joel fakes a glare. "What'd I tell you about that?"

Tommy jumps back from the car with his hands in the air and stares at Joel. "I'll tip her!" He fans his face off like he just went ten rounds with a porn star.

"Nice, Rocco." Joel shakes his head.

"She gets me all flustered." He turns to Megan. "I wasn't cheating I swear."

My sides hurt, and we've been here all of 30 seconds.

Megan is staring at him with her hands on her hips. Her foot is tapping the ground, but there's a smile on her face. "You're out of control."

Joel walks over while the two lovebirds flirt with each other. A lump grows in my throat the closer he gets. Damn this beautiful man and his gorgeous car.

"Hi." He looks at me and then gestures towards Tommy. "Sorry, I don't even try to compete with his sense of humor."

"Yeah, he is one-of-a-kind."

"That's the truth. You look great by the way. I mean absolutely beautiful. Just, you look wonder—Jesus, I'm shutting up now. Sorry."

There he goes being awkward again. I like it. I relax a little, knowing he's not perfect. Nobody could live up to dating someone like that. Wait, are we dating? Are we hanging out as friends? My mind goes into a tailspin and needs to right itself. I fake a chuckle at Joel. Not to be mean, but to buy some time and compose myself. I'm still a little hot from seeing the car and I keep staring over at it.

"Eyes up here. She's not a piece of meat."

I genuinely laugh this time, and look over at her and smile. "Sorry, I meant no disrespect. I just missed you."

"Everyone always misses the car." He sighs and gives me his best dejected look. I wrap my arm around his without even thinking about it and look up at him. "Aww, poor baby. I missed you too."

What happened to slowing things down? Just being friends? It just feels right with him, and yet I know I'm heading down a road that ends with me getting hurt.

"Thank you for taking pity on me." He bats his eyelashes, and I want to jump on top of him.

My thighs tingle, and my heart thumps rapidly. I try to snap out of it when I realize I'm biting at my lip.

Do not sleep with him, Quinn.

God, I hope he has some will power, because I don't think I can hold out now that I've rid myself of Olivia.

"You guys ready to watch me go all Bill Murray in this bitch?" Tommy stares at us.

Joel releases my arm, and we start toward the entrance.

"We don't have a cow. We have a bull," Joel hollers back at him.

Echoes from their laughter ring out through the parking lot. Megan and I stare at each other, apparently unaware of the inside joke.

"What the?" Tommy bugs his eyes out. "You haven't seen Kingpin? We have to culture these women, Herbert. I'm telling you, they need an education in proper cinema." It looks like he's karate chopping his palm in time with each word.

"I concur," says Joel.

We walk through a hallway back toward the lanes, weaving through a sea of kids running wild, parents chasing them, teenagers trying to look too cool to be there. The walls are painted like graffiti murals with bowling themes, and 80s rock is blasting over the speakers, making it difficult to hear each other. There's a faint sound of air hockey tables and an arcade that grows louder with every step. Suddenly, it comes into view, and lights are flashing with mostly boys beating on machines, completely engrossed in their own little worlds.

Stale beer and pizza with a hint of cigarette smoke permeates my nose. It's not too overwhelming, but it's familiar, and reminds me of coming here when I was a kid. This should be fun.

I glance around and see at least three boys standing in front of their mothers with big smiles, holding their hands out, asking for money to go play games at the arcade. I look up as Megan takes it all in. We both look forward at the same time, then look back at each other and die laughing.

The two boys that came with us are standing in front of us with the same looks on their faces, only they don't have their hands out. We both know what's coming before they even ask. Joel lets Tommy do the talking.

"So, umm, babe, do you think it would be okay if—"

She sighs and looks at me. I can't stop thinking about how when put in a certain setting, men automatically return to their childhood. It's cute and keeps things fun as long as they can be serious when needed. I'd like to think Joel and Tommy are that way. They're both very smart and have professional jobs.

"Go ahead boys. Do you need some quarters?" asks Megan.

"How do you know what we want?" Tommy cocks his head slightly to the side.

She stares at him for a moment, and he concedes.

"I promise we won't be long. Just one game. I swear."

"Mmhmm." Megan draws out the sound.

The boys run off before we change our minds, both cheesing. I was never much of a gamer, but I can tell Megan was. She looks as if she wants to join them.

"You can go if you want."

She chuckles. "It's okay, really. I've stolen quite a bit of their time together. Joel's been really cool about it. They can go play a couple of games together."

We stroll to the front desk, pay for the lane, and grab some shoes. It's by far the most casual date I think I've ever been on in my life, if it's even a date. We set the shoes over by our lane, and Megan taps me on the shoulder, then motions for me to follow her.

We peek around the corner and she breaks out a pretty impressive Australian accent. "Observe the males in their natural state with their young counterparts."

I nearly choke on a laugh. Tommy and Joel are focused intensely on the game, other than the occasional pause to talk trash to one another. There are about 10 boys standing around—probably aged six to nine—locked on the game and pointing at the screen. Half seem to be rooting for Joel and half for Tommy.

Suddenly, Tommy buries his face in his palms as Joel's arms fly toward the ceiling and he starts high fiving all the boys that are on "his team." They all begin taunting Tommy as he shakes his head. I get the feeling Joel doesn't beat him at video games very often, so this must be a special moment.

"You cheated!" Tommy receives support from his own team of bystanders.

"How dare you!" Joel stares down Tommy and bows his chest out.

Megan and I can barely breathe. They have no idea we're watching. We lean back around the corner. It's obvious they're halfway joking. It'd be pretty sad if they were actually serious. At the same time, I always find it a little sexy when men act like boys. They know how to have fun, and guys I've known like that usually make awesome dads. It's an attractive quality.

We walk back over to the lane and get everything set up on the screen. The boys finally show up.

"Hey guys," I say. "Have fun?"

Tommy frowns, and Joel beams with pride.

"Oh, we had a blast. Didn't we Tommy boy?" Joel pats Tommy on the back.

"Yeah. It was great." Tommy's words come through his teeth.

"You don't look too happy, Tommy. Did he hit the power button on the Nintendo right when you were about to win the game?" I ask.

Tommy looks as if he might explode, and Megan is grinning wide.

"Oh what do you know about a Nintendo? You don't know the struggles, Quinn. You don't know what it's like to have the frozen block screen, blowing into the cartridge to get it to work, memorizing the code to Contra."

Him and Joel look at each other and immediately start reciting it in unison.

"Up, up, down, down, left, right—"

"Boys!" Megan glares at them.

"Sorry babe." Tommy shoves his hands in his pockets as they both stop immediately.

When Megan turns away, they both finish the rest of it under their breath. Joel sits down next to me and smiles. "You guys want some beer? Something to eat?"

"Pizza sounds good to me. Megan, you want something?" asks Tommy.

"Yeah, pizza is good." She finishes typing a name on the screen.

Joel nudges me with his elbow. "Wanna come with?"

"Sure." I don't think it through before answering.

I'm operating on autopilot right now, and I'm not sure how I feel about it. I really need to think before I just agree to things. I keep telling myself to take it slow, but I want to live in the moment too. Trying to think back, I can't remember the last time I've been out and had fun. Tonight seems like it's going to be a good opportunity. I decide to just go with the flow, but I need to be straight with Joel before I can do that.

We head toward the snack bar, and I pull him over to the side by a wall. I pull on his shirt harder than intended, and he runs into me. His chest pressed up against me sends a tingling sensation through my whole body.

"Shit, I'm sorry." I take a step away.

I expect him to make some kind of cocky comment, but he just smiles.

"What's up?"

"I want to let you know I just want to have some fun hanging out with everyone tonight. I don't want to have to constantly worry about taking things slow, or being cautious about whatever the hell is going on here." I waggle my finger back and forth between us.

"Okay. That's fine." His smile disappears from his face, and his shoulders drop slightly.

I'm not sure I got my point across very well.

Say something, Quinn. You're crushing the guy.

"What I meant was that I want to have fun with you. I just want to be careful too." Much better.

"Okay, well I want to have fun with you too. I don't want you to regret hanging out with me—I mean us."

I'm making him nervous again. It's totally throwing me off. He's still fucking hot, but he needs his confidence back, and I have something else I need to get out of my system.

He turns to head back, and I spin him around by his arm, put my palms on his cheeks, and press my lips to his. His eyes widen for a brief moment, and then he reaches up with his hand and runs it through the back of my hair, sending a shudder down my spine. It's not a long kiss but it sure seems like one. I don't mind at all. I bite gently on his lower lip to tease him, before moving away and staring into those emerald-green eyes of his.

"Was that you being cautious?" He laughs.

"If you can do it so can I." I wink before spinning around and heading toward Tommy and Megan. I give Joel the familiar ass shake he saw the first night we met. Sometimes the hunter just needs to remember how to hunt. I'm still not entirely sure what just came over me or why I did that, but I'm glad I did it. I had to know what it's like to kiss him when I'm not angry or hurt. It does kind of shoot my whole "taking things slow" idea all to shit though.

He catches up to me as we walk up. We grab our shoes and start to put them on.

"Where's the fucking pizza and beer?" Tommy asks.

Joel and I both freeze. It's like the kiss erased our memories.

Tommy looks at me, then Joel, then back at me again. Wheels are spinning in his head. He taps on Megan's shoulder, still staring at us with a huge smile on his face.

"What are you grinning about?" I ask.

Megan turns and faces him.

"They kissed again."

I turn to Joel. "Seriously, how the fuck does he do that?"

"I don't know, but you get used to it. He's a freak."

"It's the Jedi way, and Herbert knows it. Now, we gonna bowl or what, ladies? Oh, and Quinn?"

I drop my mouth open and gasp like I can't believe he just said that. Megan socks him in the gut, and he doubles over.

"You're all going down, as soon as I can breathe again—and get the feeling back in my stomach. Woman punches like a freight train. Seriously though, you two hillbillies need to go get the pizza and beer. Don't come back with hickeys either."

Joel stands up. "I'll go."

He's only gone a few minutes and comes back with the beer. Tommy glares.

"They have to cook it, fat boy. Damn. They're going to bring it out when it's ready."

Tommy does his best to hold his stare without laughing. "Yeah." He nods. "They damn well better, Herbert!"

Joel is slowly getting back to his old self. He's brushing up against me every time he gets the chance. I might be encouraging him. I'm trying not to giggle and flirt too much, but he makes it difficult. If I do end up dating him, I want to enjoy all the fun stuff in the beginning—getting to know one another, butterflies in the stomach, falling asleep on the phone, not wanting to be apart, ever.

We're having a blast, and the night couldn't be going any better. We bowl a couple of games, and the usual hilarity ensues. I get the feeling Joel is doing the same thing I am. He's pretending to be interested in the group but really just wants to focus on me. I'm glad we did it this way though. God knows what I would do to him if we were alone.

We finally finish up our bowling and decide to call it a night. It's obvious that Tommy wants to go home with Megan, and I'm deathly afraid of leaving with Joel, especially in his car.

Tommy looks at us. "Hey buddy, I think I'm gonna catch a ride and stay at Megan's place. You good?"

"Sure, no worries."

"Quinn, why don't you let Joel give you a ride?"

Megan elbows him in the ribs. He's oblivious to his crime. While a savant when it comes to book smarts, he's sometimes hopeless when it comes to romantic intuition.

"What the hell, man? Sorry. What'd I do?" He grabs at his side and arches his back.

"Just hush." Megan growls at him.

"Yeah, it's fine," says Joel. "I'm good. Just gonna head to the house."

"It's okay. I can ride with Joel. If you want?" I stare at him.

What in the flying fuck are you doing, Quinn? Bad idea. Every red flag and alarm bell is ringing in my head, but apparently I'm thinking with my body now.

Joel tries to give me an out again. "You don't have to humor me. I'm a big boy. I have driven alone before."

Ride with Megan and Tommy. Don't be stupid. Please don't be stupid.

"Nah, it's okay. I'm going with Joel. You guys have fun."

I can't believe I'm doing this. I need to zip tie my legs shut. They'll spread for this man if I don't do something.

Tommy and Megan say bye. Concern fills Megan's stare and Tommy looks excited, knowing he's about to get laid. My entire body is numb. I keep biting at my fingernails and wiping my sweaty hands on my thighs. Without thinking, my hand goes down to his and our fingers interlock.

He looks over and smiles.

"Does this feel a little like junior high to you?" I grip his hand tighter.

"No, not at all."

I'm puzzled. Usually he plays back when I joke with him.

"I haven't given you my ID bracelet yet."

I giggle like a teenage girl again. I need an intervention. "Wow, I forgot all about those."

"I gave mine to Tabitha Swanson in seventh grade, and I'm pretty sure that bitch lost it."

"Oh yeah? Did you guys have a long and serious relationship?"

"Hell yes. It was like, three months. That's like a 30-year marriage in junior high."

We walk through the front door and toward the parking lot.

"It definitely is. I bet you planned your dream wedding with Tabitha. Was it in a church, or outdoors? I bet the reception was nice."

He laughs. "You're funny. You know that?"

He tickles my ribs and of course I giggle and flirt back. Fuck me. His fingers have magical powers when they touch me. I want to jump in his arms and wrap my legs around him.

I spy the Fastback as we walk up and the arousal hits me full force. Goddamn it. I head toward the passenger door.

"What are you doing?" He tosses me the keys and my heart attempts to explode from my chest.

"I can't. This is your baby. Just—no, no."

"I'm serious. Get in there and fire her up."

I can't believe he's letting me drive this car, especially after how things went down last time. He must really like me. As far as I know, Tommy has never even driven it. I might just have to tell him.

"Don't you fucking tell Tommy either!" He gets in the passenger seat and looks around the car. "So this is what it looks like from over here."

He adjusts his seat and settles into unfamiliar territory.

I press in the clutch and turn the key. The energy rushes up through my legs and between my thighs as the frame vibrates and shakes everything in the car. I'm so fucking wet.

Joel smiles at me as I pull out my cell phone and snap a selfie of me behind the wheel.

"What the hell are you doing, woman?"

"Hang on a second."

I say aloud what I am typing into my phone.

Quinn: Man, this thing drives like a beast. You'll have to try it sometime.

I press the send button and the picture heads to Tommy's phone. "Okay, you ready?"

"Don't you dare send that. I'll be in the doghouse for months."

I look over and wink at him. "Too late."

"You're some kind of evil, you know that?"

I shift into reverse and back us out of the parking spot. "You knew it was going to happen."

"You drive her straight to your house, understand? No funny business with my baby."

I really should do what he says, maybe even park down from the house, to avoid Joel and Olivia seeing each other. My body makes a different decision. I pull out of the parking lot going the opposite direction of where I live.

"Aren't you back that way?" He turns and points out the back window.

"Shut the fuck up, and enjoy the ride." He's lucky I haven't punched it. Yet.

His phone beeps, and he laughs.

He holds up the phone, and I glance over.

Tommy: WE ARE DONE! BENEDICT ARNOLD!

I grin and work my way through the gears.

Joel squirms in his seat, but I think I'm driving pretty conservatively. I'm still not sure what I'm doing, where I'm going. I've never just lost control of myself like this.

I get on a ramp to the highway and glance at Joel. He's finally smiling and relaxed. His window is cracked, and his hair waves slightly back and forth with the wind.

Time to make him sweat a little.

My dad taught me how to drive, and I'm not unfamiliar with muscle cars. I catch Joel in my periphery as he looks at something we just passed.

I drop from fourth to second gear and hammer the gas, sending us flying back into our seats. The engine comes alive under the hood. Joel immediately reaches for anything he can to grab hold of. It ends up being the dash and my right arm. He squeezes tight. He tries to play it off as I punch the gas harder.

"I see you know how to drive."

"Dad taught me. Dodge Charger." My eyes stay locked on the road.

"Oh yeah?" He stares at the speedometer and his fingers dig into my arm when we pass 100.

I push harder on the gas pedal. We weave around a few cars and get in the right lane to exit the highway.

"Yep. The same model McQueen raced against in Bullit. Didn't work out well for the Charger. Good thing we're in the Fastback, huh?"

I can hear him nearly panting, but he doesn't make me stop. He has no idea where we're going. Hell, I'm not even sure I do. But the wind in my face and the power in this car sends me into a different world. I could definitely get used to it.

Finally, I slow back down to a normal speed. I hear a sigh of relief and Joel sinks into the seat. I can't help but notice his cock bulging in his jeans too.

I knew that shit was getting him all excited and worked up.

I downshift as we go around a turn. "You don't like it when someone else is in control. Do you?"

"No. No, I sure don't." He hasn't fully caught his breath.

"Good."

I hammer the gas again and fly through the gears, racing down a backroad into the dark of the night. It's not busy, and I know these roads like the back of my hand. It's where I grew up.

He jerks back into his seat once more. "Where the hell are you taking me?"

"You'll see." I head down another dark street and pull off the road into a parking lot.

He looks out of the window, trying to figure out where we are.

I grab around his bicep and yank him over to me, mashing my lips against his. I can't help myself. I want him so fucking bad. Everything in the universe feels right when he puts his hands in my hair, around my neck. I slide my hand across his chest and up over his shoulder before attacking his neck and licking to his ear.

We both struggle to breathe while exploring the other with our hands.

Joel grabs me and separates us momentarily. "We shouldn't be doing this."

I slap my palms on the sides of his face and stare into his eyes. "Shut the fuck up and follow me."

I get out and hurry around the car as he opens his door.

"Damn it. You really need to let me open the door—"

I shut him up by pressing my lips to his again. His mouth is a strong drug, and I can't get the monkey off my back.

I finally release him. "Follow me."

I grab his hand and lead him across the parking lot. I don't know what's gotten into me but adrenaline is coursing through my body.

"Where are we going? What is this place?"

I ignore him as we near our destination.

"Is this a football field?"

I turn back to him once more. "Didn't I tell you to shut the fuck up and follow me? Yes, it's the football field." I point to a building across the way. "That's my old high school."

He's still staring at me like I'm a calculus test. I pry the locked chain link gate as far as it will go and squeeze through. He follows behind me. His hand grabs me by the arm and I smile.

"Are you going to tell me what we're doing here? Why the fuck are we at a football field?"

I spin around and lift up on my toes to get in his ear, and my right hand grips his big fucking dick that's bulging in his jeans.

"I've never taken a boy under the bleachers before."

CHAPTER 9
QUINN

I WANT HIM more with each step and I can't believe I'm about to finally do this. Everything in my brain says I'm making a mistake. That I'm going to get hurt. This is all he wants and then I'm just another one of his conquests, no better than Olivia. I don't care though.

I look back at the moonlight striking the side of his face, the spark growing in his eyes, and I can't take it. My want outweighs my rationale.

We move somewhere between a walk and a jog until we're underneath the bleachers, and we head to a dark corner. He starts to say something and I shove him up against a support beam, put a finger over his mouth, and slowly move it down his lips. He's trembling. I know he's used to being in control, but not with this girl. My hands have a mind of their own as they explore his broad chest and shoulders, and I stare into his green eyes.

I lean up and kiss him once more—slowly—as I run my hand back down to his cock. I need to tease him—make him sweat—before giving him what he wants. I run my hand across his belt buckle as if I'm going to take it off, but then brush my hand back across his cock in a smooth motion, lightly caressing the tip through his jeans. I look up, and his eyes are closed momentarily before locking back onto mine. They're simultaneously filled with excitement and also the fear that we might be discovered. I know he wants this as bad as I do. I can feel it every time I touch him. The anticipation works through his body.

I move back up toward his mouth and bite playfully on his lip as I run my hand along the side of his neck and brush my fingers through his hair. Still staring directly into his eyes, my fingernails lightly tease at his scalp, but my lips don't touch his.

I grab him by his shoulders and forcefully spin him around so that he's now pressed face first against the beam. Exhaling into his ear, I massage his pecs, and eagerly run my hand down to his cock. I take his hand and guide it between my thighs and up between my legs.

"Is this what you want?" My words are a breathy whisper.

He nods.

I squeeze his dick and then caress the length of him again while nibbling on his shoulder. "You like a woman who takes control. Don't you? Tells you what you need? Rubs your fucking cock just right? This is exactly what you want. Isn't it, Joel? You want to turn around and take control, but you know that's not an option."

I dig my nails into his chest and unbuckle his belt. His hand is still between my thighs, caressing my pussy through my jeans as I breathe softly in his ear. I unbutton his pants and work my hand down his abs into his briefs. He shudders when I grab a handful of his stiff cock and begin stroking it, teasing the tip with my thumb. It sends a wave of nerves coursing through my body, and they all land in one place—the pussy that now belongs to Joel.

I yank his pants and briefs down, releasing his dick. I continue to stroke it slowly while whispering into his ear.

"You like feeling my pussy, Joel? Can you feel how hot and wet it is for you?"

"Yes." He's barely able to speak.

I slap him playfully on his cheek. "Don't fucking talk. Just sit there."

He nods again, his eyes still closed. I watch him obey everything I say like a good boy.

I release his cock from my hand and run my fingers up his shirt, slightly dragging my nails across his skin.

"What do you want me to do with that dick?" I whisper.

He does his best not to answer. Maybe he's learning after all. I reach back down and run my hand next to it on his thigh, before cupping his balls and squeezing as he tilts his chin up to the bleachers. I rub my other hand over the top of his while he continues to feel me through my jeans. Moans escape my lips and fall in his ear as my pussy heats up at his touch.

"You won't last 20 seconds in that pussy. Will you?"

He starts to answer and I flip him around and take him in my mouth. I dive about halfway down his shaft then come back up, before swirling my tongue around the head of his cock. I inch my way back down until I'm cupping his balls and have his entire length in my mouth. I suck hard, wrapping the inside of my cheeks around him. His head swells in the back of my throat, then I slide back up and release him, teasing at the tip with my tongue.

Wrapping my fingers around the base, I begin stroking him while I look up into his eyes.

"Did you like that?"

He nods.

"You like the way your cock feels in my mouth, Joel?"

144

He starts to answer and then nods again.

I stare up at him with doe eyes. I want to tease him all night, make him wait for it. My pussy needs his dick inside of it, but I know he wants it even more, and I like having that power over him. I can practically feel him shoving it into me and the mere thought of it makes me moan. Knowing anyone could walk by and catch us sends a wave of pleasure up the insides of my thighs.

I continue to stroke him slowly from base to tip as I lift up his cock for a view of his balls. Teasing each one with my tongue, I squeeze and caress the tip of his rock-hard dick. I lift his thick shaft even higher and tease underneath, working my tongue between his balls and his asshole. His hips fly back momentarily.

There's the spot. Every guy has one and it shifts them into another gear.

He grunts as I work my tongue back and forth across it and then bury one of his balls in my mouth, sucking as hard as I can, etching the memory of how he tastes in my mind so I never forget. Finally, I stop and look up at him, my hand still working him up and down repeatedly. I spit on the tip and rub it with my hand before sliding my grip down and taking him into my mouth once more, this time bobbing up and down the upper half in a quick, smooth rhythm.

His cock tastes like heaven, and I love how it feels in my mouth, and watching the expressions on his face, knowing how bad he wants me. There's something about being outdoors that is just primal and raw. He needs to take me and hammer his cock inside of me. I know it's going to happen soon, and the thought of it has my legs quivering. He needs to be pushed past his breaking point, and release those animalistic instincts that are built into his DNA.

I slide his cock out of my mouth and rise to my feet. I grab the back of his hair and yank his head back, sucking on his neck as I grab his hand and slap it on my hot little pussy, rubbing it back and forth as I nibble on his ear lobe.

I exhale into his ear once more. "Get on your knees and eat my pussy."

He immediately drops down and does as he is told. I know he's wanted it for a long time, ever since I put on a show for him in the car. He's dreamt about this moment over and over, and now he's finally going to get it.

Butterflies rush through my stomach. I've heard the stories about him. He's the ultimate woman pleaser. I haven't seen much yet, but he just needs to be goaded a little.

His hands grip my ass as he kisses my stomach and I reach down and pull my shirt up over my head, revealing my breasts corralled by a royal-blue bra. I massage them for a second before I reach down and dig my nails into his scalp, pressing my tits together with the insides of my arms.

"Eat that fucking pussy, Joel. Take my pants off and do it, now."

He unbuttons my jeans and I slap him lightly on the left side of his face. It's time to tease again, make him work for it. "Not like that!"

I shove him away and turn around, giving him a view from the back. I unbutton my jeans and slowly work them halfway down my hips and look back at him, watching him study every curve of my body.

"You like the view?" I smirk. "Stroke that fucking dick for me."

Watching him rub his cock while ogling me, sends pulses of heat ripping through my body. I kick my sandals off and work my jeans down my ass. They drop to the ground as I step out of them, now wearing nothing but my bra and panties.

Joel strokes his cock slowly and I bet his balls are about to explode. I back up to him and pull his hand off his cock. I grab his other wrist and wrap both of his arms around my torso, placing his hands on my breasts.

Him pawing at my perky tits sends my head flying back as I work my ass slowly up against his dick, feeling every inch of it slide back and forth between my ass cheeks, soaking up my wetness through my panties.

"Does my ass feel good against that big fucking dick?"

"Fuck yes." He growls his words.

I need to push him harder. He's still being compliant, and I need him to take me and fuck me stupid.

I turn around and glare, wanting him to lose control, to the point he fucks me so hard I can't walk straight. I want his tongue on me, his hands exploring me.

"Get on your knees and eat this fucking pussy!"

He drops down to his knees and takes my panties down to the ground. My thighs are glistening from his touch. He knows how wet he makes me. His face brushes up against the inside of my thigh and energy radiates into my pulsing clit. He slides his hand up and caresses my slick folds, running his hand back and forth on me. His thumb works towards my clit as it tries to peek through.

"That's it. You know just how to touch me."

He slips one of his fingers inside me as the tip of his tongue makes contact with my clit.

I moan. "God, right there."

His finger explores inside me while his warm tongue flicks on my clit and I'm about to lose my shit. Excitement grows inside him, realizing he's gaining more control over me.

"You like that?" He stares at my eyes, and his face disappears between my legs.

"Yes." I gasp as his tongue begins to snake rapidly over my clit and he works another finger inside.

"You going to come for me?" His tongue speeds up.

I pant and nod. "Uh huh."

My wetness streams down the sides of his face as he swirls his tongue on my clit and fully submerges his fingers into the depths of me, hitting my spot just right. I squeeze around him and squeal.

He has me.

"You going to come?"

"Yes. God, please don't stop."

He smiles and begins ramming my needy pussy to the hilt with his fingers, and sucks forcefully on my clit. It sends me past my breaking point. I see fuzzy stars as raw sexual energy shoots from between my legs to every limb in my body. I convulse as my legs stiffen. My thighs squeeze around his face. I reach down and grab the back of his head, digging in with my fingers as my hot core squeezes around his fingers. I hold his head in between my legs, bucking my hips up and down against his face.

He tries to pull back, and I dig my nails into him harder, practically smothering him. I feel tension building in his shoulders. I need his cock in me right now, but I need him to take it.

He's almost there and he looks up at me. I slap him harder on the side of his face. He stares, knowing what I need. His eyes widen, and he stands up.

It's time.

He grabs my hips and flips me around, shoving me up against the beam. He leans down by my ear and growls, before slapping my ass, hard. "Little goddamn tease."

I giggle a little, still trying to tease him. "Fuck you. Don't talk to me like that!"

He fists my hair. "You're a dirty little cunt aren't you? Teasing me with this fucking pussy." He slaps his hand on my mound and runs his fingers through my slick folds.

I squeal. The man has arrived.

He runs his hand through my ass crack and slaps my swollen pink pussy again. Goddamn, I might come again before he's even inside me.

"Naughty little bitch." He shakes his head and yanks my head back by the hair. The sting makes my legs quake. "You like to tease?" He slaps his prick across my ass cheeks and then starts to press the head up against my asshole. I can't take much more waiting. I have to have it now. It's time to submit.

"Yes."

The head of his cock presses harder against my asshole.

"Bet you like it in the ass too. Like a little fucking slut." He slaps me with it again and wraps his hand around my throat, turning me back to look at him.

"I want you to fuck me, please." I push my ass back into him.

He smacks the fuck out of my ass and the sting rips through me like an electrical current. "Yeah." He teases me with the head of his cock once more. "You couldn't handle this dick up your ass. You'd scream like a bitch."

He shoves it underneath me and coats it with my wetness. When it strokes over my clit I bite my lip.

His cock goes back up between my ass, and I grip the steel beam, closing my eyes.

He wraps an arm around me and palms one of my tits, then yanks me up so that his chest is pressed hard against my back. "Take this fucking dick." He bites down on my shoulder and shoves into me. I squeeze my pussy around him as he pumps into me like a mad man, plowing every inch of that huge cock into the depths of me.

His hand grips my hair and pulls my ear up to his mouth as he squeezes my ass firmly with his free hand.

"Is this what you wanted?" His teeth grind together and his hips speed up. He twists one of my tight nipples between his fingers and smacks my ass so hard it has to be dark-red.

"Yes."

"Can you handle more?"

I look back and he grins, then I nod at him.

"We'll see." He grabs me around the waist with both hands, his fingers destined to leave bruises.

He yanks me into him as he thrusts in time. The sound of his thighs clapping against my ass echoes under the bleachers. My eyes roll back, and he's fucking me so hard I might pass out.

"You want it harder?"

I don't think it's possible, but I tell him yes.

He digs one set of fingers into my shoulder, the other still on my ass as he somehow increases the tempo. I'm about to come all over his dick.

He whispers into my ear, "You want me to pull your goddamn hair and fuck you harder? While you scream my name and come on my dick?"

"Can you fuck me harder?" My words already sound like a stutter from his ridiculous pace.

His eyes widen and he slaps my ass once more. I moan.

His fingers twist through my hair.

"Don't say I didn't warn you." He bears down with his knuckles against my scalp and starts yanking me back into his cock. My eyes roll back and my thighs are on fire as nerves shoot through my body.

"Fuck, Joel." My toes stiffen and curl. I start to seize on his cock, and he speeds up.

"Fuck!" It's meant to be a scream, but it comes out as inaudible gibberish.

I squirm, trying to push myself off of him. It's too much to handle all at once, my senses are overloaded, and I am about to come harder than I've ever come in my life.

"I'm gonna come."

"Come on my fucking dick."

Jesus, his filthy mouth.

I start to say something else and his palm crushes my mouth. He speeds up somehow, fucking me so hard I nearly forget my own name. "Fuck." I cry out against his palm.

He smirks and leans down to my ear, his hips keeping the same pace. "I said come on this fucking dick, you little bitch."

My eyes widen, and I can't control what escapes my mouth. I buck my ass into his hips, taking him all the way inside of me as he hammers right back as hard as he can. I start to get light-headed to the point I might pass out.

I'm on the edge, about to lose it when I feel his breath in my ear once more.

"Come on my fucking cock. Now!"

He pushes his thumb inside my asshole, his huge cock pounding into my core.

My eyes fly open, and I scream his name. My world blurs as more than one orgasm rolls through my body. I clamp down on him and everything goes into slow motion. I squeal against his hand as I come over and over on his cock, squeezing as hard as I can, trying to hold it inside me. The last one finally rips through me and he releases his hand from my mouth.

"Jesus Christ!" I gasp.

I pause for a moment, still in a daze, trying to regain my composure.

I want him to feel what I just felt, but I don't know if it's humanly possible. Perhaps it is the competitive side of me, but I'm now on a mission to give him the best orgasm of his life.

I swing around as he slips out of me and go to my knees in one smooth motion, gripping his cock in my palm and taking his balls into my mouth, stroking his dick hard as his head flies back.

I release him from my lips for a moment. "Your turn."

I take all of him in my mouth again and mash my lips against his pelvis, his cock jamming into the back of my throat as I shake my head back and forth on him.

"Goddamn." His hand snakes through my hair.

I nod back and forth on him, sucking my cheeks in and letting his big dick slide against the roof of my mouth while I swirl my tongue around it. When I look up, his eyes roll back.

I pull him out of my mouth and start licking his swollen head from every angle.

He has to be close to blowing his load. I need to help him get there. He looks down at me staring at him, while I trace the crest of his head with my tongue.

"My pussy tastes so fucking good on your dick." I dive back down on him, taking him whole.

That should do it.

"Fuck." He grabs a handful of my hair and releases, shooting his warm salty load straight into the back of my throat. I swallow each wave as it comes, sucking and closing my entire mouth around him.

His thighs tremble and he grunts repeatedly as his hips thrust into me one final time.

I swallow the last little bit that he deposits on my tongue and I slide my mouth up to the head of his cock, wrapping my hand around the base of his shaft, stroking at a slow pace and milking every last drop from his balls.

His eyes work their way open as he comes back to reality and a huge grin covers his face.

"Holy shit."

I don't think either of us knew that was possible. We fit together perfectly, and it was by far the most intense fuck of my life. I'm still tingling to the touch as I rise to my feet and put my palm on his cheek. We kiss, our lips locked together in the steamy night air.

I slowly pull my lips away and whisper in his ear, "Joel—"

"Yeah?"

"I'm naked—at my old high school, under the bleachers."

He looks down at my quivering body, breasts hanging out of my bra, the rest of me completely exposed to the night air. We both laugh.

"I see that."

I know I should put some clothes on, or be worried about being caught, but I hang my arms around his neck and stare at him, pressing my forehead against his, looking deep into those green eyes of his. I know I'm in love with him. Hell, I probably have been since the first time I saw him. I can't tell him that, though.

"What in the hell are we doing?" I ask.

"I don't know, but it feels right." He brushes his fingertips down the back of my arms and caresses my upper back, causing me to shudder one last time. Every square inch of my skin pebbles.

We must sit there for at least two minutes before we pull away from each other. Why is it so difficult to let go of him? Reality sets in fast and I don't feel regret, but I definitely feel like we are moving at light speed when we both agreed we should take things extremely slow and be cautious. I don't want to ruin this. We need to talk, discuss how we want this to progress.

It's nice to have my brain back, but I would be lying if I said it wasn't the best sex I've ever had. By far. It frightens the fuck out of me to make myself so vulnerable.

We've only been on one double date for fuck's sake. Still, I need to say something. I start to open up to him when he says, "I want you."

Jesus Christ, this guy really is a machine.

"There's no way I can—"

He laughs and wipes some of the sweat from his brow, pulling me close and wrapping me up in his arms.

"No, I mean I want you. I want to be with you. You're all I think about."

I completely freeze. Say something, dummy. Tell him you want the same thing.

"Look, Joel—"

"I'm sorry. I know it was too fast. Too much to drop on you all at—"

"Will you just shut up." I shake my head at him and put a finger over his lips. "I want to be with you too. Okay?" I blush. "But, we both know we need to take it slow, okay?"

We both die laughing.

I can't believe I just said that after I drove him to my old high school football field and let him rail me under the bleachers. But, this whole honesty thing is working for us at the moment.

"So what are we doing then?"

"I'm standing here with my tits hanging out of my bra, showing the whole world my ass."

We laugh again.

"It's a sexy fucking ass though." He gives it a quick little playful slap.

I turn bright red, but he still has not let go of me to put my clothes on. I glance back to my ass that is still exposed for the world to see. "It is, isn't it? Now, you're going to have to let me go before we get arrested and charged as sex offenders."

"Every man in the country will move to your neighborhood."

I give him a flirtatious slap on the arm.

"Will you let go of me so I can put my fucking pants on? I won't run away. I promise."

He lets go, and I yank my pants up over my hips and throw my shirt on. We meander back toward the car, holding hands and gazing at each other before we squeeze through the gate.

We approach his car, and I run my hand across the hood as he gets in to drive this time.

"Sorry you had to see that. I know you had him first."

Joel checks his phone as he's climbing into the driver's seat.

He fires up the engine, and I feel the energy rush into my hand. I could listen to this car all night.

"Get in the car, Quinn!" he screams it at me.

I can't make out what he's said over the engine.

"What? Don't scream at me like that, asshole!"

I say it half playfully, but I don't appreciate being talked to that way. What is his problem?

"Get in the fucking car! Now, goddamn it!"

What the fuck? I yank open the passenger door. He's pissed off the wrong girl at the wrong time. What is his fucking deal?

When I open the door he has tears streaming down his face and is almost hyperventilating—like he is having a panic attack. My heart goes from zero to terminal velocity as it accelerates directly into my stomach.

"Joel, Joel, calm down. What is it, babe?"

"It's my mom. We have to get to the hospital. Something—"

"Get in the passenger seat. I'm driving us."

"No—"

"Do it, now!"

He's in no condition to drive, and I know these roads far better than him and he knows it.

He sprints around as I climb over into the driver's seat.

"What hospital?"

"St. Thomas—"

It's all I need to hear as I pop the clutch and we blast out of the parking lot into the night.

CHAPTER 10
JOEL

QUINN GRIPS MY leg with her hand while keeping her eyes focused on the road. I don't know what to think. I don't have any information other than Mom collapsed at home. I can barely breathe, and it feels like I might vomit. She's driving remarkably steady for how fast she is going. It is like she can feel what I am feeling and is not bombarding me with questions, even though I know she must have a million.

"We'll be there soon, okay? I'll get us there as fast as possible. Everything is going to be fine."

I keep trying to talk to her, but my throat closes every time I try to say something. "Thank—" I gasp.

"Don't say anything. You're having a panic attack. We have to get you relaxed, okay babe?"

She's staying completely calm even though she must be going crazy on the inside. Every possible scenario plays out in my head. What if she is gone? What if she tried to call me, and I didn't answer? The guilt is crushing me from every angle.

"Lean back and roll your window down, you need air. Give me your phone."

I do what she says, and she calls Tommy as the air blasts me in the face when I roll down the window. It is helping. I can feel some of it making its way into my lungs.

"Tommy!" I hear her yell. "We're on our way. Yeah, five minutes out. Okay." She hangs up the phone. I can't turn my neck to look at her.

"What'd he say?"

"Sit back and relax, babe. You have to breathe. Just breathe in deep breaths, okay? We'll be there in a minute."

I nod and lean back in the seat, trying to take in air. My chest is thrust back into the seat, and then my whole torso is yanked to the side as I hear the engine tacking out. We fishtail around a corner, and I can see the hospital coming up.

"I'm dropping you up at the front of the ER. I'll be in right after I park, okay?"

I nod again, my chest is caving in the closer we get, and I'm starting to suffocate once more.

She starts stroking my hair. "Just try and breathe, slow and deep. Deep breaths."

She flies through the parking lot to the entrance and comes to a stop.

"Go."

I jump out of the car and sprint through the doors as she pulls away. I see Tommy down the hall, and it feels like I'm running in place. The harder I try to run the slower I seem to go.

CHAPTER 11
QUINN

I'M FREAKING THE fuck out. I can't believe I remained calm like that. I have to get back in there before Tommy gives him the news. He made me swear not to tell him in the car. He's going to be a mess. It wasn't my place to tell him he just lost his mother. Staying collected and not crying or breaking down in front of him was the hardest thing I've ever had to do.

I park the Mustang and sprint toward the entrance as everything starts to surface in my mind. He is going to blame me. His mother had a heart attack and died while I was off fucking him under some bleachers. He'll never forgive me. It's no time to be worried about myself right now though. I just want him to be okay. As long as I know that, I'll be happy.

I see them at the end of the hallway, and Tommy has his hand on his shoulder. He hugs him as Joel goes limp in his arms, barely able to stand. The tears are flowing down my cheeks as I run toward them. Megan is covering her mouth. Her eyes are watery and red. Tommy is on the verge of a breakdown as well. My poor guys, I want to take their hurt away.

Joel lightly pushes Tommy away from him and turns and sees me. He's standing as if he's being held up by puppet strings, like every ounce of strength in him is gone.

His eyes meet mine and this time it crushes my soul. He is completely helpless, defeated, hurting more than he ever has and probably ever will. His face turns pale and his eyes roll back. He collapses on the hospital floor as I run up to them. I dive on top of him and everything happens so fast it's like I'm in another world. I hear voices coming from different directions but it sounds like they're in a tunnel. I know I am screaming but I can't tell what I am saying. In my mind it is all happening in slow motion, but everything is a blur around me as I make sure he's still breathing.

He is, and I can tell he has a pulse. He must have just passed out. He had to have been so overwhelmed with emotion coursing through him, all of his senses simultaneously shocked. I look up and Tommy looks like he might do the same, he looks like a zombie. I holler at Megan to take care of him and she runs over and wraps her arms around his shoulders.

Some nurses and a doctor rush over and call for someone. They haul Joel off on a stretcher, but will not let me go with him because we are not related. Tommy's skin appears to be turning back to a slight pink hue, and he's able to talk.

I grab hold of him and hug him as he grips around my back. Megan hugs him from the other side so that both of us now have him wrapped up, squeezing his trembling shoulders.

I'm bawling my eyes out, still completely confused and praying it is a bad dream. I've never met Joel's mother, and now I never will. I want to go and make sure Joel is okay. I just want to see him, but they still won't let me.

The best I can do is to be there for Tommy until they come and get us.

"It'll be okay, Tommy. Just breathe, sweetie."

He's gripping me tighter, and Megan is rubbing the back of his head and neck, telling him the same things, trying to calm him down.

"She's gone. Mom is gone." He stares off at the wall in disbelief.

"Just relax, babe," says Megan. "Just try to breathe for us, okay?"

He nods, but I'm contemplating calling for a nurse. Megan presses the button.

"Sweetie, you need to let them check you out too. Maybe get you some oxygen. Okay?"

He appears reluctant, but Megan nods to him and he agrees.

A nurse approaches, and she walks Tommy away.

When he's out of sight, I hug Megan and really lose it. I don't do well with death, and I hate seeing people I care about hurting.

"It'll be okay," she says. "They'll get through this. It'll be okay."

"I know." I nod. "I know, but Megan, he's going to blame me. It's all my fault."

"Bullshit!" She grips my face. "No it isn't. You didn't do this. You have to be strong for them, okay?"

"Okay."

About 15 minutes pass, and they call Megan back. I watch her disappear around the corner, and I assume she's going to see Tommy. I asked to go back but they said only one could go at a time and that Joel is still recovering. The next 10 minutes are the longest of my life. I'm pacing back and forth, crying, worrying. I didn't think I'd be stuck out here all alone. I want to see Joel. I want to go hold his hand and take care of him.

Finally, Megan and Tommy walk around the corner. Tommy looks much better, but he is still distraught. They're both walking with a purpose. They seem to be slowing down as they near me, but I assume it just seems that way because I'm so eager to get back there.

"Is he okay? Tommy, is he alright?" I ask.

"He's going to be okay." Tommy stares at me.

"Are you okay? How are you doing, babe? Do you need anything?"

"We're okay, Quinn, I promise. Tommy will be fine," says Megan.

There's something in their tone. Something is off. I don't have a good feeling about it, and my face starts to tingle. My nose is burning, and I start to tear up before I even have all of the information they are hesitant to give me.

"Well can I see Joel?"

They look at each other, and I ball my hands into fists. Tears stream down the sides of my cheeks.

"He doesn't want to see you right now."

I start bawling. I knew he would blame me. I knew it. I fucked everything up. I'm such a horrible person.

I keep trying to speak, but the words just barely come out. "Did? Did he say why?"

"Look, Quinn. He's just shaken up really bad right now. It's going to be fine, I swear—" says Tommy.

"Well what'd he say? He hates me, doesn't he? What did I do? I'm so sorry—please—just, please tell him how sorry I am."

Tommy and Megan wrap me up in a hug.

"Don't worry about what he said. He's not himself right now. This is just how he deals. It's going to be alright."

I can't stop sobbing. Fifteen minutes ago the guy was practically in love with me, and now he suddenly hates me. I don't know if I can take it. I just don't understand why. He wouldn't have been there with her. He would have been hanging out with Tommy. There has to be something else.

I finally calm down a little and look into Tommy's eyes. I know he'll tell me the truth if I really want him to.

"Tommy—what'd he say?"

Him and Megan look at each other for a second, silently debating if he should tell me.

"I think—well, from what little he said, I think he might be upset because he didn't go see his mom for about two weeks after all the shit went down with you guys the first go around. He just needs some time, he's still processing everything. He's emotional."

It is like someone just ripped my heart out of my chest. I hadn't even considered it could be something to do with that.

"W-was, that something he would normally do when he would get upset?"

Tommy sits there, still not wanting to say anything to me. He buries his head in his palms and talks through them. Megan hugs me and I'm about to lose it.

"I umm—" He looks up at me with his sad, glossy red eyes. "I had never seen him go that long without talking to her. I'm sorry."

VOLUME 7

CHAPTER 1
TOMMY

IT LOOKS LIKE Comic Con blew a load all over my walls, and I love every goddamn bit of it. Megan walks through my apartment, and I gawk, as usual, when she comes into the bedroom. Her brunette curls bounce with each step every morning after she fixes it just right. I stare around at the greatness that is my decor and give my morning wood far less attention than it deserves. *Star Wars* shit lines one entire wall because that's how I fucking do.

Megan's fussing about with some earrings, trying to get them in, and I need to stick my light saber in that pussy real quick. I'll find a way. It's difficult to focus on Megan's hot ass and Tom's magic beanstalk sprouting from my boxers with Joel and Quinn's bullshit kicking around in my head. My brain doesn't just shut off like that.

Focus on titties. Focus on titties.

No dice.

"I just want to purple lightning the fuck out of those two. Palpatine style." My hands gesture to Megan like I'm putting Luke on his goddamned back. It amuses me greatly.

"This is serious. Stop playing around. What are we going to do?" She stares at me trying not to laugh.

"Woman, playing around is what I do. You know this about me." I scoff.

"Quinn is asking me a ton of questions. She doesn't know if she should go to the funeral? If she should call Joel? Leave him alone?"

The reminder of Mom being gone is akin to running into the end of a broad sword. Megan has a blank stare on her face.

"Did you make coffee?" I return her stare.

"Stop fucking around. What can I tell her?" She folds her arms across her chest, and it pushes her tits together.

Titties, death, *Star Wars*, relationship drama—my brain is extremely close to shorting out, along with my cock. Let's order this bullshit up by what's most important to Megan at the moment, and that'll increase my chances of a morning pussy hug by at least 110 percent.

1) Joel and Quinn cunt shit
2) Mom's funeral

3) *Star Wars*
4) Her getting to work on time
5) Treatment of Tommy's dick 'n' berries

"I'm not an employee of match.com. That is for them to decide. Don't put that skirt on either." I lean back for her to see the sheet propped up with my dick. I might even pull the covers down on the sides to make it look bigger. "Don't act like you're not impressed."

Pink rushes into her cheeks, but she remains stoic. Admirable, but it will ultimately fail her. "Seriously. I need to give her some kind of information."

"Tell her to ask him. Shit. Look at this fucking tent. I should get some kind of Boy Scout badge for this work of art." I give her my best "please fuck me" grin.

"You really are a man boy."

She decides to tease and pulls the skirt up over her tight ass. Goddamn I love this woman. I can't tell her that. It's too soon. People might start calling me The Panty Whisperer if I drop "L bombs" within the first few months. But it's a fact. Like the apple falling on Newton's pecker (how that little story went down in my mind). Don't give me that shit about it falling next to him. Apple to dick equals revelation of gravity.

"I know this."

She leans over me and bends down so I can see her skirt halfway off her ass. Dragging titties up my chest in nothing but a bra. I do believe I shall get my dick wet this fine morning. Perhaps I should solve her problem for her.

"I'll ask Joel what's up. About the bullshit." I whisper into her ear while she kisses along my neck.

"Thank you." She moves to kiss me and I wrap my arms around her and flip over so that I'm on top. Like her little tricksy tricks would work on me. I'm eye-to-eye with her and I can't wait to turn her to the dark side.

"No. No. I'm late."

"Jaysus woman! I've told you not to say that to a man. It freaks them the fuck out. It's right there with 'Can you see my dick hanging out of this skirt?'"

"Fine. You should have gotten here sooner, Luke. Your aunt and uncle are dead. Mama has to go catch a ride on the Falcon."

I shake my head at her and shove her skirt up to her waist.

"Sorry baby. It's calling to me." I bust out my Vader voice. Shit gets Megan all hot. I work down, bypassing titties because no time, but I assure them I'll do something special for them later in the evening. My head is between her legs and I mimic Vader breathing with an Oscar-worthy performance. "You are unwise to lower your defenses."

She giggles as I slide back up to kiss her.

I slip my boxers down and my cock springs free. I glance down at it in all its glory. "An elegant weapon—for a more civilized age."

She grips my hair, and I lean down and kiss her full on the lips, sinking my tongue in her mouth. She moans back into my kiss as my hand works between her legs.

"You are bad. You know that?" A moan interrupts her words when my finger finds her clit.

I lean back and remove her panties.

"You better be quick."

She's the only woman to ever reward me for a quick performance. I can get behind that kind of attitude.

My fingers stroke across her clit and I speed up on her. She's wet, and her pussy needs to be wrapped around my dick. I line up my cock and part her lips with the head. I don't think I'll have any problems living up to her expectations after checking the temperature. My hands want to rip off her fucking bra so I can suck on those titties, but that would land me in the doghouse, and not in the pussy my dick is currently teasing.

I look down and her eyes roll back as I push into her. "Fuck."

She moans as I thrust hard and deep. My cock is rock-solid and hitting her in all the right spots as she digs her nails into my shoulders.

She flips me over to my back and my cock never leaves her. "Can't be messing up my hair." She squeezes my cheeks with one hand and looks into my eyes. "Seriously. Be quick."

I hold my hands up and shrug. "I'll do my fucking best, Jesus."

Her pussy squeezes me tight like she's been doing Kegel calisthenics. Black lace titties wobble in front of me when she speeds up on my dick.

That'll help with the "blow quick" situation.

My balls press up against her ass as she grinds on top of me. I dig my fingers into her hips. "You close?"

She nods and my dick grows harder inside of her at the news she's about to come all over it. I thrust my hips into her and my thumb goes to her clit. She moans and clamps down on me.

"Holy shit." Her nails dig into my chest, and I lose it. My cock kicks and my load shoots into her in waves as she shakes on top of me, all of her muscles tense and her toes curled.

She opens her eyes and smiles. "I'm late, you prick."

"Already?"

She slaps my chest and giggles then rolls off of me. "I have to tell her something. Text me."

"I will as soon as I get done at Buy Buy Baby, buying up all the *Star Wars* onesies."

She glares as she shimmies her skirt down and throws on a red top. I watch her ass rock back and forth, curls of hair bouncing down her back as she walks toward the door.

"Hey babe?"

Her hair flips around like one of those big moments in the old movies, only it's unintentional on her part. Heat balloons in my chest every time she does it.

"What's up?" She smiles.

"You look beautiful. Have a great day at work."

She flashes a shy grin and turns a little pink. "Thank you." She blows me a kiss as she walks through the door.

When she's out of sight I catch her kiss and slap it on my Megan-flavored dick.

I sit up in bed, and stare around the room. For a brief second, I contemplate growing up a little.

CHAPTER 2
JOEL

WORK WAS LONG, and I didn't see Tommy at all. I sent him a text earlier, and we agreed to meet after work. I beat him to the bar and glance around at all the other professionals sipping their scotch and talking about work. I sit and stare out of the glass windows that line the front, giving a view of the busy street and business crowd leaving their offices. My mind races, and I attempt to think about anything that could possibly take my mind off of Mom—and Quinn.

I want to call her. I want to talk to her. But I just can't. Too much time has passed. She probably hates me, and I've pretty much decided it's over—done for. She'd never take me back now. Quinn is more stubborn than I am.

Mom would've wanted me to call her. She'd smack the fuck out of me if she saw me right now, to tell the truth. Sabotaging my own life is kind of my thing. It's just what I do.

Tommy struts in front of the glass windows of the bar and walks through the door. Thank god. I can use some laughs. He weaves through the rows of pub tables littered with men in suits. When he nears, I notice that he's glaring right at me.

"What's up with you and Quinn? I'm getting lawyered all to fuck at my house."

"Nice to see you too, baby."

"Jesus, how many have you had already? Fucking Dennis Hopper from Hoosiers over here? You gonna roofie my drink?" He bats his eyelashes at me.

"You gonna bitch to me about your day first? Before I take that ass to pound town in the woods?"

He gasps, and I can't stop laughing.

"For real man. Just tell me if you're going to call her or not. I have to give Megan something. She's relentless. Like Templeton looking for garbage at the fair."

"It's bad, huh? I don't know man. I want to. So much time has passed though. It'd be weird. I think I'm over her."

He stares daggers into my skull.

Fuck.

"Really? That's how you're going to play this?" He makes finger quotes because he knows it irritates the shit out of me. "Over her?" He draws out the syllables for the whole effect.

Dick.

I lift up my hands all awkward and slow. "I don't know what to do with my hands."

It draws a laugh, but I'm shit at distracting him. He's locked onto me like Maverick on a Mig.

"I ain't fuckin' around, Herbert. Give me something. She wants to know if she should come—well—you know." His head drops. There's desperation in his voice. Shit must be bad at home.

"Just—fuck man. Tell her no. It'll be hard enough already."

I want her there. Her hand holding mine right about now would make me happy. But if I give in, there's so much explaining to do. So much complication. She'll never trust me. It's the right thing to do.

"Okay." He actually appears serious. It's a rarity since, well ever. "How are you holding up with shit?"

He looks like he might cry, and I might do the same. Two grown pussies sobbing at a pub table. We are quite the sight.

Fortunately, the waitress intervenes. "Anything else?"

"Yes, two more of these." I hold up my near-full glass of Glenfiddich that doesn't even have condensation on the sides yet.

"Yeah, that's good." Tommy looks back at me. "Look man, it's hard for me too. You know this. We have to quit dancing around like it didn't happen."

"I know man, but fuck." My fist hits the table before I can stop and stares shoot in our direction. "Sorry." I hold up my hands to the other patrons, then turn back to Tommy. "Yeah man, it's rough. Not gonna lie. How are you doing with it though?"

"I drove down the street five times this week. Crying like a grown teddy bear. Wanted to go in and hug her, talk to her. I'm not doing well at all."

I'm fighting back tears as I guzzle my scotch. It burns going down and doesn't stop once it's in my stomach. This whole ordeal is not fucking fair. "Thanks for taking me to see her. It was good. If there had to be a last encounter. It was a good one."

"It was, wasn't it?" He smiles, and I do the same. The waitress walks up with our drinks and sets them on new coasters. "Thanks."

Tommy turns back to me. "Hey."

"Yeah?"

"Let's finish these and go hook up the Nintendo. Play some Tecmo Bowl. It's what Mom would've wanted."

I look down at the cubes melting into the whiskey and pick up the rocks glass, swirling it as the ice clanks against the rim. "Yeah. Let's do it."

CHAPTER 3
QUINN

"**I** DON'T KNOW what the fuck to do. I'm a mess." I look over at Megan. She's trying to console me. I feel terrible for her and Tommy being dragged into this.

"Tommy isn't giving me anything. I'm trying. I swear. It'll be okay."

I hate Joel for making me do this to him, and yet it breaks my heart that this happened. He has to be hurting so bad, and I just want to be there for him. The fact he won't let me has me warring with myself, and I know Megan can see it. I promised myself to never let a guy get to me like this. It always happens. Someone always gets hurt, and it's usually me.

"It's okay. I'm not going to go. If he wanted me there, he'd ask me." I pace back and forth in front of the coffee machine.

"Are you sure?"

The goddamn coffee pot is not filling fast enough, and I just want it to be done so I can get away from this conversation. I need to put everything into my work. The bitch brigade is standing over in the corner, no doubt trying to hear what Megan and I are discussing. I want to rip that fucking mole off Madeline's face right about now. Why can't life be simple?

"Yeah. I'm sure." I can smell the coffee, and it's drawing me toward it. People are racing down the halls, and I try to think of everything I have on my plate for the day to rid Joel from my mind. It's not working. Not one bit.

"Quinn?"

Megan and I look up at Sylvia. She has on black pumps and a skin-tight black dress that makes her blonde hair more blonde. She's gorgeous, if I'm being honest with myself, but all I can think about is Joel wanting to fuck her too, and I clench my fists. I reserve my anger because she's the secretary to my boss.

Her bright-blue eyes are narrowed, and she appears in a hurry as always. "Jason wants to see you. Do you have time?"

Her voice is calm, despite her appearance, and I know it's an order and not an actual request. I exhale a long breath, relieved to have a chance to focus on something other than how bad my heart hurts at the moment.

"Sure. Be right there." I turn to Megan. "Gotta go."

"If I hear anything new, I'll text you. Okay?" She stands up from the table and tries to hide the glow on her face. Tommy must be doing something right. Good for him.

"Thank you."

Her heels clack on the tile as she walks back to the building where the computer nerds reside.

I head over to the coffee and sit in front of the machine, letting the aroma swirl around me.

Focus, bitch. Knock things out at the office. Forget about him.

Easier said than done, as he's the first and only thing on my mind every day.

I fill up my coffee cup and head down the hall to Jason's corner office. Sylvia sits at her desk and nods, letting me know it's okay to go back. I walk through the door and look around to the windows that cover half the room and overlook the city. The coffee burns my tongue and I don't care, because I want the caffeine. Jason peeks up from around his computer. Pictures of his family line the walls. They're perfectly spaced apart, and a tall white bookshelf runs to the ceiling behind him. It's full of marketing and advertising books I haven't read.

"Quinn, have a seat." He motions to one of the three chairs that sit in front of his desk. I'm usually only in his office for quarterly reviews, and my collar grows tighter against my neck. I look over at a large plant against the wall and wonder if it's fake or not.

"It's real." He smiles as he looks up at me. His hair is dark brown along with his eyes, and they meet mine. He's always sizing everything (or everyone) up. His managerial style is very hands off. He lets people run with ideas. My hand trembles as I set my cup of coffee on his desk and watch the steam rise from it.

My elbow drops and I quickly recover from the awkwardness as I lean my arm toward a non-existent armrest.

Damn it.

It's like he ordered these chairs for the sole purpose of making me uncomfortable. His hair is lined with a few silver streaks, but he appears much younger than someone in their mid-forties. I spot a few trophies on a little table to my right up against the window. They're advertising awards our company has won. They have their own table so he's definitely proud of them.

"Don't be nervous. You're not in trouble."

Thank god.

The coffee cup warms my hand as I grab it and take a sip. "What's going on?"

He looks me up and down again. Everyone knows he's very religious so I'm not too worried that he's checking me out, or wants to fuck me on his desk.

"I need someone to travel a little. Do some speaking for the company. Would you be interested in something like that?"

My heart leaps through my chest. It's a great opportunity, and the timing couldn't be more perfect. I have to stop myself from jumping up and hugging him.

Play it cool.

"What type of speaking?" First rule in negotiations, never show your hand. Always ask questions and know the terms.

"Just presenting a few companies with our services. Telling them what we're all about. Also, giving presentations at corporate headquarters. I think you'd be good at that. You're likeable."

"Thank you, Sir. I mean, it sounds like a great opportunity. I'm definitely interested."

"Perfect. I'll get the wheels in motion then."

I get up and start to leave.

"Quinn?"

"Yes, Sir?"

"Everything okay? With work? Life?"

I lose my breath for a brief moment. I'm not sure what to say. He's always so distant and rarely leaves the office unless there's a problem or he's meeting with clients.

"Yeah. Everything is great." It's a lie, and I know he can practically sense my troubles.

"Sorry. I'm just. I like to let people do their thing. Let their creativity shine. But I've been working on relating to people in a personal way. I apologize if that was awkward for you."

I smile to set him at ease. "No, it's fine. I love working here, Sir. Thank you for the opportunity."

"Great. I'll have Sylvia get with you on the details then."

"Sounds good."

I want to start dancing, but I maintain my composure. I can't wait to tell Megan. This is perfect. It's a way to take my mind off of things. A way to take my mind off of *him*.

CHAPTER 4
JOEL

PAIN RIPS THROUGH me as I stare at Mom. Tommy's arm wraps around me. The chapel is silent as I kiss her on the forehead and say goodbye. I honestly thought it'd be more difficult. I'm numb to everything when I stare at her. My brain refuses to process she's gone, forever.

I look to Tommy and nod. Tears stream down his cheeks onto his suit. I'm regretting not having Quinn there. I loosen my tie, and my hands ball into fists, heat rushes into my face. I see Megan's hand on Tommy's back, and I lose it. I look to Mom one last time and put my hand on hers. When I touch her, I realize it isn't really her. It's just an empty shell of what was once the most vibrant thing in my life.

I turn and storm down the aisle and into the lobby. I want to be anywhere but here. I'm not religious, but I curse god just in case his sorry ass is real. All the stupid, horrible motherfuckers in the world, and he takes the gem out of the cesspool that surrounds me. I hate him. I hate everything. I have to take my mind off things.

Tommy walks out and wraps his arms around me. He's shaking, as am I. "I'm sorry, man."

I can barely make out his voice muffled against my shoulder, and I slap him on the back a couple of times, harder than I normally would.

He looks up at me, and I nod, wiping the tears from my face. We walk out to the car, and Megan follows. She insists on driving us. I don't mind one bit. I want to bury my mother and put it all behind me.

Megan gets in to drive us to the cemetery. Tommy climbs in the front with her. In the backseat, I break out a bottle of scotch and take a huge swig. It should burn going down, but it doesn't. A train could smack into me, and I wouldn't feel a goddamn thing. I hand the bottle to Tommy, and he reluctantly takes a pull off of it.

"You should take it easy man."

I glare at him, and he knows to back off. I'd do anything to take my mind off Mom right now. Tommy shifts around in the front seat. Megan does too. I don't normally get angry, ever really.

"Are you going to be okay with everyone coming over after?" I catch Megan's eyes staring at me in the rear-view mirror. Tommy looks at her like she's insane for asking me questions. Her gaze cuts right through the hate in my heart and tears blur my vision.

"I don't know." I break down and lose my shit right there. Tears rush into my eyes, and I begin to weep, so hard that I struggle to breathe. I hear Megan open the driver's side door, and she comes around to my side, rips the door open, and crushes me with a hug.

"It gets easier. I promise." I try to look at her but everything looks like a funhouse mirror.

"How do you know?"

She sighs. "I lost my parents too. A long time ago."

I wipe my eyes and see Tommy holding back tears. Megan is focused on me, Tommy on her. Apparently, this is news to him.

"You never said anything."

"Yeah. I didn't know that either." Tommy stares at her, and she glances to him and looks back to me.

She grips me by the shoulders. "It is and always will be hard to talk about. Okay? But you learn to manage it. It just takes time. I promise. That dagger in your stomach gets less painful every day. You start to remember the good times and you focus less on the end."

"Okay." I nod.

"Okay." She runs her hand up Tommy's cheek and wipes a tear from his eye. "Your mom isn't in that body anymore, but she's watching you. It breaks her heart when she sees you two in pain. The same as if she was still here and you were hurting. Just think of one of the thousands of good moments you had with her while you say goodbye. It will still hurt worse than anything you've ever felt. But it will help."

She reaches down and takes the bottle from my hand and sets it in the front seat. "That won't give you peace. I tried. It doesn't work."

"Okay." I nod at her again.

"Good."

She shuts the door and walks back around to the driver's side. Tommy leans over the seat and stares at me. His hand squeezes my forearm. His eyes tell me everything he wants to say. When Megan gets in the car, he turns his face to her. "I love you." He looks back to me. "Both of you."

"I love you too," says Megan.

"I love you too, baby girl." I grin at him through the tears.

"Come here you." He leans over the back seat and gives me a big bear hug. "We'll get through this." His words are a whisper in my ear.

I nod once more. "Okay."

People are everywhere in Mom's house—staring at pictures, telling old stories about her. It still hurts, but Megan's words resonate and give me some hope of comfort. I wish Quinn was here. I'm such a goddamn idiot sometimes.

Tommy walks up and hands me a beer. Mom would never approve, but it's our last act of rebellion in her house. I can practically hear her voice in my head. "Herbert and Thomas, I will pepper your asses if you take one more sip of that devil juice in my house."

Tommy must be having a similar thought, because I see a wry smile spread across his face. He looks down to his beer. "She would fuck us up good for this."

I clank my bottle into his. "Yeah, she certainly would. Wouldn't she?"

Megan keeps looking over at us. I don't think she's too excited about us drinking, but at least it's not whiskey.

"Mom sure made an impact on a lot of people, didn't she?" I stare around at the sea of people crammed in the tiny house.

"How could she not, man? She was larger than life. That lady was a fucking saint. I'm going to miss her so much."

The waterworks are about to start up again. I can see his eyes misting. Fuck. It's so goddamn hard. I down my beer and head for another. My face tingles, and I feel a buzz coming on. I'm certain it's the whiskey I pounded in the car.

I walk to the fridge and lean over to pull another beer from it. A pair of tan legs pass in front of my face in a black skirt. I don't recognize them and I never forget a pair of legs that reach for the sky like these.

I lift my head to see the rest of what she's working with, and I'm not disappointed at all. I just hope she isn't a family member. A pair of nice-sized tits wrapped up tight in black fabric meet my gaze. She has curled, blonde hair that drapes down her shoulder line.

"Hi." Her blue eyes lock onto me.

The cold beer is numbing my hand as I stand up to properly introduce myself. "Hi. Don't think we've met."

We shake hands.

"Bridget. Your mom helped me through some difficult times once. My condolences to you and your family. She talked about you all the time." She flips her hair back, and my cock springs into action against my zipper. She grins. An evil grin. I know this grin well. It's an "I want to fuck you" grin.

"Hopefully she said good things."

What is wrong with you, Joel? Getting a hard-on in your mother's house when you just buried her?

It has to be the fucking booze. It's playing tricks with my inhibitions.

"Mostly good." She giggles, and my dick grows harder at the sound.

She's gorgeous, but as usual Quinn is on my mind again. I take another drink and try to erase her from my thoughts. I can tell this girl isn't the usual churchgoer. I'm a bit flustered at Mom hiding her from me, but I can understand why. I'm sure she was vulnerable whenever she helped her through whatever problems she had.

Bridget nibbles on a fingernail. "She certainly didn't lie when she said her son was handsome."

She licks her lips and twirls her hair. Goddamn this girl. Maybe she's what I need to take my mind off of Mom and Quinn. I see Tommy and Megan eyeing me from across the room. Tommy cracks half a smile that disappears the second Megan looks up at him. She says something in his ear. He nods and starts toward me.

I appreciate everything Megan said in the car. She's a good person and great for Tommy. But I don't forget that she's Quinn's best friend. She has a vested interest in stopping me from fucking some strange, and it has nothing to do with what's best for me.

I turn to Bridget. "I need to take my mind off of things. You wanna get out of here?" I turn to Bridget and her "fuck me" eyes are already undressing me.

"You really should stay, but I'll give you my number. Call me later and we can hang out."

She's right. I need to stay and make sure to thank everyone for coming, even though we've been here for four hours already. "I definitely will."

She finds a pen and scribbles her number on a napkin, then walks off through the front door. Megan stares lasers that I'm worried might incinerate Bridget like Scorpion's finishing move.

Toasty!

Tommy strolls up to give me a rehearsed speech, in order to appease Megan.

"No, no, Whisperer, just no. Bad fucking idea, bro."

I'm still watching Bridget avoid Scorpion's attempt at a fatality. "I don't know what you're talking about. She just wants to hang out."

"Is that what the kids call it these days?" He stares at me and moves in closer, bugging his eyes out, before stepping back and nodding. "Yep. You gonna fuck her. You're going to fuck that poor girl. That poor, poor innocent girl gonna get fucked tonight. She sure is."

"Poor? There's nothing poor about what I'll do to Bridget later." I slap him on the shoulder, and he feigns a look of irritation in Megan's direction. He shrugs and walks back over to her. I see him mouth "I tried" at her.

Anxiety riddles my stomach. This has probably already gotten back to Quinn. Fucking gossip queens. I have frustrations that need to be relieved though. Bridget looks like she can comfort me perfectly. Quinn still sits at the front of my mind, and I plan to remedy that.

Soon.

I pull up in front of Bridget's house. The fastback is roaring under the hood, and I can feel her vibrations in the whites of my knuckles. It's a quiet street so I'm sure Bridget heard me pull up. I can practically feel her panties getting wet, staring out the window and looking at the mustang.

My buzz has worn off considerably after all the heartfelt goodbyes. Guilt is taking over my body, but the image of Bridget in that black dress keeps me from abandoning our little hang out session.

A fresh knife plunges into my stomach as I near her porch. When I hit the last step of her stairs, the door opens and she's standing there in a black lacy teddy. My dick nearly explodes in my fucking pants. Bridget takes notice.

"Well, we can't be wasting that out here."

When I near the door she grabs me by my tie and yanks me into the house, slamming the door shut behind us.

CHAPTER 5
JOEL

TOMMY IS SHAKING his head too much for comfort as I walk up to him at the bar top.

"What?" I ask.

"Nothing, man. Didn't say a damn thing, bro."

"Megan tell Quinn?"

He stares at me like I'm an idiot. "Herbert, I just wanna shake the ever-loving shit out of you sometimes. Quinn knew the second she walked by you and you poked your little head, yes I mean both of them, up like a turtle coming out of his shell. Megan tell Quinn? Fucking Michelangelo over here. You didn't learn shit from Splinter, did you? Fucking honorary Foot Clan member."

"It wasn't like that."

His eyes are about to pop out of his head. "Just save it, bitch. You're making my life oh so complicated. You're lucky you're a hot piece of man meat."

"But—"

"Don't!" He bugs his eyes at me again.

"I—"

"I said don't." He talks so damn fast I can't get out a word and his puffed out cheeks are trying not to laugh. His eyes open wider.

"Look—"

"You are terrible at this game, Sir. I said don't!" He's on the verge of an aneurysm.

"Fine. You are such a persistent prick. You know that? What the fuck is new?"

He looks away. So smart to have such an obvious tell. He's withholding information.

"What is it?"

"Nothing." He won't look at me, and now I have to know.

His voice gets all high pitched. He's nervous. "You see the new Force Awakens trailer? If Abrams doesn't bury that goddamned Binks clown I will murder him, Herbert. I will fuck his Facebook page with the fury of 1,000 angry porn dicks, by god!"

"Tell me what you're going to tell me." I inch closer to him.

He shakes his head. "Didn't work. Did it? Changing the subject. You can't be persuaded to the dark side?"

"Tell me. I know you want to. Join me, Thomas."

He looks away.

"Thomas, look at me." I'm the one bugging my eyes now.

He turns back to me and cackles. "Your Jedi mind tricks won't work on me, Sir. I am enslaved by the pussy of one Megan, much like Leia tied to the likes of a forty-ton gila monster. I am a Jedi, like my father before me."

I crouch down in his face. "So be it, Jedi. And now young Skywalker, you will die."

"Fine, man goddamn!"

I grin huge.

He glares back at me. "Quinn's leaving town. She's going to speak at some bullshit conference for their company. And it could be permanent if she does well." He gasps like he's been holding his breath for hours.

My heart drops into my stomach. Pain rips through my bones at his words, but I compose myself. "Good for her. I'm sure it'll be good for her career." I look around and want to rip the walls off this building and burn it to the ground.

"I'm sorry, man."

"For what?"

He looks up at the bartender and orders two scotches, then tosses me a look like I'm clueless and want to copy his calculus homework. "I'm sorry."

I give in and stare down at the ground. "It's okay, buddy. It's not like it's a hundred percent sure thing she's leaving forever, right?"

"Yeah, well. I don't know. I wish you two would stop being idiots. Everyone can see it but the two of you." He stares out the window.

I want to change the subject, but my thoughts are flying back and forth like a *Blue Angels* air show. "It's too late, man. Yeah, I love her. But I fucked it up. Can we all please move on?"

His face tightens and his jaw clenches, grinding his teeth together.

Guilt pummels my abs with a right cross.

"You didn't fuck it up, man. You could still have her. You're just too much of a pussy to do anything about it." He slams his fist on the counter, rattling all the glasses down the bar, then turns and walks toward the door.

"Dude, what the fuck? What do you care anyway? Sorry I'm not making things convenient for you and Megan." I squeeze my glass of scotch so hard I'm worried it might break.

He pauses for a second, then turns back around and walks over to me. His hands are clenched into fists. I don't know that either one of us has ever been in a fight, so I don't know what the fuck to do. He gets up in my face. "Don't pull your little mind fuck bullshit on me. Trying to make it seem like I'm looking out for me. I want you to be happy." He sighs and puts a hand on my shoulder.

Thank god. Us fighting would've been embarrassing. Our technique, not the actual action.

"That girl you're letting get away is the one. And this is the only fucking shot you got at her."

His words hit me in the chest, but I'm too proud to admit he's right, as usual. Naturally, I make light of the situation. It's just what we do. "Five hundred fights, that's the number I figured when I was a kid."

"Knockaround Guys, nice. Very obscure, Sir. I bet Vin Diesel slays more ass than ol' Herbert even."

"You're high as fuck."

We both laugh.

Tommy puts a hand on my shoulder. "I always got your back, man. Before my own."

"I know." I look away.

"Look at me, man."

I turn back to him and nod. "I know. Okay?"

"Yeah. I know you do, bitch. I gotta go though. That chick really does have a leash on my cock. And I like it."

"I know you do, buddy."

He turns to walk out the door.

"And don't you ever try to manhandle a cowboy, we'll cut your goddamn pimp's heart out. Understand?"

He flips back around in front of the door. "I'm your huckleberry."

CHAPTER 6
QUINN

JET FUEL AND car exhaust stick to my clothes as I make my way to the front of the airport. Everyone always looks all professional and put together, like they know what they're doing. I'm a hot mess. My hair is half dry and I don't know if my socks match. I nearly had a heart attack when I woke up and all my clocks were flashing "12:00." Out of all the days for a power surge, it had to be today.

I can't mess this up. This is my shot. Knock this out of the park and the sky's the limit. I look up to see where I need to check my bags, and my Starbucks cup hits the ground, exploding on the tile. His eyes are locked onto mine. My whole body goes numb, and it's like the sky is crushing me into the ground.

Joel.

He stalks toward me, and my heart wrenches. Why? Why now? I simultaneously want to rip into him and melt into his arms. *What is wrong with you, Quinn? Stay strong.*

He looks weak, defeated. It doesn't help the heat rushing into my face, and the anger coursing through my blood. I can't stop thinking about him with that girl at his mom's funeral. Him not calling. Not texting. Leaving me to worry about him.

Fuck him. Fuck you, Joel.

"Hey."

Goddamn his gorgeous fucking eyes. My body acts independently of my brain, and I slap him. Hard. Tears roll down my cheeks. He turns back to me, and my hand itches to hit him again.

I don't want him to see me cry. He shouldn't get to see me weak like this. "You should go."

"Can I just—"

"Did I fucking stutter?" My teeth grind together so hard my jaw will probably be sore for a week.

"Sorry."

He turns to walk away, and the pussy version of Quinn that's in love decides to rear her ugly head.

"What are you even doing here? Why now?" I shouldn't entertain his words. They're like poison that knows exactly where I'm vulnerable.

"I just. I don't know, okay? I heard you were leaving, and I just came."

"What did you think was going to happen? You show up, and I don't go? We just forget the last week ever happened?" God, I really want to do all those things. But I can't. Not to mention the girl. My fists clench. "And you and the blonde at your mom's? Seriously, just go."

"I'm sorry. I had to see you. I can't stop thinking about you. And the girl—"

"Fucking save it, Joel! I don't want to hear you talk your way out of it, like you always do. It's too late. I'm going."

He drops his gaze to the ground, and suddenly I'm the one who feels bad. "I-I understand." He sulks and turns to walk away.

"I'm sorry about your mom. I would've been there in an instant had you called me. I just didn't want to upset you."

He looks back at me. "I know."

I head inside for my plane and watch him walk into the parking lot through the huge glass windows of the airport. Standing there in a daze, I think about what might have been.

People are getting up and leaving the conference room after my second pitch of the day, when a man approaches me in a suit. He looks familiar, like I've seen him recently. I don't mind his presence. Dark-brown hair and bright-blue eyes. He looks about my age and happens to not be ugly at all.

"Hey." He approaches with a wide smile.

"Hi."

"You're doing a great job." He stops a few feet away.

"Umm. Thanks. This is about my third day doing this."

"I know." He smiles again, like he knows something I don't.

"Are you with the company?"

"Your company."

My stomach balls up in a knot. "Is that so?"

"Yes. I'm evaluating you, and I like what I see, so far." He looks me up and down like he's talking about more than just my job performance.

Fuck it. I have no reason for him not to look at me.

"What exactly have you seen?" I turn around to put my laptop in its case and lean farther over the table than I should as my skirt rides a little up my legs.

He coughs, and I linger for a little longer than normal before turning back around.

"Umm. You're a great speaker. People seem to like you. To the point, but in a fun way."

I toss my laptop bag over my shoulder and let the strap run between my breasts, pulling my bright-red blouse tighter against me. I smile and walk up closer, making eye contact. "Tell me more about how great I am."

I laugh to make it obvious I'm joking.

"I'd love to tell you more over dinner."

Something about him asking me to dinner sends waves of guilt rushing through my body. I'm a fucking mess. How do I get myself out of this hole I've dug?

"I wish I could. I have to catch a flight. You should know this."

He looks away and then snaps back into business mode. Thank god. I don't need any added distractions right now.

"Right. Well—here's the thing. Your boss speaks highly of you. You have the look we want. We like what we see."

"Okay. I mean, thank you. I'm just confused. What's going on here?" I waggle my finger back and forth at both of us.

"How would you like to do this type of work full-time for the company?"

I nearly squeal but stop myself.

Remain professional, Quinn. Fuck.

My face has to be bright-red with excitement. "I think I'd be very good at it. I enjoy it so far."

"You'd have to relocate. And you'd be based from our offices here." He smiles.

It all comes crashing down on me. I should be fucking giddy with excitement, and all I can think about is how hard it would be to leave. My friends and family I can visit.

But Joel.

That motherfucker. Why do I let him own me like this? Maybe this is how I'm supposed to finally break free from him. "Well, make me an offer, and we'll talk. I'm definitely excited about the opportunity. Thank you."

"I'll have it to you today. I'm—I mean, we're very excited about this."

Blue eyes turns and walks from the room, and I never even got his name. Once I'm certain he's left, I do a little awkward dance that

187

I pray I never repeat. My hand fishes into my bag and I pull out my phone to call Megan.

"Hey, what's up?" She sounds extra chipper.

"I got an offer. Well, they're going to make me one anyway. They want me to travel around and do these presentations for clients."

"What? That's incredible. Good for you. You deserve it."

"Bad news though, to go with the good." I fumble around trying to pick up my pen off the table.

"What's that?"

"I have to relocate here. Based out of corporate."

"No! You can't leave me here with these two boys—I mean—sorry. That just came out all wrong."

My nails dig into my palm thinking about Joel, but I know she didn't mean anything by it.

"It's okay. I don't want to leave. I just can't pass this up. I love the work and maybe it'll help me get over a certain someone you just referenced."

"It would be fantastic for you. I'm just being a selfish bitch. I shouldn't have joked like that. It just came out."

"The guy who made the offer wasn't horrible to look at. Bluest fucking eyes I've ever seen." Still thinking about Joel.

"Is that right?"

I shouldn't have told her that. I imagine it will get back to Joel. It was mean, but I don't care. He shouldn't have ambushed me at the airport like that. Who does that to someone?

"Yeah, it's nothing. He asked me to dinner. I turned him down." *Fuck, Quinn. You are being a real bitch.* "I think I get a chance to come home in a few weeks. I'll definitely update you before then."

"You better. I'm so happy for you."

"Thank you." I may squeal a little bit before I hang up.

CHAPTER 7
JOEL

I'M FLIPPING THROUGH old pictures of me and Mom, wondering what she'd think of the way I've handled things recently. I know she'd be disappointed, and it eats at me constantly. Why do I always do this shit to myself? I'm like a ticking time bomb, looking for a way to self-destruct. Thank god my phone rings to jar me from my self-loathing.

It's the imperial death march and that can only mean one thing, Tommy boy will be on the other end.

"What up purple rain?" I ask.

"Purple rain?"

"You know, because you're the prince of taking cock?"

"Nice, Herbert. Really fucking mature right there. I'm shaking my head, but you can't see it. So just know it."

"Prince Albert. I think that's what I'll call you. Because you like them pierced." I know he finds it funny, but he'll never give in. He never does.

"Are you finished?"

"That's what purple rain asks all the boys that have their way with him."

"Goddamn it. I make the fucking jokes around here, Whisperer. Sit in your tower, and fucking nap."

"Oh, you do love the Tenacious D. Don't you? You want more pierced D getting all tenacious with you." I'm on a roll right now, and I can practically feel the steam building between his ears. It's helping me forget about everything else as well.

"I will take Megan on a date to see *The Force Awakens* and leave you to go by yourself, Pee Wee Herman."

"You son of a bitch! You wouldn't dare!" I refuse to let him win this one. He always wins.

"Just wicking your little weed to the new light saber. Ushers shining a flashlight on you while you wail on your little guy in the corner, tucked up next to the wall."

"There a reason you called?" I decide to take an out while I'm still ahead.

"Oh, yeah. My bad. Umm. Quinn is moving. Anyway, so what are our plans for the movie when it comes out?"

"Wait, what?" I scrub my hand over my face as I process this information.

"What are our plans for the movie? I was thinking I dress as Han and you can be Luke. Naturally, because you just talk like a pussy. We need to get tick—"

"Quinn is moving?"

"Why do you focus on the less important things I tell you? Jesus, bro."

"Where did you hear this?"

"Really? You want to know where I heard this?"

"Yeah, you got a point there. When is she moving?"

"She's already there. Coming home in a few weeks to pack her shit and she's gone."

"She wants away from me that bad, huh?"

"I don't know, man. I'm hearing this second-hand. Some things could be lost in translation."

I can't believe I pushed her away like this. Sweat beads form on my forehead. "Alright, well thanks for the info, sweetheart."

"You okay?"

"I'm good man, I swear."

"I'll holler at you later then, girlfriend."

"Bye sweetie."

Fuck!

I hang up, and all the air leaves my lungs. *Goddamn it!* I can't stop thinking about Mom. All the things she said about making myself happy. How I needed to try with Quinn. I let Mom down. I let Quinn down. *I have to make this right.*

CHAPTER 8
JOEL

"**Y**OU REALLY DON'T have to go." I stare at Tommy.

"No, no. I must do it. For the good of the land." He smiles.

"Still loving my Tenacious D?"

"It's the best D in town, sugar tits." He pops me in the crotch and I double over as he walks off.

"You're gonna pay for that, you piece of shit."

All I see is his middle finger as he enters the large revolving glass door in front of the airport. I grab my bags and hobble along to catch up with him.

We check our bags and head to security. We're standing in line staring at all the random travelers. It's loud and busy as we approach the guy in uniform checking IDs and boarding passes. Tommy is sweating bullets.

"Will you hold me if we crash?" He turns and flashes doe eyes at me.

"Of course I will. You know this."

He looks over at the large machines scanning people as they walk through. "What do you think my dick will look like on their screen? I'm worried the resolution isn't good enough to capture its true essence."

I'm trying not to laugh as he hands his ID to the airport security guard. "How many megapixels is the internal camera in that thing?"

"What?" The guard looks unamused.

Tommy turns to me. "Amateur hour over here." He motions with his head to the guard.

"Jesus Christ, are you trying to get us on a 'no fly' list?"

He whispers to me, loud enough for the guard to hear. "We'll be fine as long as I don't leave my cock unattended."

That gets a grin out of the security guard so my worries are momentarily eased.

"See, Herbert. They love me." He steps into the scanner and another guard says something to him. He puts his hand over his head. He thrusts his hips as it scans him.

"Hah! Bet it don't fit on your screen." He's apparently committed to the big cock bit.

"Sir. We need to do it again. Please stand still."

"That's what she said."

Finally, we make it through security. We near our gate, and Tommy is shaking and fidgeting with shit more than ever.

"It's not the flying that I hate, Herbert. It's more being trapped with all these sweaty beings around here in an aluminum tube as it rockets above the earth at thirty-five thousand feet."

The four people near us get up and leave as Tommy stretches out in his seat. "Ahh. Much better."

"You're out of control."

"That's what they tell me."

"You think she'll take me back?"

"Yes."

"How are you so sure?" I lean in closer to him.

"Because she loves you. This is not rocket science. My fear of flying analysis is. The only one who will fuck it up is you."

"Thanks." I look down at the floor.

"I'm serious, bro. You're the one who gets in your own way. Just stop being a pussy and go for it. What the fuck are you so afraid of?"

"She's hard-headed man. She's not like the other girls. She doesn't seem like the type who gives second chances. Maybe this is a big mistake."

His hands are on my collar, and I feel him slap me slightly across the face. Everyone in the goddamn airport is staring at us. I wait for him to say something but he just sits there, staring.

"What the fuck?" I stare back at him, and I can tell he's trying not to laugh. Finally, I give in and burst into laughter.

His cheeks are huge, and his face is bright-pink as he tries not to laugh. "The Panty Whisperer isn't a fucking pussy dick."

Everyone must think we're insane at this point.

"Keep your voice down. You're going to get us kicked out of this fucking place."

"Do not look to the naysayers, for the Panty Whisperer will inherit the Earth." He slaps me across the face again.

"Goddamn it. You hit me again—"

I feel the sting on my cheek again, and I want to kill him but his ridiculous face keeps me laughing.

"Okay. *Okay*. Fuck. Just don't slap me again."

"About time your nuts dropped." He lets go of my collar.

Fortunately, our little act is cut short by a woman on the loudspeaker telling us to board. We get up and head that way. The other people waiting for the flight can't get out of our way fast enough.

Tommy is on my heels and in my fucking ear the whole way. I can practically feel the sweat beads that must be forming on his forehead.

"Joel? Joel?"

I do my best to ignore him.

"Whisperer? Psst, Herbert? Psst, Sir Whisperer?" The volume of his voice increases with each question.

"What?" I practically scream, but it's a whisper.

"Hold me."

"I told you that you didn't have to come."

"Well, like, I thought it was a good idea. But then I started thinking again about being enclosed in this piece-o-shit metal frame, maintained by uneducated laborers, hurtling through spacetime at an ungodly rate, whilst thirty-five thousand feet above the ground." He pauses and stares at me. "Well, it kinda has me shitting my fucking panties, Sir!"

I flip around and there are two kids that can't be more than ten years old that look like they might shriek. Their mother has her fists drawn up, and Tommy's goddamned shirt is soaked at the neckline. His face is pale as a ghost, and the zipper on his bag is rattling from his hands constantly trembling.

I stop us in the tunnel, much to the chagrin of the line of passengers, and wave the mom and kids past us. His eyes meet mine as my hand grips Tommy's favorite *Star Wars* t-shirt. "Jesus Christ. Even Jar Jar Binks wouldn't act like such a pussy."

"You son of a fuck! How dar—"

"Hey, can we speed this up for crying out loud?" says some impatient bystander in a business suit.

Tommy glares in his direction and shoots his arm out like he's using the force to choke this guy out.

"Oh what the fuck is this whack job doing? C'mon buddy, we're in a hurry here."

I'm so embarrassed I don't know what the hell to do. "Sorry, it's his first time flying. Just give us a second." I turn to Tommy. "They're showing *Desperado* for the in-flight movie."

There is no in-flight movie. This flight is approximately two hours and thirty-two minutes, but Tommy doesn't know this.

His eyes light up and then grow serious. "Unedited? With Salma Hayek titties and reverse cowgirl? Or is it some edited bullshit, Herbert?"

"Full titties. Promise."

"Oh, why didn't you say so?" His voice is normal as he strolls past me toward the cockpit.

We finally get seated and taxi out onto the runway. Thank god it's a smaller plane and nobody is sitting next to us, not that it matters since everyone is practically stuffed together. Tommy is looking all around the plane. I know it's only a matter of time until my ruse is snuffed out.

"Where are the monitors? To watch the movie?" His eyes are darting all over the place, and I know he's pretty much memorized the fucking electrical outlay of the entire aircraft. I decide to lie anyway, go out with a bang. Hopefully, it will buy enough time to get us in the air.

"Oh, they flip down from up there by the lights and stuff." I nod to the gadgets overhead.

"Bullshit. Those are oxygen masks in there." He peers around a bit more. "There's no way they'd wire fold down monitors, the shit is inefficient."

"That's how it was on the last plane. I don't know, man. Fuck."

He's still shaking his head in disbelief. "You said titties. Oh, I'm gonna be so mad if you made me confront my fears without those latin titties bouncing on Banderas' dick. I swear to Christ, man." He pokes at the air conditioner fans.

"Look, maybe they'll wheel out a monitor or something. It's what it said, okay?"

"Oh, we'll see." He nods his head, as if he plans to punish me severely for my lies.

He's passed the point of funny to socially awkward and unaware. Usually, he would take into account the presence of children and the elderly, but now, it's all fair game.

I spy a man strapping a baby seat to a chair three rows ahead of us and my face hits my palm before I even finish processing what he's doing.

"Look at this shit, Herbert. A baby seat? On a plane? Really?"

"Oh fuck me," I mumble. I know that's not all he has to say.

"Yeah, because a car seat will protect a toddler when you rocket this motherfucker four hundred miles per hour into the side of a mountain."

And we now have the attention of the stewardess. I turn to Tommy, and it's like fire is raging in my cheeks. "Get your shit together, *now*."

"What?" He feigns as if he has no clue what he's doing is inappropriate.

"Knock off the fucks, shits, dick grabs, titty talk, physics facts." I stare at him and grind my teeth. "All of it!"

"Well, you just went and covered everything didn't you, asshole? I'll just sit here and breathe. Is that okay with you, Herbert?"

"Is there a problem, gentlemen?" The stewardess looms over us, her arms folded as she glares.

"Oh, no problem Ma'am. Why do you ask?" Tommy smiles at her.

She doesn't return the gesture. "We've had several complaints."

I start to speak, and Tommy cuts me off. "About what?" His smile grows wider.

"Sir, I will have you removed if you don't watch your language. Not another word."

"Fine."

She narrows her brow, turns on her heel, and walks away.

"Phew. Thank god."

"Don't wake me up if we crash." Tommy flings his head back into the seat.

"No problem, sweetie."

"Love you, bitch."

"Night, dear."

Tommy reaches over without looking and pats me on the head. "Shh. Sleepy time."

Tommy wakes up as we are landing and grips my forearm. His nails dig into my skin.

"Jesus." I try to yank my arm away, but it's not happening.

"This is it, Herbert. We're gonna die."

"We're fine."

The wheels connect with the ground and Tommy bears down on my arm. I'm on the verge of laughing hysterically at his face. He looks like he might shit his pants and blow a load at the same time.

My chest heaves up and down as I try to contain my laughter. We finally slow down and start to taxi. He's panting his ass off.

His head swivels around to people conducting their business as usual. His eyes light up. "We did it. We made it guys." He high fives the toddler who stands up in the seat across the aisle. "That's what I'm talking about right there."

Tommy turns to me. "So go check in at the hotel?"

"Nope. I have to see her. Now."

CHAPTER 9
QUINN

I RIFLE THROUGH my bag and pull out a stack of packets. They're really just my Power Point presentation printed out and stapled. The conference room is surrounded by glass on three sides and the people walking down the halls keep staring at me like I'm an exhibit at the zoo.

I walk around the table and drop a packet where each person will sit. As I turn my back to the door and head down the other side, I hear my name.

"Quinn."

I flip around too fast and nearly face plant, bracing myself on the edge of the table. When I get my shit together, I glance up to see blue eyes, and he flashes me a flawless smile with a set of perfect white teeth.

"Hey there." I pause for a moment, trying to gather my thoughts and my composure. "I didn't get your name last time."

"It's Simon. You okay?" He nods toward the corner of the table that caught me before I fell.

"Yeah. I'm fine."

"Good." He starts to head around the table and walk in my direction.

Fuck.

"You haven't responded to the offer we sent over." He cants his head slightly and examines me.

I want to run out of the room. His stare and his eyes have my heart racing.

"I'm still thinking on it. Do you need an answer immediately?" I smooth my black skirt down with my hands.

He grins. "No. I really just wanted an excuse to come see you. I heard you'd be in the office today, talking to some of the managers. I'm sorry. It's inappropriate, I know."

It'd be pretty hot if it weren't for these fucking feels owning my every move. "Look, Simon. You're a nice—"

"Oh boy. C'mon. I can take it." He smiles again, but this time it seems forced.

"I'm getting over someone. And the wounds are still really fresh." I lean over to put my arm where I thought there was a chair, but my arm finds nothing but air and I stumble again. I catch my balance and stand up straight. "Jesus. See? You don't want any part of this. I can't even function."

"It's okay." He pauses. "I had to try, right?"

My face has to be tomato-red, because I can feel the tingling in my cheeks. "You're going to have to go so I can focus. I've got people coming in here soon. But I'll have an answer to you by tomorrow, if that's okay?"

"Tomorrow is fine, Quinn. Take a few days if you need it." He turns and heads toward the door.

"Thank you."

"No problem."

A few hours pass, and I'm standing at the head of the long conference table, flipping through slides on my Power Point presentation. My boss's bosses flank both sides of the table, eagerly listening to everything I say.

Butterflies roll through my stomach, but I'm used to speaking in front of people.

There's a commotion near the reception area, and I lose my audience as their heads turn in the direction of the noise. Someone is speaking with a raised voice and it's hard to make out at first but then grows clear.

"You can't go back there. She's in a meeting," says the receptionist.

"Where's the meeting? This way?"

The second voice is familiar. "Just relax lady, shit like this happens every day. No biggie."

As soon as my brain recognizes Tommy's voice, Joel and his sparkling green eyes come around the corner. He sees me and freezes, before opening the door and stepping inside.

Tommy flashes me a toothy grin and waves as I stand there, trembling.

Joel peers around the room, up to me, and then back to Tommy. "Maybe this wasn't the smartest plan." He turns back to me.

Panic mode sets in, and I can't breathe.

Tommy belts out one of those fake coughs to try and mask his words. "Tell her."

Joel fixes his gaze directly on me and starts walking in my direction. I wipe my sweaty palms down my skirt, and my breath hitches each time he gets closer. Heat radiates through my chest and into my face.

"I-I love you. I've been m-miserable without you. Please come home."

My brain completely forgets that there is an audience in the room as I stare into his gorgeous eyes, and perfect hair. Everything he does is wrong though. Coming here. Jeopardizing my job. It's about him, not about me. I tell myself this over and over. My nails dig into my thighs as my eyes start to water. My whole body starts to shake, to the point I don't have control over it any longer.

I glare at him and my eyes blur from the tears, and my makeup has to have painted me like a clown.

"I need you." He takes another step toward me and enters my personal space, crosses the barrier I've created in my mind to keep him out.

I shove past him and storm out of the office, a hot fucking mess. I head toward the elevator when all the feels hit my chest like a piano falling from a building and crushing me in a bad cartoon.

When I get to the elevator my finger hits the button repeatedly, as hard and as fast as possible and I can't catch my breath. I'm pretty sure I'm about to have a full-blown panic attack as my mind and body try to process a billion different feelings at once.

Finally, the bell dings and the doors open. I step inside and contemplate going back to my room and never coming out of it.

CHAPTER 10
JOEL

LOOKING AROUND THE room, I realize this wasn't the best plan in the world. I couldn't help myself. I needed to see her right then, but I should've waited until she wasn't at work.

One of the gray-headed men at the table is staring at me. I glance over and he smiles. "Son, this is the part where you go after her."

The others at the table grin.

"I'm so sorry for interrupting. I clearly wasn't thinking."

The man next to him points toward the front. "Umm, she went that way."

They all start to laugh, and I hear Tommy chuckle behind me. It takes a minute for everything to sink in. "Right. So I'm just gonna—" I point back toward the entrance and then take off running.

Tommy is on my heels. "Wait for me, Herbert!"

We get to the elevator, and my foot won't stop tapping the ground. Waiting for it is excruciating. Seconds seem like hours.

The door finally opens, and we head down to the lobby. We both sprint out to the front of the building and scan the street looking for her. *Nothing.*

"Fuck, where'd she go?" I crane my head up, trying to see over the top of everyone walking down the sidewalks.

"Got it! Follow me." Tommy takes off down the road.

What the fuck?

I run after the crazy bastard, trying to keep up. He's holding his phone out in front of his face.

"Where the fuck are we going?"

He's already getting short of breath and can't respond as we come to a stoplight in the middle of downtown. I'm winded too and arch my back, looking up at some of the tall buildings looming over us. Tommy nudges me with his elbow and nods when I look up at him.

I look in that direction and there she is, sitting on a park bench in a little courtyard, her face buried in her palms.

"So I'm just gonna—" I point over in her direction.

"Yep."

I cross the street and walk toward the bench with my hands in my pockets. Quinn is still in the same position, and I hear sniffling as I near.

"I'm an idiot."

Her head lifts up to meet my gaze and black tears are coursing down her cheeks from her mascara. Her eyes are tinged with red. It's like someone is punching me in the stomach repeatedly. I should leave and stop bothering her because all I do is hurt her, but instead I walk over toward the bench.

I sit down and rest my elbows on my knees while running a hand through my hair. "I'm sorry."

She stares at me. I can see it in my peripheral vision, and I sigh.

"You should go." Her words hurt more than the way she looks at me.

"I know. But I just can't."

"What about the other girl? I can't trust you."

"I didn't do anything with her. I swear. Yeah, I went to her house, but I couldn't go through with it." I wipe my hand down my pants. "All I could think about was you."

"No. You always have an answer. You always talk your way out of everything, and I end up getting hurt."

"Look, I swear—"

"Please." She cuts me off, and her face goes back to her hands. "Just go. Please don't make me beg."

"Why do you want me to go so bad?"

"B-because I m-might change my mind."

I should rejoice on the inside, but somehow the words murder me. How did I hurt her so bad? How did I not realize this? I reach over and hug her around the shoulders and pull her head up to my chest.

She reaches around my neck and buries her face into my shoulder and cries. My arms tighten around her, and I snake my fingers through her hair. "I'm sorry. I didn't mean—" I pause. "I'm sorry."

I run my other hand up and down her back and her whole body is quivering under my touch, but she nestles into me, tears still flowing.

Both of my palms move to her cheeks and I lift her head up to see her eyes, the only eyes in the world that matter to me. I press my lips into hers and hold them there for a second. An electrical charge courses through my entire body, and it's like we're connected to each other again.

Her fingers move to the back of my neck and tease across my nape as her mouth parts. Our tongues intertwine, and she tastes the exact same as the first time I kissed her.

"I missed you so much." Her words barely come out when our mouths part for a second before pressing back together. I lift her up off the park bench without a care for the passers-by who keep turning their heads. I wrap my arms around her waist and lift her from the ground. She lets out a slight squeal as I kiss her again. The buildings rotate in my vision as we twirl around in the small park, my heart thumping so hard it threatens to burst from my chest.

"Atta boy, Herbert!" Tommy's voice rings out from across the street and Quinn puts a palm on each of my cheeks and presses her forehead to mine.

I set her back on her feet and lean down to kiss her once more. I break the kiss and stare into her gorgeous face with streaks of black running down it. "I love you."

She smiles and it turns my legs to jello.

"I love you too."

CHAPTER 11
QUINN

WE BURST THROUGH the door to my hotel room, and I push Joel up against the wall. He nods toward the bed.

"No time." I yank his shirt up over his head and then drag my nails down the ridges of his abs while staring up into his eyes. My fingers work his belt loose, my gaze still fixed on him, and then I reach down into his pants and palm his hard length. "I missed you."

"I missed you too." His eyes roll back as I stroke up to his tip and tease it with my thumb.

"I wasn't talking to you." I yank his pants down and let his cock spring free before I lick down his delicious abs and kiss the lower part of his stomach. His head beats against the wall as I lick the tip and lift his dick up and run my tongue the length of him.

He groans. "Fuck, that feels so good."

"Not as good as this will." I lower him back to my mouth and kiss around the head before taking him all the way to the back of my throat. My cheeks squeeze around his cock as he grows harder.

His fist pounds against the wall and his thighs tense, the light illuminating all of the muscles in his legs. I release him from my mouth to catch my breath. "You like the way I suck your dick, Joel? Take control and show you what you want?"

He fists a handful of my hair. The sting against my scalp allows a coo to escape my lips.

"Did I say you could stop?" He grips my hair tighter and tries to move my head toward his cock. I strain against him, goading him even more. Hot tingles rush into my inner thighs, and my clit is on fire, so much that I might come if he so much as grazes it with part of his body.

I stare up into his eyes, then back to the hard dick resting in my palm in front of my face. A smile forms on my face and then I open my mouth for him. I slap his head on my tongue and his other hand reaches into my hair as well.

"You gonna fuck my mouth, Joel?" I tongue the head of his cock and watch his never ending abs tighten, but hold my head back as he tries to push into my mouth.

He grunts, and his legs tremble. My tongue is his puppet master.

After sufficiently teasing him into a rage of sexual energy, I dive onto his cock and swallow him whole. I nod back and forth on his hard length, sucking my cheeks in to give him the warm, wet friction he needs so desperately. His hands grip tighter in my hair as he pushes himself in and out of my mouth, until I'm finally sitting idle and letting him fuck into the back of my throat.

My hand slides down over one of my breasts and I palm it, teasing at my nipple. It's not enough for me and I work lower, into my pants over my panties. I circle my clit and moan on his cock, fueling the rhythm of his hips. My eyes start to water from the head of his dick hammering into the back of my throat, and I look up into his eyes.

He's about to lose control, and I want him to. He pulls his cock from my mouth and yanks me back by the hair, so that my head is tilted up to him. "Up!" His word is a sharp command, a bark.

My pussy kicks up a few degrees as I shake my head at him and smile.

"Wrong move." He grips me under the arms, digging his fingers into me and carries me three steps to the bed, before tossing me down on my back. I try to sit up and he grips my wrists and shoves me back to where I was, pinning my arms above my head.

I struggle against him and he drives me into the bed. His chest is against mine, holding me steady as his mouth lingers around my ear, exhaling warm breath down my neck that sends a shudder ripping up my spine. "My turn, you fucking tease."

He sucks down my neck, hovering around the spot between my ear and shoulder that he knows will spread my legs for him. His left hand palms my breast over my shirt and he squeezes hard as my nipple grows tight against his palm. He rolls it between his thumb and index finger and I belt out a moan. His mouth finds the magical place on my neck, and he owns me.

His hard length of cock brushes over my pants on top of my clit and my free hand claws at the sheets. He already has me moaning, and I worry what will escape my lips once he's inside me. I reach back for the sheets above my head as he lifts up from me, his upper body tense as his eyes rake across my body.

If he so much as breathes on my clit I think I'll orgasm instantly. He reaches down and hooks his fingers in my pants at the hips and yanks them off of me. I start to sit up, still wanting to fight against him and he shoves me back down. I squeeze my knees together, trying to goad him.

"Spread your legs." His voice is like gravel, his words a command.

I shake my head at him, a slight smile showing through my serious demeanor.

Without warning his hands wedge between my thighs and shoves them apart. I try to fight back against his hands just enough to keep him frustrated, but my head flies back once more, my fingers clawing at the mattress.

"Don't act like I don't know what you want, Quinn." He spreads me farther, his fingers digging into my legs, destined to leave bruises.

"What's that?" My voice is a half moan, half plea.

His hands slide to the back of my thighs and he pushes my knees up next to my head, my ass and pussy inches from his face. He flattens his tongue on my pussy and licks me slow over my panties, from asshole to clit, the tip of his tongue grazing me as he finishes. His eyes are locked onto mine the entire time, recording every reaction in his mind. My thighs quiver in his grip, and a shudder rips through my body.

"For me to rip these panties off and shove my cock where my tongue was." He drops my legs and rips my underwear in half.

I moan loud enough for the entire floor to hear. "God, you and your filthy mouth."

He leans down and cages my throat with his hand, staring into my eyes and starts to work the head of his cock back and forth on my clit, his face inches from mine. "It's not half as filthy as the shit I'm about to do to you."

His words send a jolt of electricity through me that channels into my clit, and his hard cock rubbing across it has me on the brink.

"You're about to come, aren't you?" He smiles and moves his cock away from me.

I want it back. I need it touching me. My hands grip his forearm as he applies pressure to my neck. My nails claw into his skin.

"No, let's try this first. I don't know if you can handle me fucking you just yet." He slaps his hand against my wet pussy and rubs up and down on it, his gaze never leaving me. "Let's see how long this takes."

He takes two fingers to the hilt and swirls my clit with his thumb. My hips jolt from the bed up toward his hand, and he takes his fingers deeper into me, gripping up to find my spot as I start to tremble.

I fight the waves of pleasure that are quickly becoming unable to contain as he leans into my ear. "Don't fight it. Come on my fucking fingers like a good little slut." His thumb speeds up on my clit. My breathing follows suit, especially at his words.

I try to say something, but nothing comes out. My thoughts are muddled and I'm dizzy with euphoria, everything in me trying not to focus on every nerve in every limb of my body being stimulated to alarming levels. My hips betray my mind and start bucking against his hand. I shake my head against his grip.

He leans up to look at me and the corners of his mouth turn up ever so slightly. "You asked for it."

He dives to my neck and bites down. His fingers drilling into me at the same time, and his palm slaps against my clit. The wet suctioning sound echoes through the room and my arm wraps around his head, my fingers digging into his scalp.

"Fuck!"

His grip on my throat catches my scream and muffles it. His teeth dig harder into my shoulder and his hand slides from my neck and covers my mouth, forcing my head down to the bed as my hips start to convulse on his hand. He growls into my neck, and his fingers speed up as the onslaught of nerve firings rip through my body and swirl like a drain into my pussy. I scream into his hand and my vision blurs, my body a complete slave to his touch.

When my hips finally lower to the bed, he pulls his fingers from me and leans up, removing his hand from my mouth as my breaths come in huge waves. "Goddamn your fingers and your filthy fucking mouth." I struggle to catch my breath.

He leans up, and rubs his fingers—glistening with my wetness—up and down the length of his cock. "I'm not done yet."

He wasn't this rough before, and it's doing things to my body that my brain doesn't quite yet understand.

Before I can catch my breath, he reaches down and flips me to my stomach. I squeal.

I can feel his eyes on me as I'm bent over the bed. My toes find the soft carpet as I grip the bed sheets, wondering what he's about to do to me.

I feel his hands on my ass, kneading my soft flesh. "I've missed this view."

I look straight ahead at the wall, not wanting to see what he's doing, only feel it. I try to push my ass back against his hands and he shoves me harder onto the bed.

"Don't fucking move."

I do it again.

Crack. The stinging of his palm on my ass sends a new current of excitement ripping through me. "Fuck."

Before I can react his face buries into my ass, his tongue on my pussy, licking around my entrance. I plant my face in the sheets and moan. How he's turned me into a screamer—knows exactly what to say and do—I will never fully understand. He spreads my ass apart, licking every inch of me, then slides his tongue across the tight ridges of my asshole. I'm not certain how much longer it will be until my legs give out.

Right when I'm about to come all over his face, both of his hands are on my hips, forcing me down harder onto the bed. Once more, I fight the urge to stare back at him, to see what he's doing. I want to feel it.

One of his hands slides to my shoulder, and then I feel his breath on my neck, then in my ear. "I'm not going to be gentle. And you're going to come when you're told." I feel the head of his cock teasing around my pussy. "Got it?"

I nod and try to push back into him. My body needs his cock inside of me.

He smacks my ass again, harder this time, and he eases inside just enough to tease. "When I fucking say so." He swipes my hair from my neck and licks from my collar bone to my ear lobe, exhaling warm breath across my neck. My skin pebbles at the rush of heat.

I try to hold still, but I'm losing control quickly.

"Tell me what you want, Quinn." He eases inside of me a little farther. My legs quake and my eyes close.

"You know what I want, *Joel*."

He bears down on the side of my neck at the sound of my words. "Tell me." His cock teases me, barely moving in and out.

"Fuck me." My voice is a whisper.

"I can't hear you." I feel his free hand run down my curves and come to rest on the side of my ass.

His cock continues to tease in and out of me, and I'm about to lose it if he doesn't fuck me soon. "Fuck me, Joel."

I don't have time to finish my sentence, and he's balls-deep inside of me. "Oh my god—"

He fists my hair and yanks my head back so that I can see his face as he drills into me. "Is this what you wanted? To get fucked like a naughty little whore?"

I start to nod when I feel his hand connect with my ass, and slide up to one of my breasts. He squeezes my nipple between his fingers, hard, as I hear his thighs slap into my ass with each thrust. I start to close my eyes, to focus everything on how he feels inside of me.

"Open your eyes, and look at me when I fuck you." His voice is a growl as his hand tightens in my hair.

"F-f-fuck, I'm gonna come." His cock pounding into me turns my voice into high pitched, vibrating squeals. I stare up into his green eyes, on the brink of another release.

One of his hands is still in my hair, and the other moves up to my throat as he holds my head steady, facing him. "You're going to come on my dick when I blow inside of you."

His hips speed up, and I try to hold back all of the energy collecting deep inside of me. I nod. Joel starts fucking me so hard I rely on his hands to keep my head from dropping to the bed. His fingers tense and his muscles constrict.

Smacking sounds from him ramming my wet pussy echo through the room, and I don't know how much longer I can take it.

"Okay." He nods. "Come on my fucking dick. *Now*."

I give in and pleasure courses through my veins like a river of heat. My pussy clamps around his cock and my legs stiffen. Right when my orgasm crests, he grunts, and I feel his cock kick inside of me as he comes, feeding my own pleasure another few moments. He lets go of my hair and neck, and my head falls to the bed. His fingers dig into my hips as he groans one last time and pushes as far inside of me as humanly possible.

I pant against the sheets as he collapses onto my back and drops light kisses down my neck and shoulder.

His voice is a whisper. "I love you."

CHAPTER 12
QUINN

I WAKE UP thirsty, nuzzled into Joel's shoulder, and something about it just feels right. *What time is it?* Rolling over, I snag my phone off of the night stand. My muscles ache in the best possible way. Last night was quite a "workout", hot sex, dinner, more hot sex, dessert which was basically eaten off of each other, and then more hot sex.

Comfort fills me, and it's like I'm floating around, somehow lighter. I slide out of bed with the phone in my hand and start walking to the hotel mini fridge. *Fuck.* The pain from all the rough sex reminds me of all the pleasure and I grin.

Finally, I make it to the fridge and pull out a bottled water and start guzzling. My mouth is dry and the cold water is like heaven as it goes down. I finish it off and set the bottle down, then rub my eyes trying to make out the phone screen. It's three in the morning. I head back over to the bed, wincing a little less as my body adjusts. When I start to put the phone back on the night stand, a message pops up. It's a pair of tan legs in black lacy stockings, and some black heels. *What the hell? Who the fuck is Bridget and why is she sending me half naked pictures?*

Bridget: can't sleep. thinking about our last encounter. call me. xoxo

Reality kicks in. I drop the phone on the ground and freeze in my tracks. Joel's phone.

I turn to him while he sleeps, every woman's fantasy naked in my hotel room bed. I feel stinging in my eyes, and they start to mist. I wipe them before they can be tears, because I will not cry over this son of a bitch again. Won't happen.

Part of me wants to smother this asshole with his pillow so he can never hurt me again. How can this beautiful prick who fucked my brains out all night long tell me he loves me?

My mind is racing, trying to figure out what my next move will be. I bend down and pick up his phone, set it back where it was, gather my things as quickly as possible, and get the fuck out of there.

CHAPTER 13
JOEL

BRIGHT SUNLIGHT SHOOTING through the window hits me in the face right when I open my eyes. Something is off. I turn my head to stare at Quinn, and the bed is empty. The sheets are drawn down, but I don't see her anywhere.

Maybe she went out for coffee or had a meeting.

I tell myself it's normal, but something is wrong. Something has always been wrong since I fell for her.

I reach for my phone on the night stand and pick it up. There's a new text so I check it. Bridget. Fucking great. I click on the message and close it just as fast. "Chick is fucking crazy."

I need to find a way to get rid of her, but that can come later. Focusing on Quinn is the only thing that matters right now. I get up and walk around the room and notice shit is missing. Quinn's shit. *Fuck me.*

I try to call her. Nothing. Everything is gone.

Call Tommy.

After dialing his number he picks up on the second ring. "Herbert, my bitch! You finally come up from the sea of pussy to take a breath?"

There's water and a loud engine in the background. Tommy sounds like he's getting smacked in the face with hurricane winds.

"Where the fuck are you?" My voice is loud and insistent.

"Jesus Christ. I'm on my way to Alcatraz. If you must know."

Fuck me. He's always wanted to go there. I should've known.

"Sorry for sounding like a prick." I sit down on the bed and scrub my free hand over my face and into my hair. Then I pull. Hard. "I've got a problem."

"Oh you're not doing this to me right now, you dick goblin. What did you do?"

"I'm not sure."

"How do you always fuck up and never know what the problem is? It's bad enough Episode 7 is going to suck Mother Teresa's taint. Now I'm going to miss out on Alcatraz? I planned on doing Connery's voice the whole day while you got your fuck on." He must cover up the phone because it sounds like he's farther away. "What? Watch my language? You gonna kick me out? We are in the motherfucking ocean. Go buy yourself a spray tan and a sense of humor, you pasty old fuck. I've got real problems here."

"Tommy. Focus." I chuckle a little and stand.

"Sorry about that. Someone always gets offended about *crude* language. Oversensitive pricks."

"Quinn is gone." I sigh. The words pummel my chest.

"What do you mean she's gone?"

"I mean she isn't here."

There's rustling and then the line clears. "Like she just went out for a bit? Or like gone, as in, never coming back, gone?"

I open a few empty drawers, praying her clothes are in them. They're not. "The second one. None of her shit is here."

He lets out a long, exasperated sigh. "Oh boy."

I walk over to the window and stare out at downtown San Francisco and the expanse of water behind it. "What are we going to do?"

"Well, she probably went home. Your bitch ass is going to go book us some flights. I'm going to find fucking Carmen Sandiego."

"I just—"

"Stop your goddamn thinking and let me do that. Get your shit together and get us a flight. I'll find out where she is for certain in the meantime. You owe me a blow jibber and a box of Krispy Kremes for this. I'm tired of being the goddamn marriage counselor in this motherfucker."

"Okay."

There is a long pause. I hear him breathing.

"Why aren't you getting us a flight, *Herbert*?"

"I don't know. I was waiting for you to hang up."

"I don't hang up! I wait until the other person does! Everyone knows that. Now hang up, bitch. We are on a schedule."

It gets a chuckle out of me. "Fine!"

I hang up the phone and saunter over to the bed. Opening my browser I start searching for flights and they're all full. "Fuck." I call and try to get us on any combination of flights possible. They're all booked for the holidays.

This cannot be happening.

My phone goes off, and it's the imperial death march. Tommy's picture flashes across the screen and he's holding Jar Jar Binks severed head by the ears, a decapitated body is on the ground below.

"What's up?"

"She's on her way home. You get us a flight?"

Why is she on her way home? What in the fuck could I have possibly done?

214

"No, they're all booked for the holidays." I wait for it.

"One thing, Sir. You were in charge of one thing!" There is a pause. "Let me make a call. Pack your shit."

About fifteen minutes go by, and I finally end my little pity party on the bed. I walk around the room, shoveling clothes and anything else of mine into my suitcases. It's almost noon and the grumbling in my stomach reminds me I haven't eaten anything.

Every time I think, breathe, take a step—it's like a dagger, ripping up through my guts. My entire life, the one I thought I was happy in, and had all figured out, is flipped upside down and full of regret. I can't figure out how it happened.

Tommy is an awesome wing man, but the person I really need right now, more than anything, is Mom.

It's still like I'm in a torture rack when I think about her, but the vise around my heart eases a little each day. I need her advice, her experience. A simple hug from her always solved any problem I had before, and now I'm in a tailspin that can't right itself no matter how hard I try.

I wheel my bags over and set them by the door. The silent, empty room does nothing to help keep my mind from racing. I comb through every detail, trying to figure out what I missed. At the same time, I hold my phone out, waiting for it to light up, vibrate—do anything.

Finally, Tommy calls and I answer.

"Got your shit packed?" He speaks before I can say anything.

"Yeah, what's up?" The phone vibrates against my ear from my hand constantly shaking.

"I rented us a car. Road trip mother bitch. I'm coming to get you."

"Dude, it's like a five-hour drive." My heart thumps. I guess anything is better than sitting around doing nothing. I'm sold on the idea by the time he responds.

"Well, maybe if you had your life together, we wouldn't need to be doing this goddamn shit."

"No, it's fine. I'm sold. Just hurry." Adrenaline is pumping through my veins now, and I'm pacing around the room.

"Oh, fuck you, mister first class. You ain't riding in this car now."

"I said it was fine, dickhead. Just come get me." My voice is desperate.

"Oh, look at me, I'm Herbert and I don't ride in cars like peasants do. Maybe you can put on a toga and I'll feed you some grapes, Caesar." His deadpan delivery has me wanting to laugh and strangle him simultaneously.

"Stop fucking around. I'm serious. Come get me."

215

"I've been in the lobby for five minutes, pussy. I'm not waiting much—"

I hang up and grab the bags before he can finish his sentence. When I get to the elevators, I punch the button with my finger like a woodpecker trying to cut down a redwood. The ride down is excruciating, and I may have called the elevator a few choice words like "tortoise cunt" and "fuck snail."

When the doors open, Tommy is standing in the lobby pointing at his watch. "Whenever you're ready, pussy."

I run past him with the bags and he follows out to the car. "Which one is it?"

"The white one."

I look around and the only white car I see is a hatchback that looks like it's built for circus clowns. My bags fall to the ground, and I flip around to see Tommy glaring.

"Say something about the car, Herbert. I dare you to say one goddamn thing, you pompous fuck." His nostrils are flaring and his cheeks are puffed out. It's an act, and we both know it. I play along.

"You got that shit on purpose." I grind my teeth for some effect.

"So what if I did." He holds out a hand and starts counting off all the great things about the car on each finger. "Great fuel economy, great price, and umm—"

"I don't care. Let's just go." I grab my shit and run over to the car, barely missing one of the valet drivers. "Give me the keys."

"No way. This isn't *The Italian Job*. You're not driving this bitch through all these hilly streets, Steve McQueen." He twirls the keys around his index finger and laughs as he walks over to the driver's side.

"Fuck that. You're not driving! Hand them over. We're in a hurry." I shove my suitcases into the tiny trunk area.

"Oh Sir, your name is not on this here paperwork." He holds up a few receipts, grinning his ass off. "Hop in, sweetie."

CHAPTER 14
JOEL

WE ARE TWO hours into the trip, and I've been staring hate into the side of Tommy's head the entire drive. He has the cruise control set to the speed limit and seems to be enjoying himself far too much for my comfort.

"Keep staring. I can go slower." His lips curl.

"What the fuck is wrong with you? I'm dying over here and you're making jokes. I'm about to get pissed off." The seatbelt locks up and nearly decapitates me before I spring back against the seat. "Fuck!" I yank it around trying to get it to loosen.

"Good. Use your aggressive feelings, boy. Let the hate flow through you." He brakes subtly and the car starts slowing even more.

"What is your fucking deal, asshole?" Immediately, I regret yelling. Though I still want to rip his head off.

Tommy whips the car over on to the shoulder and slams on the brakes. Once again the seatbelt digs into my chest and then I fly back in the seat. "What the fuck? You fucking maniac!"

"Get out!"

I can see the whites of his knuckles on the steering wheel. He's never yelled at me like this before.

"Just, okay. Look—"

"Get. Out." Tommy's breath is labored, and his face turns red.

He turns the car off and unbuckles his seatbelt, then opens his door and gets out. Not before slamming it so hard I fear he may have busted something in it. I've never seen him like this before.

I unbuckle my own seatbelt slowly as he paces around the car. Veins are bulging in his neck and he rips my door open.

"I said get the fuck out!" He swings his arm out to the side, so that he's pointing to the field on the side of the road.

"Jesus Christ. You're going to leave me on the side of the highway?" I glare back at him. "Why are you doing this?"

"Because it's my job."

I stare at him like he's some kind of strange alien. "What the fuck are you talking about? This is your job? You're not making any sense."

217

He rolls his eyes and starts slow clapping. "Very good, Herbert. Jesus H Christ, man."

I'm still trying to figure out what he's talking about as I lean up against the car. He still looks like he wants to whip my ass on the side of the road.

"Well, explain. I'm so stupid I obviously don't get it."

I can practically hear his jaw grinding. "Have you thought about Quinn the entire trip?" He takes a step toward me.

I try to think. Actually, I haven't thought about her once.

"Or have you been pissed at me the entire time?"

I shove my hands in my pockets and look down at the ground.

"That's what I thought. You've been pissed off at me. Worried about how fast we're going. Do you know why I'm going slow? Because that girl that you supposedly *love* needs some fucking time to think. And god forbid she get more than just a couple of hours because the goddamned Panty Whisperer isn't getting what he wants at the moment." He takes another step toward me, and his eyes are bloodshot, haunting me as I look up at him. "Oh, you can blow her off for days, and she's just supposed to drop everything for you. When you decide to come around. When you just show up at the airport, and her fucking job, busting into the middle of meetings at her work. No, you're a fucking train wreck right now and I'm tired of watching you fuck it up. Tommy will take it from here. And if it means you being a pissed off little cry baby in the seat next to me, so be it, if it keeps you from being a little clingy ass stalker."

I look at him, knowing he's right, and the anger seems to have faded with his words. I give him a slight shrug. "I didn't stalk her."

A smile tries to fight through his now fake anger. "Yes you did. You stalked that poor girl all stalkily. Stalker Texas Ranger. You could write a short story about it if you want, William Stalkner."

I turn to get in the car as he walks around the front, still staying in character as he points two fingers at his eyes and then points them at me. He opens his door and gets back in the car. Turning the key, he looks over at me.

"Go ahead, I know you have at least one more." I chuckle.

"I don't know what you're talking about." He puts the car in drive and gets back on the highway.

I reach for my phone to check my messages.

"Don't you pull out that goddamn phone." He gives me a side eye. "Fuck around and Joffrey will cut your head off, Ned Stalk."

We both erupt in laughter.

After a few minutes have passed, I glance over to him. "Thanks, man."

"Not a problem, Sir. You just have to give her a little space. Just figure out why she left. And form some kind of plan, if you really want her."

"Well, my way didn't work. So whatever you think. Just feel like I'm missing something. Like it should be obvious."

"I don't know. Her flight should be landing soon. I'm sure she'll call Megan first. We'll find out what's up."

CHAPTER 15
JOEL

TOMMY PULLS OVER to a gas station. "I need to take a piss. You want anything?"

"No man, I'm good. I think." I wipe my hands down my pants.

"Don't be a bitch. You know I'm going to call Megan first. She should've heard from Quinn by now."

I try not to look excited, but it has to be apparent.

He grins wide as he puts the phone to his ear. "Hey baby, I missed you."

His cutesy voice makes me want to vomit, but not as bad as the sounds I hear from the other end of the phone. I can't tell what she is saying, but it sounds like a female screaming version of the teacher from Charlie Brown.

"I told him. I told him. Oh, sorry. You're right, babe. You told him. I know." Tommy is shaking his head and staring at me like I'm an idiot. "Yes, he needs to be smacked around. I agree." He shakes his head at me, as if he's joking. "We're about an hour away. I'll call you when we're close. Okay. Bye babe. I love you."

As soon as he hangs up the phone, I'm all over him like a fat kid on cake. "What'd she say? What is it?"

Tommy shakes his head. "You idiot. I told you." He glances up to the roof of the car. "I told him, lord. You heard me." He glances at me then back to the road. "Quinn, got up very early this morning. And you know what? She gazed into those beautiful sea-foam-green eyes of yours—not really because you were sleeping, but this makes my story better—and in her hazy, just-woken-up state, she grabbed your phone and went to get a bottle of water. Probably to replenish herself of all the fluids you took out of her body the night before. And a certain message popped up on your fucking phone." He flips his head over and stares at me.

A lump forms in my throat. Tommy continues speaking.

"And because she thought it was her phone, she looked at it. And she got quite an eye full along with a message from that whore I—I mean umm—Megan told you to stay away from."

My fingers are tapping on my thigh a million miles an hour as I look over at Tommy. "I didn't do anything with her. I swear." I can see Tommy's face heating up again. It's worse than when he pulled

221

the car over which is worse than I'd ever seen him. "I swear to god. Just hang on." I whip out my phone and go looking for the message, glancing back up at him while I try to hurry.

"You've never lied to me that I know of. But I swear to fuck you better have compelling evidence, Herbert. Or I will throw you the fuck out of this car after the shit I've gone through. I missed *Alcatraz* for this bullshit!"

He must believe me if he's joking, somewhat anyway. I hope it was a joke and he's not really that mad about Alcatraz. The message pops up on my phone and I read through it real quick. Where I told her it was done, and that I was sorry. I shouldn't have ever gone there. I hand Tommy the phone.

He glares and then glances back and forth at my screen and the road. "You're forgiven. Though you should've never been at that chick's house in the first fucking place. You need to show this to Quinn."

I smile. "I know, I'll—"

"No. When you show it to her you do it with humility. She didn't jump to an illogical conclusion and you're not going to rub it in her face. She should have asked you about it. But fuck, given your dubious goddamn history, I can't blame her for what she did."

"So she gets a free pass?"

"Yes motherfucker. Do you know nothing about women? Or have you always just left after the first night?" A huge smile spreads across his smug face. "Oh shit, rook. You've never really done this before. You're not the whisperer. You're the padawan."

"I am not a goddamn padawan, take that shit back!" I can't help but laugh.

"You just sit there and let Obi-Tom Kenobi teach you a thing or two, my apprentice." He cackles at his own joke.

"I will not call you Obi-Tom, and you ain't teaching me shit."

"First rule, my young Jedi. You are never right. You don't throw shit in their face and think you win. Nuh uh, Sir. Those days of being a prick and having the girl wrap her mouth around your little bean bags are over. Listen to Uncle Obi on this if you want to be happy. Even when you're right, you're wrong." He slaps the steering wheel and belts out a laugh. "Oh, this is going to be fun. You have much to learn."

"Okay, okay. Tell me more if you're so wise."

"Oh shit, you want lessons now? Thought you weren't a rook?"

I stare at him. "I want to be happy. With her. For real man."

"I know. You will be."

We're half an hour from home and Tommy has *Home Sweet Home* cranked to eleven on the stereo when the power cuts out and we start coasting like a fucking roller skate down the highway. All the lights on the dashboard are blank.

"What the fuck?" He yanks the steering wheel over as we pull off the highway. He stares over in my direction as we come to a stop.

"Don't ask me, Obi-Tom. Why don't you use the force and make it turn back on."

"Nobody jokes about Obi-Tom you prick!" He wiggles a finger in my face. "Nobody!" He starts fiddling with the key, trying to start the car. He's getting no power.

I lean back and run my hands over my face before letting out a sigh and pulling on my hair. "This just keeps getting better."

"Well, get out of the car and whisper to the goddamn battery. I thought you knew shit about cars." He smacks the top of the dash a few times with his palm like it's an old television with no reception.

"Hey maybe if you blow into it like a Nintendo game it'll work."

"The jokes stop now. I'm the joker. You're the jokee listener person. Got it?" He laughs.

"It's probably the battery or the alternator, man. You probably used up all the power in this beast with your fucking Motley Crue concert."

"I didn't even get to my aria. Sad day this one is." He shakes his head.

"Yeah. That's the worst part of this day. It sure is."

We look at each other and grin.

"I'll call Megan real quick. She can come pick us up and we'll have this piece of shit towed."

"See, you still have good ideas. Find out where Quinn is at."

His eyes narrow.

"Wait, I'm not done. See if it sounds like she wants company. Or what Megan thinks I should do. I don't want to bother her if she needs more time." I remain calm and collected.

"Good. You're learning."

Tommy gets out of the car and walks along the side of the road as he makes the phone call. I get out to stretch and look at my phone. No messages or calls. I'm not surprised.

After a few minutes, he walks back over. "Megan is on her way. But she doesn't know where Quinn went. Said she was cryptic on the phone. She's going to send her texts telling her she needs to talk to you. That there was a misunderstanding."

"It's a start. I guess I'll just wait for Quinn to talk to her. I don't want to smother her."

"Oh fuck that shit, bitch. We didn't go through everything today for you not to get the girl at the end of it. We're finding her ass and making her listen to you." Tommy is bouncing around like he just snorted a Tony Montana sized mountain of coke.

"What the hell? Thought you said to—"

"Megan sent her messages. She needs to know what's up. She's had enough time to think about shit."

"You thought I fucked up really bad didn't you? That I did something awful like the last time when I ignored her." I put a hand on the hood and grab the door handle, but keep Tommy in my sights across the car.

"Don't concern yourself with my methods, Herbert. They're beyond your comprehension, Sir."

We both get in the car as if we're about to leave and realize we still have to wait on Megan.

Tommy throws on the hazard lights. "Well, that was anti-climactic."

"Yep."

"So, I know how to find Quinn, but you won't like it." He won't look at me.

"How? I'll do anything."

"When I was on the phone with Megan, I got a number."

"Whose number is it?"

He turns to me. "Olivia's."

"Oh boy." A wave of guilt crashes into me.

"Yeah."

"Fuck it. Give me the number. Let's get it over with."

"It's your funeral." I type the number into my phone as Tommy reads it to me. *God help me.* "This will not be fun." I press the button to call and she answers.

"Hey Olivia, it's Joel."

"Go fuck yourself!" She starts to hang up. Tommy is about to die of laughter in the driver's seat.

"Wait, don't hang up! Please!"

I can practically hear her huffing and puffing into the phone. "What?"

"Just, give me a minute. Please?"

"You have a lot of nerve calling. Fuck me in a bathroom. Treat me like shit. Turn my own best fucking friend against me." Her voice gets louder as she speaks.

"I'm sorry. Okay. I really am. I never meant to hurt you. I swear." I start to wonder how many other women would react this way if I called them. Bile creeps into my throat.

"Just tell me what you want. So we can end this phone call."

"It's about Quinn."

A high-pitched, angry laugh mauls my ears. Tommy starts mimicking her in the seat next to me along with her laugh that he can clearly hear. I cover my mouth and then give him a playful punch on the shoulder. I'd scold him but it's helping distract me from thinking about the other women.

"This is a joke right? I must be fucking dreaming. You did not call me to ask about that fucking bitch!"

I make a fist with my free hand and bite down on it to avoid being an asshole. Even though she deserves it. Finally, I compose myself. "Look, I said I was sorry. But, I need a favor. Please. Do you want me to beg you? I will if that's what it takes."

"God, you really love her don't you? It must've taken a lot of balls to call me asking for a favor." She laughs in a mocking tone. "You two worthless slutbags are made for each other."

My face turns red, and Tommy coaxes me into taking a huge breath.

"Please. Just, if she was upset, do you know where she might go?"

Olivia lets out a long sigh. "I don't know why the fuck I'm telling you this. Maybe so you'll get the fuck off the phone with me. But when she gets mad or needs to think about something, she always goes to the football field at her old high school. There's something sentimental about that place to her."

I start fist pumping and acting like I'll scream into the phone, but manage to control myself. Tommy scrunches up his face like he's constipated and does a couple of karate chops in the air.

"Thank you. Thank you so much." I cover the mic on my phone and high five Tommy hard as shit.

"Whatever. Lose my fucking number, you prick."

I think about yelling mean things at her, but I'm too busy celebrating with Tommy as the phone hangs up. "Yes!" I let out something like a growl or grunt that follows and shove Tommy's shoulder.

After a few seconds we both calm down and look at each other.

"So, back to waiting?" he asks.

"Yep."

Megan finally passes by on the highway and shoots Tommy the finger out of her window.

"God, I love that woman." He beams as her car passes.

"Yeah. She's a real lady of manners." I chuckle.

"Mind your fucking tongue, Sir. That's me lady you are disrespectin'."

I hold up both of my hands. "Ohh."

"Oh, I forgot to mention. She's probably gonna rip you a new asshole. Okay then, good chat." He opens the door and hops out before I can say anything back.

"Fucker." I brace myself for the abuse and get out of the car.

Tommy and Megan are practically dry humping on the side of the highway. I walk up and fake a cough, and they break free from one another.

Megan's hands are on her hips and she's staring at me like I threw her favorite shoes in a wood chipper.

"Hi Megan. Umm, good to see you." I take a step back when she starts tapping her foot on the ground.

She turns to Tommy. "That's all he has to say?"

"Oh, well, I'm sure he has more to say. Right Herbert?" He takes a step back so that he's behind her and shrugs, mouthing "I'm sorry."

Whatever. I know he's enjoying this shit.

"I'm sorry." I ease my shoulders into a shrug.

"What are you sorry for, Joel?"

Oh fuck. Questions aren't good. Usually I would deflect with some sort of compliment, but that doesn't really apply to my best friend's woman. *Fuck.* "Umm, umm—" I'm so screwed. My brain wasn't ready to be hammered with an interview. "For not listening to you." I say it slow, more like a question. Tommy throws me a thumbs up so I try to appear confident in my answer.

"It'll do for now. Get in the car. Obi-Tom tells me you've been a good little padawan bitch the last few hours." She cracks a smile.

I shoot my head up to Tommy and he's giving me the finger and grinning. He turns into a statue of serious when Megan flips around. She smiles and punches him in the gut as she walks past him. Tommy doubles over at the waist.

226

"I see everything." Her back is to us as she gets in the car.

Tommy looks like he's about to spill his lunch, and I grin as I walk by.

"God I love her." His voice is like a mumbled groan as he stands up and walks to the car.

I slide into the back seat and Tommy gets in the front. "What about the car?"

"I called the rental company. They're sending someone for it." Tommy's voice still hasn't recovered from getting socked in the stomach.

I look up and catch Megan's eyes in the rear view mirror.

"So we good to go?" she asks.

"Let's do it."

She smiles back at me. "Okay."

CHAPTER 16
JOEL

MEGAN PULLS INTO the parking lot. The last time I was here was the night Mom passed, and when I told Quinn I loved her. I try not to think about it.

I look over and see Quinn's car parked next to a light pole.

"You got this shit, man." Tommy sticks his fist back toward me, and I tap it with my knuckles.

"Thanks, bro."

"Good luck." Megan is still grinning in the front seat, and keeps looking over at Tommy.

"Well, I think this is where I—" I point to my door.

"Yep," says Tommy.

I step out of the car, and it smells like fall outside. The leaves are turning all kinds of reds, and bright oranges to match the sun that's setting behind the bleachers on the other side of the field. Walking up to the entrance, I squeeze myself between the chained gate. The same way Quinn and I did the last time we were here.

My head scans the area, looking to catch a glimpse of Quinn's familiar blonde hair. I head up the ramp leading up to the bleachers, hands in my pockets, trying to think of what to say or do. The harder I try, the more jumbled my thoughts become. All that races through my mind is Quinn, hurting.

Finally, I turn around the corner so that I can see everything. I look up the rows and my breath hitches.

There she is, sitting in the middle of the bleachers with her face buried in her palms. I freeze, unable to move for what seems like hours, but most likely is only a matter of seconds. The fading sunlight highlights all of her features, from her hair down to the curve of her breasts.

She's wearing jeans and a blue tank top wrapped in a cardigan, hair down and flowing across her shoulders. Every step I take toward her seems to grow heavier, like I'm walking in the ocean and the water is getting deeper. Will I drown when I get to her?

She doesn't lift her head from her palms as I near, and I keep moving until I'm standing in the aisle, staring at her. It turns awkward when she doesn't realize I'm there. What the fuck should I do?

229

I don't think it through, and I tap my foot on the thin metal of the bleachers.

The sound startles her. She looks up and squeals, then flies back about two feet on the metal bench. I do my best not to laugh, but it has to be apparent, and I can't fight the smile much longer.

She clutches her palms to her chest, her breaths coming in large bursts, and she smiles. Then I watch as she processes who's standing in front of her.

The gorgeous smile quickly disappears, and she starts to tense. I happen to know that the anger usually follows.

"Why are you here?" Her voice cracks a little.

I hold up both of my hands. "I just wanted to explain things. But if you want me to go I will. I don't want to upset you more." I start to back away.

"What is there to explain, *Joel*?" The volume in her voice is rising, and I can practically feel the heat radiating from her face. I start to speak, and she cuts me off. "You always have an explanation, for everything. But shit like this keeps happening."

"I'm just going to go. I don't want you to hurt more than you have to." I turn on my heel and head down the steps. Before I met Quinn I would've never given in like this. I would've been relentless until I got what I wanted.

But, I can't watch her hurt any more. She deserves more than that. I want her to be happy.

"Did you sleep with her?"

The words are like an ice shard in my back the way she says them. Maybe I'll never escape this kind of questioning. I only have myself to blame for it.

I turn back toward her and stare into her welled up eyes. "No. I didn't."

Her lips curl up slightly, but she tries to hide it. "Why can't I believe you?"

"Do you want to see the messages? I'll show you. You can go through my whole phone if you want." I pull my phone out of my pocket and hold it up.

"God." She stands up and starts pacing back and forth in the aisle. "How do you do this to me?"

I have no clue how to answer her. I start to respond, and she cuts me off.

"You drive me fucking batty. I don't know how or why." She keeps turning her gaze to me and then looking away. "You transform me into this clingy, insecure—weakling." Quinn makes some weird gesture with her hands flailing around when she says "weakling." She looks back at me for another moment. "It's just, ugh—"

It's insanely cute when she gets worked up, and I want to smile, and run up and kiss her. But I'm torn, and I don't want to make things worse. "I don't want to make your life more complicated than it has to be. It's why I offered up the phone. I want you. I have since I met you. And I fucked that up really bad. I did shitty things. And yeah, I should've never gone to her house. But the message you saw was bullshit. I told her to leave me alone, that nothing was going to happen. She sent that message anyway. I haven't been with anyone else, since before the night we went bowling."

Her lips start to do the half-smile thing again, then they flatten once more. Her arms fly in the air and she makes a flustered sound that's something like a growl.

Fuck this Joel, shit or get off the pot.

I know I've done nothing wrong this time, and I won't ever do anything to hurt her again. Knowing that, fuels my steps as I take off up the stairs toward her.

When I'm about three steps away she says, "What the hell are you—"

Both of my hands go into her hair and I crush her mouth with mine, slanting over her as our lips meet in the middle. She's frozen stiff, but almost immediately loosens, and then her mouth parts and our tongues intertwine, rough at first, but then into a smooth rhythm like that first time at her work and at the bowling alley.

When our mouths finally part, I drop a kiss on her forehead and then press my forehead to hers while staring into her eyes. My hands move from her hair to her shoulders and I caress them up and down. "I love you. I want to be with you."

"I want to be with you too. And you know I love you." She looks away.

Fuck, I can't win with her. "Look at my messages. You'll see I told her to fuck off. It was a mistake going there, but I realized it as soon as—"

She silences me with her index finger over my lips. "I believe you."

I start to say something else, and then her words resonate. "Here, let me—"

She stops me from reaching into my pocket. "No. I trust you. I have to do that if we're going to make this shit work."

"I'm sorry. For everything I put you through. The airport. Your job."

Her lips are on mine as I finish my sentence, as if she's trying to shut me up. I don't mind at all. She finally releases me from her grasp. "We'll figure it out, *Herbert*."

EPILOGUE
QUINN

3 MONTHS LATER

I'VE NEVER BEEN so happy to get out of a room full of nerds in my life. We stroll through the lobby of the movie theater, and there are grown men everywhere, dressed as characters from *Star Wars*. The stale popcorn smell wafts across my nose as I look over at Megan. She's dressed as Rey. Big mistake on her part that I'm sure she regrets, because she's being ogled by every forty-year-old man in a costume.

"Babe, you look so fucking hot in that tee shirt." Joel wraps his arm around me and the light saber strapped to his hip digs into mine.

I wince a little.

"Shit, sorry babe." He shifts away.

"It's okay." I wore a plain black and yellow *Star Wars* tee shirt just for him. "As long as you plan on force choking me later."

A passer-by wearing a Bobba Fett helmet starts to cough like something is lodged in his throat when he hears it. I can't believe I know all these characters' names. What has become of me?

I look up at Joel in his Luke Skywalker get-up and my question is quickly answered.

"That can be arranged." He smiles.

"They made me a pussy!"

We both flip around, along with Megan. Tommy is behind us in authentic Kylo Ren garb complete with voice synthesizer and everything. His words are deep and eerie sounding.

"Calm down, Kylo. Always getting mad about something." Joel snickers.

Tommy rips the mask off of his head and tucks it under his arm. "You probably liked that abomination didn't you?"

"Well yes. What? You didn't?" Joel nudges me.

"Oh I liked it the first time I saw it. You know? When we watched episode four together?" He's huffing and puffing like he's either worked up from wearing the mask, or it's from his anger toward the film. Probably a little of both.

"They weren't that similar." Joel grins at me again.

"Weren't that—" Tommy gasps. "Don't even get me started on fucking Finn! And you!" He flips around to Megan, but apparently

233

he's treating her as if she's Rey. "You just magically—" He waves his arms about in the air. "—know how to use a fucking light saber and can battle someone who's been training with Jedis his whole life." There's a pause. "Poppycock!"

Tommy storms off and stops in front of the large cardboard cut-out advertisement for the film.

"Oh shit." Joel removes his arm from my waist and starts toward Tommy. He's too late.

Tommy throws his mask and hood back on, and wields a three-pronged, red light saber from his hip. "Ahh!" He starts pummeling the character cut-outs, effectively knocking down the whole display and keeps whacking it with his light saber.

"Jesus Christ, Tommy!" Megan and I stop at a distance and she folds her arms across her chest.

"Should we do something?" I ask.

"No, no. Boys will be boys."

I watch Joel try and pull Tommy away as the movie theater workers scramble around frantically. Joel finally pulls him off of the display and shakes some sense into him. They both peer around the room, then giggle like children, and haul ass for the front door through a sea of people.

I turn and look at Megan. "Did that really just happen?"

We hook arms and stroll toward the parking lot, laughing.

"Psst!" The sound comes from the side of the theater away from the doors as we walk outside.

We poke our heads around and it's Tommy.

"What the fuck are you doing?" Megan waves her arm at him, motioning him over.

"Are we good?" His voice is a whisper.

I can hear Skywalker's muffled laughter behind him.

"Get the fuck out of here. Seriously. You're acting like children." Megan tries to mask her laughter and is failing.

The boys saunter over to us, and we walk out toward the cars. I stare at the Mustang. It's become my baby now, much to the chagrin of Joel. He humors me, but I don't mind teasing him a little bit.

I stare at the sharp curves of his beautiful car as the light from the parking lot reflects off of the shiny paint. So much power under one hood.

Joel walks up next to me, and I feel his hand slide down into mine. Our fingers intertwine. No matter where we are it feels perfect. He's perfect.

We take a few more steps. Megan and Tommy are play fighting about his behavior in the theater. All at once, Joel's fingers threaten to break the bones in my hand as he grips my hand tight.

"What the fuck!" His scream echoes through the parking lot, stopping the rest of us in his tracks.

I try to make out what's going on, what he's yelling about, when he takes off running. Pure instinct kicks in, and I take off behind him. Someone is yanking furiously on the handle to his car and a host of profane threats come from Joel's mouth.

Oh shit. They fucked with his car.

I'm on his heels and see someone step out in front of the mustang in a Sith robe, dressed as the emperor.

What in the fuck is going on here?

Joel slows down to a jog but is heading right for the shadowy figure. Before I know what's happening, I launch past Joel and tackle the guy. We crash to the ground and my fists start flying out of nowhere as the guy covers his face with his arms. My blows are all connecting with his forearms but he's not going anywhere.

"Quinn! What the hell?" Joel's words come from behind me, but I'm too focused on beating this guy's ass. I'm not sure if I'm trying to protect the car or Joel. Everything is a blur.

"Dude, what the fuck, Joel? You didn't pay me enough for this shit!" says the hooded man.

I freeze up and stop my assault on the guy. "Who the hell are you?"

"Joel, a little fucking help here. Please. She hits like a fucking man!" The guy is shaking underneath me, and I can hear Joel laughing his ass off behind me.

I spring to my feet and flip around, staring lasers at the three of them. "What the fuck is going on?" My eyes start to sting when Joel takes a step toward me.

He's trying not to laugh. "I'm so sorry. I didn't know you'd react like that. I'm trying to find the words right now."

"What's happening?" The collar of my shirt seems to tighten around my neck, cutting off my air supply.

Megan is standing by Tommy, who still has his mask on, and she's smiling, grinning a big cheesy grin. I turn back to Joel. "What is this?"

"That's Brock, from my office. I paid him to pretend like he was stealing my car." He smiles.

"But why? And why the fuck is he dressed like Palpatine?"

"We were supposed to have a light saber fight that we choreographed and rehearsed. But you went all Ronda Rousey on him."

"So, it was just for fun then? Just as a joke?" I turn to Brock. "I'm so sorry. Seriously, I didn't know."

Brock looks at me. "It's okay. But you should turn back around."

"What? Why?" I flip around. "Why did you—"

Joel is on one knee a few feet away from me and a heat wave rushes over me so hard I get dizzy. My face heats up like embers in a fire. I cover my eyes with both hands but then peek between my fingers as Joel extends his arm toward me, holding a solitaire diamond ring.

"So I can ask you something."

"A-a-ask me what?"

You bumbling fool, Quinn.

"Ask you to join me. And together we can rule the galaxy as husband and wife."

I don't think I've ever cried at a fucking *Star Wars* quote in my life, but this one does me in. I'm an official mess.

"Will you marry me?" His eyes and his bright white teeth are on full display as he looks at me like I'm the most beautiful thing he's ever seen.

I can't speak. Every nerve in my body is firing off at random, like celebratory gunfire. I drop my hands from my face, smile, and nod furiously at him. I take a step over and he slips the ring onto my finger.

I look over and Kylo Ren and Rey are both clutching their hands across their chests and swooning. I'm sure Tommy's antics are sarcasm. I hope anyway.

Once the ring is on, I run my other fingers over it. It's perfect.

Joel stands up and puts his palms on each side of my face, and stares into my eyes. "I love you."

I gaze back at him, the man who is everything I've ever wanted. "I know."

OTHER WORKS BY SLOANE

Novels by Sloane Howell

The Matriarch: An Erotic Superhero Romance
The Matriarch Trilogy, Book 1

Betrayal is easy, sex is a weapon, and information is power. Maggie Madison sits in the lofty towers of her city during the day, but at night she lurks the seedy underbelly, looking to snare the man who stole her innocence. Her simple quest becomes complicated when she meets a man who is as light as she is dark, as straightforward as she is deceptive. When a villain rises and sets her world alight, she must weigh her need for revenge against the good of the city she vowed to protect.

Cleat Chaser
Co-authored with Celia Aaron

Kyrie Kent hates baseball. She hates players even more. When her best friend drags her to a Ravens game, she spends the innings reading a book... Until she gets a glimpse of the closer—a pitcher who draws her like a magnet. Fighting her attraction to Easton Holliday is easy. All she has to do is keep her distance, avoid the ballpark, and keep her head down. At least, all that would have worked, but Easton doesn't intend to let Kyrie walk so easily. When another player vies for Kyrie's attention, Easton will swing for the fences. But will Kyrie strike him out or let him steal home?

Coming Summer 2016
The Matriarch Trilogy, Book 2

Coming Summer 2016
Cleat Catcher (Co-authored with Celia Aaron)

Coming Winter 2016
The Matriarch Trilogy, Book 3

Shorts and Novellas by Sloane Howell

Chloe Comes For Christmas, An Erotic Holiday Novella

James lives in the friend zone. His best friend and fraternity brother Mark, the All-American cornerback, has always found a way to get the girl going back to their teens. When James meets Chloe first and falls for her, Mark swoops in once again.

This time is different though. James has his sights on teaching them both a lesson for making him look the fool.

***

Bad Boy Revelation
The Alpha Bad Boy Series, Book 1

Daddy told me not to even look at the man in the corner. He's troubled he said. I wanted to do more than look at him.

I grew up in the church. I was raised better. And I was broken. Oh, was I ever broken. I had a sexual appetite that couldn't be filled. A thirst in me that only sin could quench. I needed him, the man in the corner, to claim me, dominate me, own me.

I'd do whatever it took. Goad him if necessary. I needed that man like I needed air or water. I needed the bad boy.

Bad Boy Prospect
The Alpha Bad Boy Series, Book 2

Fighting, f***ing, and winning. It's what I do and nobody will stand in my way. It's how I live my life on the field and in the bedroom. I make hitters fear me. If they're scared, it gives me an advantage, and I capitalize on it. People say I have an attitude problem, that I'm a bad boy. It's exactly what I want them to think.

Until I meet Elizabeth, the psychiatrist Coach makes me see. She specializes in pro athletes. There's something about her. Maybe she'll be the one who finally cuts through my layers and sees the real me. Who knows?

Bad Boy Brawler
The Alpha Bad Boy Series, Book 3

Devyn O'Dare is the Ultra MMA world heavyweight champion. He destroys opponents. He doesn't like to be in the public eye. One day he makes a bad decision that will alter his life forever.

In the hospital he meets Carly, single mom, nurse, struggling day to day. Devyn feels he can right some wrongs from his troubled past. He can change Carly's life and end her struggles, prevent her son from the same type of childhood he experienced. But Carly must decide if she wants to trust Devyn and put her pride aside, or soldier through life alone with her son.

Bad Boy Con Man
The Alpha Bad Boy Series, Book 4

Grayson is a con man. If he sees an opportunity, he capitalizes. When the score that can set him up for life comes along it's too much for him to resist.

Then he meets Amelia. Intelligent, funny, gorgeous, and a lover of comic books. She's everything he's ever wanted. But, at the end of the day he has to make a choice — hurt the woman he's crazy about, or take the money and leave his old life behind.

***

Payne Capital
The Payne Capital Series, Book 1

Devyn White and his fiancee Meredith—the perfect All-American couple—have just moved to New York City following his acceptance of his dream job working at Payne Capital, a private equity firm ran by Rebekah Payne, a billionaire math and finance prodigy. Devyn soon realizes his dream isn't all that he imagined as he is thrust into ethical dilemmas involving an ex-husband, an out of control boss, the operations of the firm, and his own personal relationship with Meredith. When the heat is turned up he must soon make difficult choices that will affect the rest of his life and possibly hurt the people he loves in the process.

ACKNOWLEDGEMENTS

This anthology has been quite the ride. Producing a book is not easy, and it takes a team of people to do it properly. If I thanked every person individually, this section could be its own novel. The one thing I fear more than a gaping plot hole in a book that I've published, is forgetting to thank someone. If I do forget, I sincerely apologize. It's not intentional. I'm just so blessed to have so many people who help me out.

Family is first, and I could not do this without Mrs H and the boy. They get me through everything. They ARE everything. I love you so much and thank you! Also, I suppose I'll throw Lil Bro in the family section. Thanks buddy. Your "buy his shit" mantra is pure marketing genius. Love you!

Celia Aaron, my writing bestie. You're the shit. You know this. You'll remind me of this. I'm quite certain. I couldn't get through some of the hard days without you. You are a workhorse and the best writer I know. And you make me better. Thank you!

My publicist and PR rep, Neda Amini, with Ardent Prose PR. She is the best. Literally. When I worked with small businesses before becoming a full-time author, I would always start to pick up on patterns. Every single successful client always had a few traits in common. They surrounded themselves with people who were experts at things they weren't. But not only that, they surrounded themselves with experts who shared the same goals and visions as they did. I feel so comfortable knowing I have a publicist who has my back at all times, and also shares the same loves and visions as I do: reading (even though her tastes are not as refined as my own, *runs*), not forgetting where you came from, building your brand organically through hard work and personal relationships and not throwing money at it for temporary gains, helping others who are just starting out. She's taught me so much and I can't see myself anywhere else but with Ardent, as long as they'll have me. Thank you!

Stacey Broadbent at Spell Bound. The greatest proofreader of all time who also happens to be an author and a fan. But more importantly, a friend. Thank you so much! You're a rock star.

Rachel at The Saucy Owl and Vivian at Beaute de Livres. KSBAFCM! You ladies are amazing! Seriously. I don't have words to describe how, in Rachel's terms, motherfrikkin shiznitting awesome both of you are. The teasers, organization, book trailers, swag planning... I could go on and on. They still find time to read my own and others' books and write reviews, serving the indie community without asking anything in return. You both mean the world to me. I'm sure you already know that. But thank you!

Laura McHale and Lauren Lascola-Lesczynski. My other duo who are admins in my group and inseparable. I heart both of you so hard. Day in and day out, I can always count on them spreading the word about my books (and others), keeping the group interesting and hilarious while I'm busy with things, or hanging out with boy or Mrs H for the day. Lauren constantly finds new ways to promote my books, or she's raising money for charities near and dear to me. Laura is always posting something somewhere about my books, or on her Facebook blog page. This is on top of everything they already do. They're both just incredible. Thank you!

My ninja pimps, Ciara Hunter and Paro. My god, these two. They are freaking machines. We have a chat and a ninja pimp group that Rachel and Viv set up. It's super organized and amazing. Ciara and Paro show up in the chat and it's like I'm reading the news wire at the stock exchange it's moving so fast. And it's not just release day, it's every single day. They are out there hustling for Celia and I, rounding up others, entering us in contests, posting teasers, making teasers, making gifs. I just want to hug you both so hard. Thank you for all of your hard work. I can't say enough good things to do you justice.

Thank you to Mr. Aaron. Not only is he Celia's husband, giving up time with her for us to work on our books, but he's a graphic design virtuoso. He did the cover for this book and also does most of Celia's. Cleat Chaser is his design too. He's like the digital Da Vinci of romance covers and ab pictures. Thank you, sir. You saved my ass last minute on the PW cover and it's fucking incredible.

All of my good friends at the Harem. I just wanna hug all of you. There are too many to list out, but thank you so very much. I have so much fun daily and it's the best group I could hope for. You are amazing, and I don't think I can say enough about all of you. My heart is so happy that you all take the time to read my books and help spread the word about them. I'm going to leave it at that, at the risk of crying at two a.m. as I write this. I love you all, so very much! You aren't fans. You're friends. I truly mean that. When one person is down, we pick them up. When one person is up, we lift them up higher. It's just what we do. You're all incredible and lovely. Every last one of you.

Helena Hunting and Christina Santos over in the den. Thanks for letting the wood come hang out (see what I did there?) and fangirl all over Helena. I love that group so much. It's a place where I can escape being an author (most of the time) and just be a fan like everyone else that loves to read and gush over books they love. And do it with an often inappropriate sense of humor. *insert heart emojis and shit*

To all the bloggers who work so hard for so little to spread the word about my books. Thank you so much! Cecily Bonney, Sissy, Smuttt, Ellie and Petra at Love N. Books, Morgan Cross, Holly Shields, Avephoenix, Laura Martinez, JP Uvalle, and many more. All the Shhluts, SueBee, War, Ebru, Jabby, Kay, CC, Carlene, Snow, Timitra, Dawn, Lloyda, Kay, Elizabeth... Gahhh, I know I'm forgetting some, and I'm so sorry. All the bloggahs. Much love from this guy over here. Thank you, thank you, thank you. You make this industry run! Thank you!

All my fans... I often don't know what you see in my writing sometimes, but you see it, and I thank you for it. Maybe the self-doubt just comes with the job. But you are amazing and I can't thank you enough. You make it possible for me to stay at home and do what I love. For that, I am eternally grateful.

To anyone I have forgotten, thank you so much! I will get you next go around. I promise.

Sloane

Made in the USA
San Bernardino, CA
11 June 2016